DOMINATION DOLLS

Poor Reynolds was the last of them to hold out, which is probably why the girls were so hard on him. But eventually they tired of the flogged, wet wretch with the bin on his head. They needed fresh sport. Eyes still wild with drink and a strange lust, clothes dishevelled, breathing hard so their breasts rose and fell inside their silky blouses, they gathered around my chair to stare at my two boys – Creech and Brown – tethered beside their mistress's desk.

Crossing my legs at the thigh, so neither man could fail to see that their boss's sex was naked above her black stocking tops, I said, 'Go ahead, ladies. It's Christmas. Treat yourselves.'

DOMINATION DOLLS

Lindsay Gordon

For Marilyn Manson

This book is a work of fiction.
In real life, make sure you practise safe, sane and consensual sex.

First published in 2004 by
Nexus
Thames Wharf Studios
Rainville Road
London W6 9HA

www.nexus-books.co.uk

Typeset by TW Typesetting, Plymouth, Devon

Printed and bound by
Clays Ltd, St Ives PLC

ISBN 0 352 33891 1

Contents

1	Passenger	1
2	Archivist 1	24
3	The Women in his Life – Wife and Maid	42
4	Archivist 2	80
5	Mother	88
6	Archivist 3	105
7	Doctor	113
8	Archivist 4	138
9	Manager	166
19	Archivist 5	191
11	Diva	200
12	Archivist 6	218
13	Lady	223

You'll notice that we have introduced a set of symbols onto our book jackets, so that you can tell at a glance what fetishes each of our brand new novels contains. Here's the key – enjoy!

cp (traditional)

cp (modern)

spanking

restraint/bondage

rope bondage/hojojutsu

latex/rubber/leather/enclosure

fem dom

willing captivity

medical

period setting

uniforms

sex rituals

1

Passenger

Written Statement. Submitted December 2002. Archive number 8968.

Following items also submitted: one latex mask; one animal print and one imitation fur coat; two pairs of leather boots; one black and red corset; assorted foundation wear (six pieces); three used pairs of black, fully fashioned, seamed stockings; one pair leather gloves; three rubber dresses; one leather bag containing assorted implements – collar and leash, crop, ball-gag, rectal plug, cuffs, crop, flail.

It is midnight in the middle of winter and my journey finishes in Prague.

Outside the window of my hotel room the snow is falling. I hear no voices or cars from the street. No noises at all. Even the radiator next to the bed has stopped its trickling sound. Time has paused. Space has changed. The whole universe has suddenly got smaller. Nothing exists other than this room and the waiting I must endure inside it.

They will be here soon.

I am a thief. I stole something of great value to certain people. And now they want it back. It was loaned to me with precise guidelines on restricted use.

I ignored the instructions and used it too many times. Even after having it in my life for so short a time, there was no way on earth I was going to give it back.

I am wearing it now, on my face. During the night when I wear it most, you would never guess I was wearing a mask. Only under strong lights or a bright sun can you see there is something unnatural about my beautiful features: a certain sheen to the skin that is impossibly smooth and unblemished, like the glossiness you see on a very fine rubber. But if you were to compare a photo of my face now with a photo of the girl I used to be, you would be shocked by the alteration. So much more has changed beside skin tone. What has happened to her features? you would ask. How have her eyebrows become so thin and arched? Her cheekbones so defined? Lips so full? Eyes so clear and cold as arctic water? Surely, surgery is not so advanced as this? How is it possible for an ordinary girl to become this creature, this painted doll, this pretty thing of the night?

I have fallen in love with this face that looks back at me from the many mirrors and reflections I gaze into. I have worn this clinging, discreet skin for months, not hours as they prescribed. And now it does not want to come off.

But this, I guess, is how it ends for all of us who dare to wear such forbidden things from private collections. Now I understand. Ultimately, it is we who are collected. It is we who are exhibited. It is our most intimate and secret selves that are put on display.

Perhaps they are surprised I made it this far when they were watching me the whole time; waiting, anticipating my readiness, knowing all along that the mask would remove me from any kind of life I may have known before.

Red lipstick is thick on the filter of the cigarette in the cheap ashtray. How long will it be before I smoke another? Will I even want to inhale smoke when I become that other person again: my old self who first put on the mask?

I pour another three fingers of Johnny Walker Red into my tooth glass. My pouting, lavishly painted mouth has left its mark on the rim of the highball glass also. I add ice to the whisky. Then I stand up and take a last look at my reflection in the long, dark windows of my room. Black and bobbed with a straight fringe, my hair alone has transformed me into something you only glimpse from the open doorway of a Berlin cellar nightclub, or through a limousine window on a rainy, downtown night, or partially captured in a grainy photo taken in a cheap motel in 1950s America – some flop-house outside of suburbia where actresses are known to go, where reefers are smoked and where singers overdose. Like this place: the fusty hotel room where I have come to make my last stand. It can't have changed much since the 50s. Yellow painted walls, thin orange curtains, a Formica headboard on a fuck-pad bed, imitation walnut finish furniture, an unread bible in the bedside drawer. Uncannily, with all this make-up on my latexy face, this place and I complement each other. Applied with such precision, one layer upon another, it gives me a new identity. I look like the kind of woman who instantly fills any room with tension and the smell of strange perfume. I barely remember what the girl underneath looked like. Pale and timid and mousy, I think. Not like this. Crimson lips down-turned to a sullen pout. Slut-black mascara and indigo eye-shade. Charcoal eyes that have seen too much. Bruised rouge. Eyelashes too long for even a

3

doll. Beauty spot. A face that draws eyes, is leered at by the camera, is hidden in secret places by desperate men . . .

Standing up, I unzip my leather pencil skirt and let it fall to my feet. Claret nails work my silky blouse free and then toss it on to the bed. It lands without a sound beside my leopard-patterned coat. Keeping my shoes on, I approach the mirror. Under my Cuban heels the carpet feels thin and dry as if I am walking over a big slice of cheap bread. Beneath the beam of the 100-watt bulb, hanging inside the pinkish shade like a UFO in a bad sci-fi movie, I admire the exquisite details of myself this final time.

Destiny: I belong in black and white. Dressed up in pin-up nostalgia, smoking a long cigarette and sipping Scotch in a cheap hotel. Make-up and heels and nylons and dyed hair, startling as a fresh tattoo at first glance: this new identity whenever she hugs my face. With her, it has always felt as if a long-held fantasy has become real, but with all the euphoria of the dream still intact. I'm contained inside my own vision: a pretty butterfly from long ago, trapped in the celluloid of a private screening for ever.

Once I step out of my slip, a second skin of black nylon shimmers over my breasts, buttocks, sex and legs. In between the sheer fabric of my underwear, my skin is the colour of fresh cream. To the touch, it is soft as a sheared lamb. Once unwrapped, you will find it fragrant like the flesh of a rich lady taking tea, or cock, at the Dorchester. Turning left and right and rising on to my toes, I am pleased by the way my stockings shimmer. Every movement of my legs makes the nylon brush my shaven flesh like a black feather. Inside my brassiere, my pinkish nipples tingle against their see-through pockets. Dropping my head back, I tease them through the gauzy cups with my finger tips, make them hard and insolent. Slipping long fingers under my garter belt and transparent panties I finger my pussy. Sticky candy under a glossy wrapper. Shorn and downy, my floss feels like moleskin. It has taken a lot of grooming to create this little pelt. And she is already damp.

Dizzy, I move back to the bed, keeping my eyes on the girl in the mirror. I would like to see her fucked now. She's been teasing me for the last three months while I've watched her smoke and drink and run around Europe and the high seas, unable to stop indulging herself, getting her own peculiar fix. Every time I look at a reflection in a mirror or window, she's there, staring, defiant; tall and white-skinned and clothed in black like a witch.

Sitting on the end of my bed I ever so gently circle my finger around my clit, sometimes brushing the underside of my cool fingers across my lips. Soon I can just detect the salty aroma of a girl hopelessly aroused and shamefully expectant. I can't help it. I close my eyes. Just the thought of the unspeakable acts I have committed while wearing the mask transforms my whole being into the familiar hunger that can never be sated. Tiny pictures, like outlawed subliminal messages, flash from my memory until my skin gooses and my legs shake. I replay so many of the situations I have manipulated, and so many of the wicked things I am guilty of, and would repeat to infinity if allowed.

Now I reach the end of my life with her, the strange desire for confession in me is greater than anything else. This flimsy transforming skin of latex on my face is not merely content with instigating wayward compulsions inside me, she also wants me to tell my tales. It's as if my life lived through her is a testament to her power and her beauty. The heat and intensity of the moment is not enough for her; she demands immortality through erotic narrative.

I have dominated men. I have used men. But I am her servant. Her doll.

1. New Face

The first time I wore the mask outside the apartment, I knew I would misbehave.

Previously, hidden away inside my warm and darkened flat in Bloomsbury, London, I only wore the mask for short, intense periods, always remembering to take it off after a few minutes as instructed, despite the pleasure of the dreamy visions I enjoyed and the sense of empowerment that thrilled me to the marrow. But, in time, I became careless and greedy. I let her tighten on my face for far longer than was safe. And I began dressing up, like a naughty girl in her mother's clothes and cosmetics. Wearing increasingly bizarre outfits and soon finding myself closer to the front door of my apartment after each session with her on my face. Later, teeth clenched and chin raised, after gently peeling that thin, artificial skin off my head, I often found myself wearing lingerie and long boots under a fur coat, while twisting the stem of a thin umbrella handle between my gloved fingers. I would be in shock at my uncharacteristic loss of control and stunned by what I had been compelled to wear. To my horror, it was as if I were making preparations for some kind of illicit liaison. Not only, it seemed, did the clinging mask have the power to reshape my face, it also possessed the power to transform my will, my very character.

After removing the enchanted face it was as though I had experienced an intense daydream. But when fully conscious again, and standing in the hallway with those delicate, transparent features draped across my palms, I would be aroused in an unusual way. There was something savage about my excitement. I would find myself in the grip of angry and vengeful emotions, as if I needed to inflict pain or humiliation on a victim. I was emboldened by something cruel and irresistible. Complete in my mastery. An evil, painted dictator.

And how could I account for the eerie residue of curious impulses left behind each period endured under the hot rubber? While that second identity smothered my real features, I felt as if some clever mesmerist or hypnotist had implanted weird suggestions deep in my subconscious mind. Increasingly, when shopping, I found myself drawn toward leather garments in window displays. In shoe shops I would pause by the highest heels with the thinnest ankle straps, or the tightest boots with the most severe spikes. Soon, I was trying them on, making purchases. Drawn into Soho after work, I then found myself engaged in reckless spending sprees, buying tight rubber dresses and even more outrageous heels that I would never previously have purchased or had occasion to wear. Tight pencil skirts that reduced my stride to teetering baby steps, complemented by well-cut jackets of silk, became my uniform for work. Trips to the hairdressers and beauticians increased, eventually becoming obsessive. I was never happier than when a pretty girl in a white uniform was on her knees before me, engaged in the painting of my toenails. When a male podiatrist in Kensington, with warm hands and an attentive manner, recreated my feet into the softest and most slender shapes, I found myself profoundly affected. Suffering a hot flush, and becoming shamefully damp between my thighs, I wanted to punish the man. Suddenly, I wanted to slip my long feet inside a pair of cruel shoes in order to tread on him. To squash him. Crush the bastard. I could almost feel his skin and muscles oozing under the tipped heels and leather soles of my shoes. Just the imagined discomfort etched on his face brought me close to climax.

Men began to interest me more than they had ever done before. But to interest me in a different way. I've always found myself manipulated, sometimes bullied by men, my shy and diffident nature often being mistaken for weakness. And yet, within weeks of wearing the mask, I was under the spell of a new confidence. A quick temper replaced my infuriating habit of repressing anger when slighted or mistreated. An uncharacteristic imperiousness straightened my spine and pushed my shoulders back as I walked. A noticeable coldness in my manner soon had my male colleagues on the retreat at the office. Many were surprised by the dramatic changes in my appearance and attitude. Defensive postures were adopted after nothing more than a look from my heavily painted eyes. Stammers began when I crossed my legs in meetings. Others were taken by my severity. They had never noticed me before. At best, they had been dismissive. Now I was in my new suits and high heels and excessive make-up, they thought me worthy of their attention; as if I were pandering to their desires, hoping for their attentions. Those foolhardy enough to ask me out were left speechless by the impact of rejection. I burned them with ice. It wasn't long until someone called me a bitch; I laughed in his face. On the street I took to using my elbows to move along; I shaved twenty minutes off my commute, both ways.

Those prodded, struck, or knocked off-balance by me, who would turn with a curse ready on their lips, would suddenly be confronted by a tall woman in a dark suit, her face exquisitely painted, her stilettos gleaming, nails blood red, stockings sheer and sea-med, eyebrow raised above a stern expression; and they would apologise, excuse themselves, stare like imbeciles.

After racing home, able to think of nothing but the mask, I would draw the curtains, latch the door and flee to my room. On the top of my closet space I would rummage for the hatbox in which I kept her safe. Hands trembling, I would remove her and then luxuriate again in her most special coating.

Soon, I had no defence against her. No longer content to recharge me after a demanding day in the city, she insisted on coming to work with me. She took me outside. She took me to places I had never been before. She and I did things together. Terrible things.

2. First Time; First Taste

Face to face with a stranger on a crowded under-ground train: blue eyes full of surprise, cheeks flushed with arousal and embarrassment, he found his lips no more than a few inches from the pale face of this curious woman who wore dark glasses, a headscarf and a long fur coat. A woman whose slender fingers were coated in tight, but soft, black gloves. Discreet-ly, these leather hands had gone to work inside his trousers. They clung to the skin of his thick erection; they massaged the rocklike muscle.

Jostled by the other passengers, squashed against us with their newspapers, sneezes and umbrellas, my prey was frozen with surprise. Too shocked even to speak. There was no room to pull away had he

9

wanted to. His movements were restricted; he was compelled to stare into the beautiful, smooth, wicked face of the stranger who had just helped herself to his cock. Faint with arousal from the touch of that expert hand, he became hypnotised by my patent mouth, permanently moist. The red paint on my lips was so glossy it looked wet, as if I had just dipped a kiss into a spoonful of fresh blood. The pale forehead and chin were too perfect, untouched by sun or blemish. His obedient face was reflected in the opaque lenses of my glasses as his body gently rocked with the train and accepted the insistent, uninvited ministrations of my leathered hand.

He first saw me on the platform before we boarded the train at Kings Cross. Slinking through the crowd looking for prey, I caught his eye. He stared at me, looked away, then returned his gaze to the woman with the headscarf tied tightly under her chin. Unmoving, her painted face maintained a single expression of haughty indifference, the concealed eyes marking him for later.

Then, before the train stopped at Hyde Park Corner, I moved deftly through the carriage towards him. Expensive perfume clouded from out of the black fur of my coat, paralysing him as if it were irresistible pollen from a flesh-eating plant. He turned, saw me, and at once offered himself. An instinctive susceptibility to a certain kind of older woman was at work inside him, the way it always had been since his first sexual awakenings. Unable to remove his eyes from my alabaster face, rouged high on the cheeks, its countenance stony as a marble face on a temple door, his pulse hammered inside his skull, his mouth dried, his sleepy manhood awoke. Not a leer, or lascivious grin on his innocent, shy face, but a look of longing and adoration, of utter subjection to this unusual, dollish beauty.

Masked, I could not resist such a vulnerable morsel on this first foray outside the apartment. So I took my pleasure in public. Tugging at his shaft, the lapels of my coat concealed his hips and the activity between them. From an idle glance, it would appear the woman in the furs was merely trapped against another passenger with her hands crossed at the wrist before her stomach. Only a determined inspection from above would detect the quick, jerking motion of my forearm above his belt buckle.

Peering down, he saw a string of pearls around a pale throat and a silk blouse open to the sternum where the edge of a lacy bra-cup could be seen. He dared to peek further down the long body of the woman who had taken control of his journey to work. Near the shadowy floor of the carriage, he caught a glimpse of a tight leather skirt, shapely knees re-skinned in black nylon, and the pointed tips of patent leather knee-boots.

Who was she? Some exhibitionist wife of a million-aire from Knightsbridge? A nymphomaniac duchess from Chelsea? A crazy widow from Sloane Street?

The lights of the carriage dimmed and then cut out for a moment. Blue sparks erupted outside the windows; a shower of sparks from some subterranean workshop on the road to hell, where scented demons serviced the cocks of the damned. And, as if this brief blackout was willed by me, the doll face moved closer so he could smell my make-up, and something reminiscent of the surgical fragrance that issues from a powdery latex glove when it is squeezed over long, skilled fingers. A voice whispered through the humid darkness. 'Let me taste you,' I said to him. My tone

11

of voice was both stern and tense with contained excitement.

'Yes,' he whispered.

Lurching from side to side, the train approached Knightsbridge station. The lights flickered back on. Around his thick meat my hand increased the speed of its pull and shuffle while loosening its grip. Stifling a moan, he pushed his groin into my open fur coat. Not long now.

An anticipatory energy surged through the commuters as the platform came into view. Some began to push toward the doors, but we remained face to face, bonded by the intensity of our inappropriate behaviour. Transfixed, he stared at my mouth, his eyes dreamy, lost. 'Now,' I said. 'Do as I say.'

His face darkened with hot blood. Feet scuffled. Bags rustled. A pre-recorded announcement sounded throughout the echoey tunnel. 'Come, you bastard,' I whispered under the white noise. 'Give it to me.' His body tensed under his overcoat and suit. His breathing sped up and condensed like fog on my plastic face. The doors slid open. Limbs relaxing, chin dropping, forehead beaded with sweat, his whole body hung from the handrail fixed into the ceiling. In the palm of my leather hand I felt his cock pulse. Five jolts followed by the immediate softening of his rigidity. Cupping my hand over the end of his phallus I collected what I could and then withdrew my hand from his trousers. His shirt became untucked. Without another word or even a final look, I bowed away from him, found a slipstream among the alighting passengers and disembarked from the carriage. The doors closed behind me.

Looking up and peering through the window of the carriage, he caught a final sighting of the beautiful white-skinned woman in the headscarf and furs. Eyes still inscrutable behind the lenses of the dark glasses, she looked back at him and held a cupped hand across the lower half of her face as if pinching her nose between thumb and forefinger, or eating from the palm. Bemused and exhausted, he watched her pass from sight as the train pulled away from the platform.

It had been my first day outside the apartment with her, that see-through loveliness in latex, so clingy on my face. And from that day forward, I could remember everything we did together in precise detail. The daydreams became real memories. My eyes through her face. Together. This was the birth of an erotic life for this sweet-smelling creature in the mask. It was the beginning of the compulsion to seduce and be seduced in the transient, anonymous world of the traveller, where the paths of strangers briefly cross and then part, and where the intimate moments of contact are made all the more ferocious because of situation, fear of discovery, mystery.

I took time off work. She made me. I took money from men. She showed me how. We travelled.

3. Discipline at Sea

Together, on a passenger liner that crossed the Atlantic, we stalked the decks, the bars, clubs, restaurants, theatres and the casinos of this vast floating city. But, by day, I was nothing more than a simple passenger who read books in deckchairs, who always dined alone and slept late within the confines of her cabin. One who walked on deck in silence, often pausing to look out at the blue-black immensity of hidden depths and slow waves, her mind distracted by dreams as she waited for the night when she and her mask would be one again. Even by day, maybe I seemed overdressed when it was hot. Pale and too tightly wrapped; constricted by foundation wear beneath my elegant suits and dresses, always remaining aloof, side-stepping the suspicious and ignoring the inquisitive among the other passengers and crew.

She slept below, carefully concealed inside an airtight container disguised to look like a simple, elegant hatbox. Waiting in her own, private, rubbery darkness, longing to cling, impatient to reshape a face to her will and to make a body do her bidding.

All day I would struggle to suppress the nerves in my stomach; the tingling anticipation of finding myself in strange berths, or under darkened stairwells, or striding down narrow passageways, or working a crop above a body huddled into a hot space that smelled of diesel. Craving to fill and satisfy the void, deeper than the oceans we traversed, that existed inside me whenever I enhanced my face with living, accursed latex.

And after the sun set, I would hurry down below and then prepare myself for the destination of her choosing. Dizzy with excitement, thrilled by the scent of her skin against mine, I would smooth her into place – into my eye sockets, over cheek and chin, nose and lips, her delicate flesh sculpting my own in her image. Slowly, carefully, gripped by the suspense that precedes all female transgression, I would then dress to her exacting specifications. Bind my middle with tight black girdles. Sculpt my breasts into hard, streamlined peaks. Draw long black nylons to the top of my thighs. Zip my shimmering feet and calves into stiff, mummifying boots of patent leather with spike heels. And over this inner sheath of nylon and silk and whalebone I would then squeeze my slender contours into a latex dress, its fabric as light and thin and glossy as the skin of my new face. Gloves to the elbow and a long coat to complete the ensemble.

Gripped by a new confidence, a stillness of mind, a determination to ruthlessly seek satisfaction, my entire body would shiver. Every muscle, limb and inch of skin under latex, every toe trapped inside patent leather would suffuse with an electricity destined to earth itself on the flesh of others.

At the end of a quiet, darkened bar they would find me perched on a stool, legs crossed and one foot forward as if to invite a kiss. Prowling the quieter decks, the fading gunfire of my heels would draw them in; subordinate rats running after a perfumed piper. A tall woman in black, riding the mirrored elevators down; a peek of patent toe from under a hem, catching the eyes of those with a peculiar weakness, with a specific curiosity about the illicit treasures that can exist under the beguiling folds and wraps of these rare and unobtainable women.

Mostly, they would follow me in silence; dreaming of contact and yet praying I would not discover their stealthy stalking. It was not the overly assertive baboons or the ageing Lotharios we had a use for – though occasionally it was interesting to break one. No, we sought the company of those haplessly enamoured and made submissive by the power of our imagery – the spikes, leather, whispers of nylon, glimpses of latex, the cold, painted beauty. They could be found everywhere. Those that needed to serve, to worship, as they surely knew they would in the company of one such as I. The stammerers, the blushers, the nervous: it was they we needed most for our pleasures, for our power.

Inside my black leather handbag I transported my tools like some deranged female surgeon: collar and leash; ball gag should I need to silence their pitiful cries; eye mask should their nervous or pleading eyes offend me; butt-plug of cold steel should a recalcitrant streak of stubborn masculinity survive the lash of whip or crack of cane. And it is with great fondness I recall their use.

A young steward in his dress whites was our first selection. He brought the evening meal to our cabin most nights. I believe he insisted on the job; he was weak for me. I had already seen him flirting with matrons and divorcees above deck, craftily in pursuit of women twice his age, as if eager for guidance, experience, discipline, a firm hand. Just the sight of his innocent, smiling face in the half light of our cabin during those warm evenings was enough to set us off. But it was he who gradually made things worse for himself. He could not just deliver the trays, bow and leave. No, he had to loiter; to try his luck. 'You're looking very glamorous this evening, miss,' and, 'Is there anything else I can do for you, miss? Anything at all?' And all the time he was looking at my legs and boots as they peeked out from under the long, strange shiny gowns I wore; garments he had never seen before, neither at sea nor ashore.

'Are you under the illusion all this is for you?' I said, in a voice that was quiet, but all the more assertive because of it, as I rotated a boot under the cabin lights to make it shine, and stroked my glossy knee, emerging from the slit in my dress. 'You think I'm one of those desperate creatures that come on cruises to sleep with young sluts like you? You think you're some kind of stud?'

'No, miss,' he said, stammering and blushing. 'It's just . . . It's just that you are so beautiful. I'm sorry. I can't help myself staring. I've never seen a woman like you before.'

'That's right. And you'll be a damn sight better off if you never do again.'

'Yes, miss.'

'I'm not your miss, you little shit. And your service stinks. I should complain to the head steward. Unless your behaviour and attitude improves drastically, I believe I will.'

'Is that necessary?' he said, his voice choked up, his eyes full of loathing for the tall woman in black he had so recently admired. 'I've always gone out of my way to please you.'

'Well it's not good enough. I doubt you ever will be good enough. I doubt you'll ever be able to please a woman of any taste and intelligence. You are presumptuous. Overconfident. Obsequious. Your leering is inappropriate. It may work on the tarts in the Coconut Island Lounge Disco, but not with me. Do you understand?'

'Yes, madam.' His face was sullen, his tone of voice surly. Unaccustomed to rejection, his pride was injured. He was hurt. But all this time the front of his white, pressed trousers had been bulging with the hard meat of the truly servile. Confronted by a pretty face, a raised voice and a spiked heel, the poor devil could not help himself. In my opinion, though, he had not even begun to ache. Or to learn any useful lesson. Or to correct his ways and adopt the total respect and subservience his position truly required, especially in my cabin. More was required. Much more.

'Come here.' I pointed at the floor before my chair.

Sulkily, he minced closer. 'What is this?' I pointed one long finger at the thickness between his legs. 'Is this an appropriate thing to display before a first class female passenger?' I stared right into his eyes. 'You are filthy. Disgusting.'

17

Left eye twitching, bottom lip quivering, he reddened and began to plead. 'I'm sorry. I'm so sorry.'

'You dirty little shit! You dirty little cocksure shit!'

'Sorry. Oh, madam, I'm sorry.'

'I am not your madam, boy. I am your mistress!' And I was on him in a heartbeat.

White uniform trousers around his ankles. Underpants strung like a hammock between the trunks of his lean thighs. My latex hand fisted into his prettyboy hair. Face down to my boots I held the wretch; the subservient, overly helpful boy whose eyes lingered too long on her whom he could never afford nor impress. Over his back my arm swung, crop held high. Its thin shaft whipped the air below deck, then cracked across his rump. Forty lashes for the sailor. Crying out with surprise and pain, them whimpering into the carpet, he took every streak of lightning. Red with the shame of his belittlement and disgrace, I kept him on all fours with striped arse raised and genitals on display to a stranger. Jutting out between his hips, a dark cock quivered and reached for the shiny uppers of my pointed boots as I introduced him to this new concept of customer service.

Gagging him with a rubber ball, I then made him salivate like a dog. Despite his tears of humiliation, his whimpers, and the white-hot brands of pain delivered with precision from my crop against his taut backside, not once was he able to remove those watery eyes from my boots and legs. Irrespective of the demeaning postures I made him assume, he could not steal his gaze from the smoke of my nylons, the mirrors of my toes or the silver tips of my spikes. So, after his caning I paid him a gratuity. Only his tip came in the form of a trampling. Angry at his utter acquiescence, drunk on my own power, I spiked that man-kitten around the floor until he was forced to crawl under the bed, dragging his thick cock and leash into the shadows.

And before I let him cringe from my cabin to soak his wounds in the crew's quarters – his initial correction a mere entree for a banquet of punishment I would inflict on the other polite, liberal, sensitive male passengers until dawn – I made sure to milk the young steward's seed into a chilled champagne flute. And what a thick and filling draught these young things can produce. A beverage I sipped through my rubber lips as he kissed the dirty soles of my boots and apologised for being overly familiar with the female passengers during the execution of his duties.

By no means was this the last of my dealings with him on that cruise. For the entire duration of the single day off work he was granted each week, right up until we reached our final destination, he served me exclusively: laundering my delicate under-things with careful hands, polishing my shiny footwear, cleaning my cabin, running my errands, pandering to my every whim, most of the time naked, save for a collar, and lashed to the furniture on an extendable dog's lead.

There were others too; so many others we had use for aboard that ship.

A married man once followed me from my favourite bar to a nearby pool deck. Deserted at that late hour, but chilly and exposed nonetheless, it was perfect for what I had in mind for his impertinence.

I would not tell him my name when he approached me. So he called me 'madam', and that was fine, but anything more would be too familiar, I informed him. 'No, you cannot kiss me,' I told him. 'No, I don't even want you to sit next to me. I'm not interested in how long you have wanted to speak to me. And I don't particularly care what the sight of my thigh boots does to you. Or how much you need to know whether I am wearing stockings under them, or tights. How dare you! Sorry is not good enough. Do you think I am a barstool slut you can fuck while your wife sleeps below? You're too old and useless for me,' I said while examining my crimson nails. 'And you're too ugly. Your cock also, would never satisfy me. I can barely see a bulge,' I added, refreshing my lipstick before the mirror of my compact.

'Yes, you're right, madam. You're right. I am pathetic,' he replied, as something long and thin tented the front of his khaki trousers.

'You are pathetic. Your poor wife must be so frustrated. She should be harder with you. More demanding. I can see that.'

And when he sank to his knees and tried to cradle my spike-heeled foot in his trembling hands, he said, 'Oh, yes. She should. She doesn't understand me like you do.'

'I'm not here to understand you. I'm not interested in your pathetic wormlike existence. Now, get your hands off my boot.'

'Please. Please. Just a touch. Just a taste, madam.'

'When you're dressed like a history teacher? Never,' I told him. 'Get those boring textiles off and we'll see what you're good for. That's it. Everything. Get those ugly, shameful pants off. Ugh! You have no style. No idea.'

And he folded his clothes on the sun-lounger next to mine and then stood before me with his shoulders stooped, head bowed and hands covering his genitals. 'Now can I? Just for a moment. Please. Let me touch your boots.'

'Turn around,' I told him. 'Prove yourself to me. Prove you really adore me, and then we'll see what you are worthy of touching.'

And when he turned I plugged his anus with thick surgical steel.

'Make a noise and you'll attract attention to yourself. A pathetic naked old man with metal up his ass. What would they think? What would your wife think? I need a strong man,' I told him. 'Someone who can grit his teeth.' Then I struck the back of his thighs with my short flail. The leather made a wet sound on his skinny legs. 'I need a man who can grin and bear it,' I said. I struck him again, and again, and again. I lashed him until he started to dance to the percussion of his own strangled cries. 'I don't trust you. You haven't earned my trust. Your hands are undisciplined. You always want to touch things that don't belong to you. When your hands are secure, maybe then we'll be able to attend to your cravings, your needs.'

'Oh, yes, madam,' he said. 'Of course, madam,' he muttered as I cuffed his wrists to the sun-lounger and manacled his bony ankles together. And there he lay, prostrate, his eyes wide in the moonlight, his lips moving, his manhood engorged. 'And there you will stay,' I told him. 'To cool off. To think about how inferior you are. How you should lower your expectations and not expect tall, beautiful women in black seamed stockings and sexy boots and corsets to have anything to do with you.'

And when I returned three hours later, walking a retired gentleman like a dog on all fours – his throat collared, his naked body kept tersely at heel, his casino chips jingling inside my leather bag – I was pleased to see that no one had freed my slave from the sun-lounger. To my surprise, his erection had not wilted either. And neither would it, considering how I made him watch me relieve myself into the open, gasping, gulping mouth of my doggy. So much champagne and orange juice and cool night air – I was bursting. But not a drop for the moon-lounging gimp. Not a drop, or so much as a brief touch of my leathered legs. For his pains I gave him nothing but a shadowy glimpse of my stocking tops above the patent thigh boots. Milky skin above nylon and patent shininess. A dark triangle of bitch fur. A silvery rope of midnight mineral water disappearing between the open jaws of my puppy dog. Nothing but a peek for the man in chains. And then I was gone, letting them make their own way home, their own explanations.

4. Epilogue

On a Boeing 747, businessmen sucked my hot toes in first class; pretty air stewards found themselves in toilets, tied down and spanked for amusement; on long train journeys, single men choked on my fresh panties inside their hot bunks; the hairy back of a concierge at the New York Hilton became a carpet for my platinum heels; a manager of a designer shoe store in Singapore shed tears over the stocking that tied his erect cock to his neck; a cycle cop in LA rode his own night-stick while his tongue tickled my fancy; a top chef in Moscow ate fish eggs from the soles of my shoes; a famous football player went missing for a week; in international airports, elderly men carried my luggage on their backs; in limousines, playboys took stiletto heels deep between their lips, or worse: I was wild and hungry and hot under that latex face. I enjoyed a freedom I could never have imagined. But now the dream is over. I have made my first statement. I will make further detailed confessions when all charges are dropped.

They're here now. I can feel them outside in the hallway. They were just waiting for the typing to stop. I want to use the gun, the Beretta I took from the politician's bodyguard, to give this dream a chance to continue. But they are too many, even for me. I shall have to give her back to her rightful owners.

Damn them. Damn her.

She used me. She used me. She used me.

I love her for it.

So come in and get me now. My nails are sharp. I bite.

2

Archivist 1

Twice I stumbled. My heels clattered against the marble floor of the long corridor and echoed into the distant reaches of the museum. I lost co-ordination before the many artefacts, pressing against me from every side. Anxious, but too excited and curious to turn back, I teetered further into the collection, telling myself to move on, calm down, take a breath, just get the job and there will be plenty of time to admire these . . . these things. Admire? Study? Stare with an appalled mystification? What would have been appropriate? And did I want a job among such icons and devices and symbols of the depraved?

All of them mounted on green felt and displayed behind the glass of the oak cabinets that stretched up the walls to the ceiling. Cuffs, canes, collars, whips, crops, chains, underwired lingerie, erotic costumes, provocative clothing: all carefully preserved and presented in a stately manner as if they were treasures from a fallen civilisation renowned for its culture and decadence. I paused to look at a pair of silver cuffs with a hallmark, and their sparkling adjoining chain, crafted to limit the mobility of slender hands and feet. And no one but a true sadist would own so many canes, the handles inlaid with precious metals and stones to depict the little figures of young men on the handles, naked and supine. Studio light glinted off their bent or kneeling shapes, as if tiny souls were trapped inside the cruel implements to be forever fondled by their mistress's fingers.

And were such garments ever worn by women? These were sinister contraptions as much as they were items of designer fashion. Which waist could be cinched so tightly by the corsets? Were the pale backs of women ever constricted by the crisscrossing laces of this foundation wear? Some were fashioned from leather, others elaborately embroidered from whalebone and silk.

Briefly imagining my own slender feet mounted on the cruel spikes of the shoes, sandals and boots caused a momentary loss of balance and I was forced to right myself against the dark wood of a display case exhibiting a shiny sarcophagus, fashioned in the shape of a man. I covered my mouth in shock; this indecent casing for the warm and living contours of a male body promised a permanent night-time of captivity from his jailer: no apparent slits to see with, no connection to the outside world save the discreet grill beneath the nose for his hurried breaths, and the tailored apertures over sex and anus to allow her access. As I stood beside this terrible suit, I experienced a shortness of breath preceded by a tightening of the chest and a perilous tingling in my stomach as if it were occupied with my own prisoner, vulnerable and catacombed in the inflexible rubber shell.

I shuddered and looked away, only to have my eyes settle on a score of staring faces on the other side of the hallway. Who had worn these masks? Cold, beautiful, astonished faces crafted from ceramic and latex to resemble pale, smooth, lifelike flesh. Why were the open mouths painted to entice? Why did they all peer at me with black, lifeless eyes? To what purpose were they ever put? Which identities did they conceal?

Beside each exhibit, a single white card presented the title, date, source, a brief explanation and the catalogue number of the piece, but my vision was too jumpy and my mind too startled to read much of anything at this point.

At the end of the corridor I found an archway and moved into a larger rectangular chamber with a stone floor as before. Dumbstruck, I hesitated on the threshold of this cavernous chamber. Lit by two enormous chandeliers suspended on brass chains from the domed ceiling, and by wall-mounted lights with scallop shades of green glass, I immediately understood that what I had just passed through was nothing more than an antechamber, an introduction to something greater – perhaps a deterrent for the faint-hearted or virtuous. This open-plan space was two storeys high, with a wooden balcony protecting the catwalk of the first level. From flagstone to ceiling, more of the oak cabinets, fronted with polished glass, were filled with thousands of these curious relics. In two aisles on the ground floor there were display tables with glass tops from which issued the dull gleam of leather, the smoke of sheer fabrics and the sinister glint of steel. I looked up. Around the walls of the second level another audience of pale female faces stared down at me. Hundreds of inscrutable faces; beautiful, some heavily painted with cosmetics, others clear, but all clinging to the smooth, glass pedestals in the shape of heads on which they were presented. Instinctively, I presumed that the faces were watching over the many artefacts below, like collectors admiring their secret hoard.

'Those must be the tipped heels of Ms Canada Lisle's shoes, beating such an uneven rhythm on the floor of the Doctor Neretva Memorial Room.' It was the same cultured voice of the Director; the elderly man I had heard through the intercom of the front entrance, while I was still outside in the street, somewhat more innocent than I would be only minutes later. A sonorous, distinguished voice, bereft of static and authoritative inquiry now I was inside the secret world. The tone of his voice had changed; it suggested intelligence blended with a paternal kindness. It took the edge off my nerves.

At the far end of the main gallery, I could see an open door leading to an office. From here the voice had come. Walking towards the office, I saw part of a large desk, a wine-coloured carpet and walls completely covered with hardback books.

Before entering the office, I quickly turned to face an upright cabinet to check my reflection. My spirits fell. My jacket and skirt suddenly looked, and indeed felt, flimsy. It was as if they could easily become caught on the sharp things under glass and torn away. My court shoes, increasingly tight and hot around my feet, were also drastically miscast here; dull, ordinary, neutral. Just like my cheap and functional undergarments – the flesh-coloured tights, white panties and bra – embarrassing me as if the scornful eyes of the beautiful masks above were capable of seeing through my suit. I cursed myself for not possessing a more commanding outfit: something black with hard lines and tailored to hug my every contour. I suddenly wanted my milky skin to be thrown into sinful contrast against a sheer, black fabric. And I wanted shoes with thin heels that would ricochet off the stone floor and cast sparks into the

eyes of those foolish enough to stare without permission. My reflection immediately dissolved before
my eyes to be replaced and mocked by a pair of long
boots with invisible zippers and pencil-width heels.
Who had worn them? And had she walked so well it
was essential they were preserved behind glass?

What was I thinking? What had just come over me?
I chided myself for my instant susceptibility to the
things on display in these private rooms. I was here
for an interview, I scolded myself; for a job I
desperately needed. I must remain professional, calm,
articulate, alert.

After steering myself around a table revealing a
glistening collection of braces, belts, plugs and phallic
shapes with a surgical appearance, I entered the
Director's office.

'Miss Lisle, thank you for coming. And welcome to the
Doctor Neretva collection. Forgive me for not rising, or
greeting you at the door.' He wafted a slender hand over
the wheelchair in which he sat. 'May I call you Canada?'

'Certainly.' I leant across the table and gave his
fingers a brief shake. Long and cold and manicured;
I could not imagine these posed, feminine hands in
everyday use. Perhaps idly engaged on the keys of a
grand piano, or employed at writing with a priceless
fountain pen. On the third finger of his left hand, I
noticed a heavy gold ring embossed with the same
saturnine face I had seen on the ornamental door
knocker outside the building, and then again above
my head on the stone feature of the porch; its
grinning face watching the street as the face on the
ring now watched me with delight.

I smiled into the Director's angular face. Pleasant,
studious features were lit from the side by a stylish

Edwardian lamp. Thin delicate lips were surrounded by a well-groomed, white beard. Elfin cheekbones drew attention to his clear blue eyes, sparkling beneath the high brow from which his thick, white hair was swept back. Quickly, dismissively I felt, these clever eyes looked over my outfit. Though it may have been nothing more than my paranoia, in them I intuited a kind of disappointment at this contemporary uniform of the disgruntled office worker. I sank into a chair and tried to obscure most of my body under the desk.

The director wore a red dressing gown; the kind favoured by gentlemen in nineteenth-century portraits, and dramas I had seen on television. It struck me that everything about him suggested antiquity, as if he too were a survivor from a distant culture, an eccentric preserved by the austere interior of this building and its curious churchy smell of incense, wood polish and floor wax.

'Well?' he asked, and then reclined back into his cushioned chair, his eyes mischievous.

I cleared my throat. 'A fascinating place, sir.' I had not called a man 'sir' since my schooling, but his voice, his manner, his very presence seemed to require its use. 'I can honestly say I have never seen anything like it. I couldn't even have imagined such a place.'

My remarks pleased him. He chuckled. 'But how did it make you feel?'

The look of shock and embarrassment and guilt on my face answered his question.

'Forgive me, Canada. I have a weakness for playing devil's advocate.' Smiling, he spread his fingers over my CV and letter of introduction that lay in front of him, as if stroking the paper. He peered down through the elegant spectacles that hung

29

around his thin neck by a gold chain. 'I summoned you to interview because your work as archivist for the university poetry library, and indeed your time spent as curator of the surgeons' museum, interested me greatly. Especially the latter. Was the material fascinating also?'

The question perturbed me; I was unsure of its meaning in the context of my being present in this strange gathering of sexual artefact. 'I took an interest, yes. History is a passion of mine,' I replied, as if innocent of any ulterior motive he may have had for asking me about the scalpels, bone-saws, syringes and preserved body parts I was currently archiving.

He smiled, amused by my reticence. 'Indeed it is, Canada. A first in ancient history and a masters in heritage management speaks for itself. I think I may not be presumptuous in saying that the contemporary world does not ignite your passions in quite the same manner as the ancient and the esoteric?'

I nodded, smiling, flattered by his intuition.

'Your own professional history is all very impressive, though I think you have been suffering the same fate as those dedicated souls who preserve our national treasures.'

'Sir?'

'An appalling and unjustly low salary.'

I smiled. 'Perhaps, sir. But one can be rich in other ways.'

He laughed, softly. 'Indeed.'

'May I ask who recommended me for this position? I mean, how did you even find out about me?'

'Aha. The head-hunted requires the name of the head-hunter.' The Director chuckled, obviously enjoying my mystification. Following a written request from the Director for my CV two weeks earlier, I had been offered an interview for the position of archivist of this collection that I had no prior knowledge of. The post included a generous salary. 'You may have guessed that we never advertise our vacancies,' the Director added. 'This collection is a purely private concern. Of which I will tell you more in good time. But, as a result of our anonymity, all of our employees are handpicked. We are very careful in these matters. And I'm afraid I must apologise for all of this subterfuge, and for the fact that I must keep the name of your patron a secret. It was he that requested confidentiality. Sadly, his involvement with such a collection as this could harm his reputation. All I can tell you is that he is a member of the medical profession who is very impressed with the research work you have carried out on his behalf. He is a friend of mine and when I told him of my vacancy for a librarian, your name was mentioned.'

Alarm bells had been ringing inside me from the first moment I stood outside the front door of the Neretva collection, but something – a cocktail of curiosity and greed perhaps – made me continue, even as the peculiarity of this situation increased. 'I see,' I said, appearing as guarded and cautious as I could. 'When I received your letter I found it all very mysterious. But, I'll admit, the remuneration package was the main reason I am here. I've never seen such a generous salary offered in this field.'

Again, he seemed delighted by my response. 'Welcome to the private sector, Canada. Shall I say, the very private sector. We do things differently here, my dear. The handsome rewards are but one indication of this.' He beamed at me. Again, I was struck by a suspicion that some further information was being imparted by the director's mischievous smile.

31

'And you require an archivist for ... for this material.'

'Precisely. To preserve and catalogue our treasures.'

'I cannot imagine it presenting me with any great difficulty.'

'That is why you are here. But don't be fooled, Canada. It may appear to be a civilised working environment. But the work can be demanding, the hours often long. Would travel be a problem?'

'Oh no, sir.' My eagerness immediately embarrassed me.

He smiled and studied my face for a while, as if trying to see behind it, to read the thoughts, my true reaction to his crazy world. Appearing satisfied, the Director then wheeled himself out from behind his desk. 'Come, Canada, if you would be good enough to follow me hither and thither, I will show you more of our pieces. And I can tell you more about the situation. Maybe answer any questions you have. But be candid, my dear. We are not feckless here, but we are frank. And then coffee.'

For twenty minutes we moved among the exhibits and I knew he was watching my reflection the entire time, gauging my reaction to what I saw behind glass. I tried to maintain a constant frown of scholarly interest as a means of suppressing the shock I suffered before so much of the collection. There were times when I wanted to close my eyes, or to stare agog at a particular piece, or to speak out loud to decry the purpose of an implement. Perspiration broke across my brow, my pulse raced. Twice I was overcome sufficiently to murmur, 'Oh, surely not. That cannot be.'

When the Director finally glided to a halt beside a display of vintage undergarments, hobble skirts and long gloves, he looked up at me, his face sincere, serious. 'Many people, Canada, would take objection to our collection. They would find it distasteful, repulsive even.' He raised an eyebrow. 'They would want it destroyed. Indeed, at times in its own history, its existence has been in grave danger.'

'No,' I said, my voice a hoarse whisper.

'I'm afraid this has been the case. It is why the Neretva collection can only exist as a myth. Such is the fate of the misunderstood. It can never become a public exhibition. It must remain, as it always has done, a private concern. As a custodian of the collection, I am as discriminating about visitors as I am about staff.' His voice lowered to a conspiratorial murmur and, momentarily, his eyes became sad. 'We have made mistakes in the past.

'Only those capable of admiring these artefacts in the same way that an art lover is transformed when he admires a masterpiece at the Royal Academy can ever be admitted. We operate by invitation only. And most often in the evenings. You would not be permitted guests or friends here under any circumstances. And even the very nature of your work here – the very collection itself – must never be disclosed to a soul. This is no place for the garrulous, the indelicate, Canada.'

'I quite understand, sir.'

He looked at me with a fresh scrutiny I found unnerving and I barely managed to maintain eye-contact. 'I paid close attention to your references, Canada. You possess all the right qualities for a curator. Attention to detail, dedication, purpose, an enthusiasm for your subject matter.'

'Thank you, sir.'

'But even these are insufficient without discretion, and without empathy for the artefacts themselves. I

33

took a chance, you see, even opening the door to you.'

'Yes, sir.'

'Even the most excellent references and impressive, detailed work history can tell me little until I see the individual's reaction to our hoard.' He smiled; his eyes penetrated me. I felt tense, then a little dizzy. As if hypnotised by his voice, I knew I could not lie; any deceit, even of thought, would immediately have been recognised by his intuitive eyes. 'A face can tell me more in an instant than any letter or voice. And in your handsome features, Miss Lisle, I see astonishment, but not horror. Wonder, but never revulsion. An innocent's fascination, but not a cynic's sneer. I see a historian's curiosity and an aesthete's delight in the beautiful. I have seen all I need to see, Canada. I do believe my judgement to be sound in the matter of your potential as an archivist here. Am I wrong?'

'No, sir.' My voice was dry and weak.

'Am I going to be mistaken?'

'No, sir. Absolutely not. I would be delighted to work with your collection. It would be a privilege. I would treasure it, keep its secrets and –' He stared at me again until I was sure I would have to avert my eyes; I sensed him inside my head, reading every memory file and testing every impulse. I felt naked, vulnerable, silly, angry at myself for being so susceptible. 'And I think I would be challenged. I need to be challenged. Stimulated. I could learn too ...' I no longer really knew what I was saying. I was jabbering like an imbecile, a child desperate for approval. But the Director smiled and I felt, at once, as if many ropes had been loosened from my limbs; my muscles and tendons were suddenly permitted to relax. I breathed out, my mind exhausted by anticipation, tension, hope.

'I have no doubts, Canada.' He finally looked away and then pushed his chair past a set of prosthetic female legs, all shod in preposterously high-heeled shoes. 'Should you decide to join us, there are papers to be signed. Matters to be taken care of. But coffee first. I feel you need to be revived. This place can be taxing for the uninitiated, my dear. Taxing.' This was said with resignation, and over his shoulder like a tired aside to a weary companion.

A contract of employment was set before me, beside an elegant china coffee cup and saucer. It was a strange manuscript on thick, expensive paper. He'd produced it from his desk drawer in the shape of a roll tied up with a black ribbon, like a diploma.

My eyes quickly scanned the many clauses on discretion and information protection that comprised most of the contract while the Director spoke in his quiet, educated voice, his expression remaining grave as if I were signing a peace treaty, a will, or adoption papers. 'Before you commit yourself, Canada, I feel it incumbent upon myself to warn you of a somewhat unusual feature of this job.' At once, his confiding tone summoned back my initial unease at seeing the artefacts. 'It is difficult to describe, and I fear you may fancy me foolish for mentioning this matter. But, nonetheless, I think it necessary that you realise that your predecessors all proved susceptible to the powerful ... how should I put this? Yes, the powerful influence of the collection. It may surprise you, but throughout its long history, the collection has been attributed with supernatural qualities. Some have said it is charmed, others cursed. Do you believe a place can be haunted, Canada?'

Uneasy, I found myself unable to answer.

He chuckled to himself. 'There was once a young lady who swore the entire gallery was psychically charged.'

Had I not felt something myself, when surprised by the sarcophagi?

'As well you know, Canada, an immersion into any professional discipline carries a risk of over-involvement. The neglect of one's personal life. Perhaps, among those of us concerned with a particular genre of history, we sometimes experience what some would consider an unhealthy attachment to the subject matter. And the collection certainly possesses its own unique magnetism.'

His remarks were made as warnings. But I found myself at a loss to put his mind, and now my own, at ease.

His voice softened. 'It's important, Canada, that you steel yourself against it at times.'

It was as if he was talking about a seductive but manipulative entity; something with a peculiar kind of life force and intelligence. I began to wonder if he were completely sane. But despite the penetrative power of his gaze, I felt no threat from this benign, kindly, scholarly paraplegic. He was eccentric, that was all, I told myself. A kindly misfit. I had met many like him in the world of academia. 'I understand your caution, sir. I will endeavour to remain . . . objective.'

The Director relaxed and chuckled; his eyes smiled. 'A capable and wilful young woman. How compatible you and the collection will be. I have every confidence in your resolve. I only felt it appropriate to suggest that the preoccupations of many powerful personalities are concentrated here. Who is to truly know if the spirit of their creators, or former owners, endures in their relics?'

I smiled, suddenly thrilled at the thought of the salary, the long hours of silent contemplation down here in my preferred environment, the secrecy and mystery of it all. A curator of sin, an archaeologist of the illicit – I liked the sound of that. 'I have no reservations in accepting the position.' I signed the contract with a flourish, my hand watched closely by the Director.

But I was soon to lose all sense of my growing confidence in the Director's company. Despite my initial shock at the size and scope and subject matter of the exhibition upstairs, it seemed insufficient preparation for what I experienced in the basement.

A vast archive of manuscripts had been fitted into one half of the large and heated basement conversion. They were all bound in leather and stored on shelves in a mobile library in which an aisle could be created by turning a wheel at the end of a column. Among the leather-bound manuscripts, there were also treasury boxes tied shut with ribbons. There was a microfiche system and a computer database beside the paper archive. Three systems were run simultaneously as if the museum was terrified of one system failing. The space dedicated to administration was situated in another corner of the basement. A simple, tidy affair with desk, chair, computer. Beside the office area was a viewing monitor and a bank of the latest, digital beta, video and DVD players. The remainder of the area was filled with wooden packing crates. Some were open. Styrofoam and straw spilled from them. These would be the new exhibits awaiting investigation, cataloguing and preparation for display upstairs.

'I'm not as active as I once was, Canada. I now prefer to direct proceedings rather than work hands on. And as some considerable preparation is required for each new piece, you will find yourself quite busy down here. Every object has a corresponding history, mostly in manuscript form. This practice was started at the very beginnings of the collection in the late 1890s, so that each piece would tell its own human story. There are journals, diaries, letters, some photographic material. All of indispensable historical importance. And in recent years we have taken receipt of electronic media also. The collection must move with the times.'

'Of course. I am fully conversant with both tape and film.' I began to talk about my early experience in a film library.

'I'm sure,' he said, as if impatient. He seemed tired again. An odd vacancy entered his stare. In hindsight, I realised how distracted he had seemed from the very first moment we entered the basement.

'I can't wait to get started,' I said, wanting to regain my momentum, for my enthusiasm to become infectious.

'Yes. Quite,' he said, and then, as if to himself, 'You could become lost in here. Lost.'

Again, I worried for my new employer's state of mind. Amassing a hoard of intimate confessions, photos, films and depraved objects seemed, and not for the first time that morning, utterly absurd to me and I fought to suppress a smile. And to think the Director had the audacity to warn me of becoming too close to this bizarre antiquity, while it was he who now gently rocked back and forth beside me, perhaps in awe of this massive tribute to the erotic he so carefully guarded.

Only when I asked him from where the material originated did he snap out of his trance and become alert again. All the material of the collection, he explained, was purchased on behalf of the museum, or donated, by a wide and well-established network of agents, antique dealers and private collectors; all members of the exclusive society who were patrons of the collection. In time, I would meet most of them. I humoured him with nods and smiles and gentle frowns of concentration, indulging a brief moment of superiority after seeing him diminished by the brief show of vulnerability. But no sooner had I begun to enjoy my new confidence than I experienced the most intense and unusual sensation, both physical and mental and emotional. I suddenly found myself unable to move or speak or hear a word of the Director's commentary.

We had come to be standing in a space between the office and the archive when I noticed a black door fixed into the painted brickwork of the basement wall, partially exposed between several packing crates. Or rather, I felt that the door noticed me. As if struck by a sudden, subterranean draught, chilled through earth and stone, I began to shiver and clasped my hands to my arms. Cold air, moving like the brush of wintry hands, goosed my skin from ankle to scalp. Again, my suit and accessories and underthings felt especially thin. I became certain my skirt had blown upward and that my nipples had exposed themselves through my flimsy blouse, like insolent and wayward indentations. It would explain the icy presence I felt against my breasts and then my panties. An uninvited intrusion between my shivering thighs, a rough hand drawn across my nipples to set them tingling. Then a sharp, yet intangible prod of air against my anus that forced me to gasp.

Slapping one hand down against the front of my skirt, I suddenly regained composure and took a quick step out of the draught. And yet, when I looked down, my skirt was undisturbed and in its place; the hem fell to my calves and my chest was still concealed by the double-breasted jacket. The exposure and intrusion was all imagined.

I nearly collided with the Director's wheelchair. Before I could apologise and use my reason to lay the blame for these strange sensations at the door of an old building and how it played on my heightened imagination, I heard laughter. And not from the Director. It issued from behind the black, wooden door. Mirth filled with an unpleasant glee, as if some practical joke had met a successful conclusion.

'What is it, my dear?' the Director asked. 'Canada?'

'The door, sir. What is behind that door?'

'Nothing,' he said, at once, clearly unsettled by the surprise and fear in my eyes. He cleared his throat. 'I believe it was once a coal cellar. I hoped to use it as storage, but a surveyor warned me against the idea. A problem with damp. A tributary of the river runs close here. We keep it locked. It is vitally important it remains so. Some of our papers are quite frail with age.'

'Of course,' I said, feeling more foolish than afraid. 'It should be sealed,' I added, without thinking, still shaken by the cold.

It was only a draught. Of course. One of those strange air currents that snakes beneath old London town, combining with my heightened sensitivity to the dark nature of this museum to give me a fright. Nothing more. Eagerly, I followed the Director back to the elevator and upstairs to his office. No more was said of the little black door and I tried not to think of the impending hours I would spend down here, working so close to it, alone. And until I reached the ground floor, my flesh tingled from where it had been touched by the draft.

I would begin a three-month probationary period at the Doctor Solomon Neretva collection once the notice period for my current job had expired. After leaving the premises in Farringdon, I took a taxi straight to Bond Street, fingering my credit card all the way. Never again, I swore, would I feel cheap and insubstantial under the Director's scrutiny or in the presence of the collection. In anticipation of the new salary, I was determined to make my attire worthy of rivalling anything they had preserved behind glass.

But how was I ever to know there was nothing innocent about this impulsive desire of mine to improve my appearance? That it was the first evidence of my succumbing to the powerful influence of the collection? Little did I know, but a great and ancient force had set in motion a change in me that would soon render me unrecognisable.

3

The Women in his Life – Wife and Maid

Written Statement. Submitted January 2003. Archive number 8969. Following items also submitted: two latex masks; two pairs of high-heeled sandals; two pairs of boots – one knee-length, one thigh-length; two corsets; two used pairs of fully fashioned, seamed stockings; one maid's uniform; one long silk gown; one leather collar; one Victorian mouth gag; one antique wheelchair with wrist, arm, waist, leg and ankle straps; one cane; one horse whip; one cat-o'-nine-tails; one pair of steel cuffs; one large latex penis.

Under the tartan blanket, pulled up to his chin, Sir is naked from the waist down. His arms, legs and waist are belted by leather straps into the wheelchair. Just a quick tug of the blanket, and I could leave him in the middle of this park, blushing and stuttering with cock and balls on display. Although he remains terrified of exposure as I push him through the park, detection is unlikely unless I wish it; I am careful in the way I secure his bonds and cover his disgraceful state of undress. But it is good that he remains wary of me because then my entertainment is unimpeded by his obstinacy, and my power over him is complete because he can think of nothing but me, and all those things I may choose to do to him, at any time outdoors, in this public place where couples lounge about, young men play football and the joggers huff and sweat past us.

His wife is pleased with this arrangement: in fact, she encourages me.

Last week I left him on the shore of the Serpentine for an hour. Under the blanket he was trouserless. Sitting alone he attracted attention; an elderly couple stopped to talk with him, and three dogs all paused to sniff at the blanket. But usually he is safe from prying eyes as I push him along the paths and into the little cafés, because most people look away from the disabled out of consideration. Only the children stare. 'What's wrong with the man in the wheelchair?' I have heard them ask embarrassed parents, before the inquiry is silenced by an adult with an early lesson in discretion. But the true answer to their question is simple: Sir is in the wheelchair because I put him there, and he cannot get out of the wheelchair unless I unbuckle the straps about his waist, thighs, calves, forearms and biceps. There is nothing wrong with him physically; any physician would consider him able bodied and in good shape for a man of fifty. His problems lie elsewhere.

The chair was a present from Madam to her husband. She made the purchase shortly after she and I acquired that wonderful facial treatment from the women's institute of Mayfair, of which she is a member. The chair was bought from an auction when an old asylum for the criminally insane was closed in East London. And now it is my employer's only method of transport outside of his house in Belgravia. Neighbours and friends think it is a tragedy, 'a dreadful shame', that such a tall and fit man should have been struck down by this debilitating condition of the nerves when so young. His wife and I nod our heads in sympathy and thank them for their consideration. We smile to ourselves when their backs are turned.

'Here will do fine,' I say, and park his chair beside a bench facing the Serpentine. As a tree provides shade, I take my black silk parasol down and tuck it into the pocket on the back of his chair, where the rubber things were once kept when the chair was hospital property. My complexion is white as milk and I want to keep it that way. And Madam will never leave the house unless the clouds cover the wretched sun.

'You're not going to leave me today, Alice?' he asks in a timid voice.

I adjust my little black hat and veil. 'Depends.' Then I check my make-up in a compact: it is immaculate. I smile and watch my features move from the usual dollish mask, but only for a while before the muscle and tendons in my perfect face are compelled to contract back to the usual, stern expression. I was once considered pretty, but with the new method I am imperious.

Two young men in suits look at me as they pass. One of them smiles. I wither the oafish leer from his face with a look he has not seen since boyhood, in fairy-tale picture books where witches eat children. But what an elegant couple we must make: well-groomed, handsome Sir, stiffly arranged in his chair, with his beautiful young maid in the black livery and shiny boots, ever attentive at his side.

'Depends on what, Alice?'

'Depends on whether you displease me, Sir.'

He swallows. 'You must tell me. If I do something wrong, I assure you it is accidental.'

I clench my little gloved hands. Holding the tip of my tongue between my teeth, I close my eyes to let the feeling pass. I speak softly to him. 'Perhaps. But we tire of your ingratitude. It shows itself in almost imperceptible ways, Sir. It is a burden on your wife. You have such needs, Sir.'

'I don't see how. I can do much more for myself than you can imagine.'

Slowly, I cross my legs and watch him from the corner of my eye. Unable to control himself, Sir looks down at my black stockings and boots before I arrange my long dress to cover everything but my high heels and the uppers of my feet, shod in tight leather. 'No, Sir. You are wrong. We are not lacking in the faculty of imagination. We are well aware of what you are still capable of, Sir. And for this reason, it has been regrettable but necessary to remove even more of your privileges.'

'But this has gone on for far too long. I am better. The doctor said so. She said I had responded to the treatment well. That I was making excellent progress.'

'Your doctor does not supervise you twenty-four hours a day, Sir. Your wife and I are far more intimate with your . . . predilections, Sir. Did you not notice how upset your wife was this morning? At breakfast, she couldn't bear the sight of you.'

He is getting exasperated and red in the face. 'Whatever have I done this time? Haven't I suffered enough?'

'She notices how you still slip, Sir. And this is not about your suffering, Sir. This is all a matter of your rehabilitation. Your condition has been worsening, unchecked, for many years. We must be sure you are recovering, before we can progress to the next stage. And Madam has her doubts about the treatment's efficiency.'

'But I have changed. I swear to you!'

'Do not raise your voice to me, Sir!'

'Sorry. Sorry, Alice.'

'You should be. You're a big old Silly Billy. Getting yourself all excited and agitated. What will people think of you? And, as well you know, Sir, Silly Billys can quickly become Billy-No-Mates when they get left all on their own in the park.'

'No. Not that. You go too far, Alice. I beg of you, not that.'

'Then let's have no more of this silliness, Sir. Or that wretched self-pity. It is unbecoming of a gentleman. I only meant to mention to you that your wife was upset over an incident she observed yesterday with your physical therapist. It reminded Madam of your past, Sir. How you made her suffer, Sir. And she is a very caring, understanding woman, Sir. You should not test her so. It is she who has suffered enough.'

'But what did I do this time?'

'It wasn't so much what you did or said, but the way you looked at your therapist.'

'Preposterous –'

'Your tone, Sir! I will not remind you again.'

'Forgive me.'

I sigh. 'You are crafty, Sir. But we are not fools and we are not to be trifled with. We were both in the room when the therapist treated you, and you humiliated us with your behaviour. Peeking into that white dress-coat as it parted over her chest. Perhaps

46

even trying to inhale the scent that rose from her perfumed breasts.'

'No, Alice.'

'And how you watched her legs as she moved around the table. Did you think her legs pretty? Mmm? In those white stockings and pretty court shoes? You wanted to touch them, didn't you?'

'Never. I swear. I was merely being friendly. And grateful. She's very attentive.'

'Friendly, ha! Grateful? You fool no one but yourself, Sir. Were you being friendly to those tarts you used to meet at the Hilton? While your wife played bridge, or anxiously waited for you to return home, only to have you enter the bedroom in the early hours reeking of drink and other women? Was it gratitude in the casinos and bars and on golf trips, when you stuck yourself into the waitresses and call girls and air hostesses?'

'That is all in the past. I'm over it. I swear. I am a changed man. Reformed. Devoted to my wife.'

I turn to him and silence his protestations with a look that makes him flinch. 'We have decided it is best if the blonde girl does not continue your physical therapy. We will find a more suitable therapist.'

His voice is tight with frustration and sarcasm. 'As you wish, Alice.'

Smiling, I remove the long black glove from my right hand. The skin is ghostly, the nails dark red and shiny. 'Oh, look at that, Sir. Isn't she pretty. That girl who is walking our way.'

'Where? I don't see her.' Sir follows my eyes to the willowy redhead who drifts through the trees, her long skirt parting to show a naked, shapely leg, freckled on the calf. 'Oh, her. All right, I suppose.'

Deftly, I slip my bare hand beneath the tartan blanket. Sir gasps when my white fingers crawl over his thighs and then grip his erection. His cock is magnificent – thick and long with the softest sheath of skin to cover it – and it has been appreciated by many women in his life. But, for the last ten years of his marriage, his wife has rarely seen it. 'Just "all right", Sir? Are you quite sure?'

Red in the face, his brow moist, he swallows but cannot look me in the eye or think of anything to say. Gently I begin to caress it up and down while it contracts in the palm of my soft hand. 'Aren't her breasts wonderful? Firm and white with pinky nipples, I bet. Oh how you'd like to play with those, Sir. And her sweet, sweet sex. I can almost smell it. Can you? Through her silky white panties. Your mouth down there, Sir. In her softest most secret part. We know how you liked to eat the young, pretty things between the legs. Don't forget we've seen the photos. And with this one, right in the park, you'd lick her through the silk and then tear the panties aside to get your big, wolfy tongue up inside her. Yum, yum. Eat her all up, Sir. Kiss her toes and legs and feet. Lap her sex. Hold her slim young waist with your strong hands and –'

'Stop! I beg you.'

'Pull her on and off your big cock, Sir. Shake her about like a dolly while your thick cock is shoved inside her. It would hurt her, thrill her, give her so much pleasure. All at the same time. Does that sound nice, mmm? Well, is that what you were thinking?' Speeding up the motion of my hand, I throttle and shake that hardness in my palm until his body rises up in the chair and pulls against the leather straps.

'Yes. Yes. Yes. I want her.'

'Oh yes, Sir. You do. And what a slut she would be for you.'

48

'Yes, yes. She'd love my cock.'

'I think she'd lick it and suck it.'

'That's right. She's a slutty tease and she wants my cock!'

'She'd just stuff it inside her.'

'Oh, oh yes, Alice.'

'Like the pretty blonde therapist. Is she a slut too?'

'I know it.'

'The way she rubbed your body and sneaked little peaks at the towel around your waist? Maybe she heard about your reputation? About your tremendous cock? About how you used to get through at least three little tarts like her every week? Leave them exhausted and satisfied and sticky, all over town?'

'Yes!' Under the blanket, his cock chugs its thick soup all over my dainty little hand. I remove it from the blanket and wipe it clean with a handkerchief. Then I mop Sir's brow and resettle his blanket.

When he gathers himself, he looks up at me, his eyes full of guilt. 'But I am getting better, Alice.' There is no strength to his voice now.

I stay silent but show him a superior smile. I rise and then stand behind his chair.

'Aren't I? Much better. It's just that ... the younger ones. It reminds me.'

'You have a long, long way to go, Sir,' I say, and push him away from the bench and then re-open the parasol. 'And we've had quite enough excitement for one morning. Your wife will be expecting you.'

'Well, Alice, was I right?' Madam glides down the staircase toward the hall where I stand with Sir after returning from his walk. She looks magnificent. A ruthless queen one would never wish to displease. Her thick blonde hair is immaculately coiffed on top of her head. Sharp cheekbones and cold green eyes are given prominence by the regal make-up. Lips the colour of a bloody slit in pure flesh. The complexion flawless and pale as a recently dead star of the silver screen. Pearls about her slender neck. Her black dress tight on her thin body, hugging her gentle curves to the knee, from where her slender calves shimmer in flesh nylons to her patent, black, sling-back shoes with the spiky heels. She is so handsome, so cold, so untouchable. And to think she has been so injured by this wretch in the lunatic's big black chair.

Sir looks up at me, his face twitching with nerves, his eyes wide and pleading with me for clemency. 'Alice, for the love of God, do not tell her,' he whispers to me from the side of his dry mouth.

I sigh and shake my head and stare deep into Sir's pale blue eyes. 'Madam, I am afraid that you were right.'

'Alice!' he pleads. I take my eyes from him and look at his wife, who has paused on the stairs and holds a hand against her heart, where the scars are still fresh. She has closed her eyes to gather her wits for a moment. 'The therapist. He could not take his eyes from the slut. I knew it.'

I nod my head. 'Yes, Madam. He confessed. And, to make matters worse, there was another too. In the park. I caught him looking. He was all excited again.'

Resigned to the awful truth, Madam composes herself and offers me a thin, grateful smile. 'Go on, Alice,' she says in a soft voice. 'Tell me everything. I have to know.'

'Alice, no!' Sir wrestles with his bonds and begins to shout.

'Gag that bastard fool!' Madam cries out.

From the back of the chair I retrieve the dummy-gaga-gag she also bought from the auction and try to stuff it into Sir's mouth. I am forced to clamp his nostrils shut with a vicious mouse-trap peg first, because he won't part his teeth. Opening his mouth to gasp for air, his face now purple with apoplexy, I stuff the dummy-gaga-gag into his mouth and then secure its rubber straps behind his head.

Madam takes a deep breath and speaks in a soft, sweet voice. 'Alice. Go on.'

'There was a girl in the park, Madam.'

'And was she young?'

'Yes.'

There is a noticeable hardening of Madam's mouth. 'How did she look?'

'Long hair. Too much leg on display. A good tight bust. Young skin, freckled by the sun. Pretty eyes.'

'Showing herself?'

'Of course.'

'And he was weak for it?'

'I'm afraid to say so. He was like the basest sort of animal. I was afraid he might howl, so I sedated him and brought him home. Down there, Madam, there was so much of it. So much. This blanket will have to be dry-cleaned.'

'So predictable. So damned predictable. Take him to the wall, Alice. Take that bastard down to the wall. We will go back to the start, Alice. My dear, we must start all over again. His progress was mere trickery.'

There are muffled shrieks of protest from behind the dummy-gaga-gag. I wheel Sir to the stair-lift and make ready to take him down to the wall.

Stretched on the rack, Sir's long body is secured in a vertical position so that he faces the wall of his own shame. Wrists and ankles are strapped with black leather into the corners of the vast frame. A royal carpenter and saddle-maker both contributed to its manufacture. On his head is the rubber pig hood with the snout and funny ears. His body is naked. Inside the hot mask, his eyes blink and peer out at the evidence of his past disgraces.

A selection of the many photos taken by hidden cameras, and by the detective Madam hired to record his crimes, have been enlarged and mounted and fixed on to the brick walls of the wine cellar where the racks are empty after she sold his vintage stock to raise money for charity. All my favourite pictures are on the brick wall; I helped pick them out for enlargement.

Sir with his face between the young duchess's legs at Ascot: her polka-dot dress ruffled around her waist; her pretty face hot and red, with long strands of blonde hair stuck to her cheeks; lipstick smudged; the pale colour of her skin tinted by the green of the tent's canvas, where he took her, behind the boxes of champagne; her sheer, nearly-black tights ripped at the gusset to allow that big tongue access to her salty folds of velvet skin; one high heel missing from a tensed foot as a long leg climbs over his back. She gave birth to his second illegitimate son nine months later.

Then we have Sir with the waitress in the toilet stall of the hotel in Edinburgh: her hands against the wall; her face creased as if to cry – all the emotion of one who has tried to resist but cannot – etched on those young features; the white blouse open, the brassiere pulled down, the milky breasts streaked red by the long mauling fingers that have been there; one of her sheer, black hold-up stockings, running with a ladder from the lacy top, down her milky thigh; brown hair in disarray from where it has come undone from all the clips and pins in her bun; those tanned buttocks raised and parted by his big hands, so he can thrust into that little pinky mouth down there; and just a section of his cock – the thick root – as it withdraws, naked and gleaming, from her womb. One of my favourites – he got this one pregnant over a toilet. Madam had to be revived with smelling salts after seeing the picture. I swear the colour has never returned to her cheeks.

Then beside that picture, we have Sir with the air hostess at Heathrow: a Czech girl with dyed-blonde hair, still in uniform. He did not want her to undress. Ankles gripped by his hands and held apart; fingers of one of her hands stuffed inside her shameful, smudged mouth; one white stocking ruffled down to her left foot, the other pulled taut at the top of her right thigh; her blouse torn open; panties thrown to the bed like a wet dish rag; one breast exposed and shiny with his saliva. Sir had no patience, was so eager, never thought of whether she too could have been ovulating. They had to sell the house in St Tropez to raise the hush money this time.

And there are another six portraits of his disgraceful conduct, dotted about this wall. Just a handful of his affairs that were captured on film. The actress with her mouth and throat stuffed with his cock, as though she is a python swallowing a young deer. A call girl in Monte Carlo into whose arse he grinds his swollen rock-meat, her tanned body bent over the red bonnet of an Alfa Romeo Spider. A beauty therapist speared from behind in the shower right here, in his home. His psychotherapy counsellor thrust across the floor of her clinic with her black tights all caught up around her ankles and her glasses skewed on her painted face. A pretty blonde socialite with her bottom mounted on a marble coffee table as he thrusts and makes her squeal. And, finally, the mother of one the girls he impregnated the year before. She's biting on her pearls and her mascara is running as she peers into the mirror behind which Madam had a camera installed. Behind her crouched-over body, his broad torso can be seen, heaving itself, burying the prized organ deep into another friend of his wife. We now know that he had them all – every one of her closest friends over a ten-year period.

And now he must pay again, for another of his indiscretions, down here, before the wall.

Beside the rack, I stand and polish the canes and flails and instruments of torment that Madam has been collecting in secret for years, always knowing she would have a use for them, one day. 'Well, Sir, you only have yourself to blame again. If you could control your cock-a-doodle-doo, Madam wouldn't get so angry.' I have to speak; my excitement is making my body tremble on the high, high heels I can barely balance on, and in the shorter maid dress I always put on for the cellar. Sir gruffly grunts.

And when Madam enters the cellar, I turn and admire her. Shiny thigh boots and black stockings, a naked and close-cropped sex, a leather corset and rubber gloves to her shoulders: she looks dangerous and I know she will be hard with him.

She walks before the rack so her husband can see her body so wonderfully presented in black. Between his legs, his hopeless, treacherous cock moves between his thighs, gradually stiffens and then juts out toward his wife's stomach. She spits on it. 'Pig. Pig fucker,' she says in a low, tense voice, then moves behind the rack so he cannot see her finger the tools.

'We'll use the Marquis with the silver handle first,' she says to me. 'It cuts hard and deep.'

More of the muffled sounds come from out of the piggy-wiggy mask. He knows what's coming. This will be the worst flogging he's had in a long time.

I hand the long black cane to Madam and stand back, out of her way. Four times she whips it through the warm air and nods her approval at the hissy sounds it makes, as if there is a serpent in the cellar with us, eager to bite into flesh. On the rack, Sir's body tenses. Muscles define themselves on his shoulders and down his spine. His buttocks clench. Then he takes big, deep breaths in preparation for hell.

Ssthick! Ssthick! Ssthick! Ssthick! Ssthick!

Madam steps back and takes a breath. Across her husband's white buttocks, five red lines rise, inflamed. On his shoulders his head roams and circles. There is a gargle from his throat.

'Pig fucker, hear me! For twenty years I have endured your weaknesses, your habits, your disgrace. And I have tried every conventional tactic a woman has at her disposal to draw you back into my arms, and each time I have failed. But you have never left me. You are unable to leave me. It seems you cannot exist without me. Can't get me out of your head. Why is that, darling, when there have been so many others? So I have no alternative but to reform you the old-fashioned way, the secret way that women of breeding have had at their disposal for centuries. And know this is your last chance, darling. Fail me again and I will use the most sacred method of all to break you so you cannot be fixed. Do not ever underestimate what I can do to you.'

Sssthick! Sssthick! Sssthick! Ssshick! Sssthick!

I replace the Marquis when Madam has delivered these preliminary strokes. Then I hand her the horsewhip with the beaded tails for his back and shoulders. And it is a joy to watch her agility and grace, this former champion of lawn tennis, as she administers this leather fire to her husband's broad back. I have to sit down, I shiver so. Yet my face is flushed, so hot and stifled I feel. Between my legs too, there is warmth and such sensations that I fear I will climax if so much as a finger was to touch my tender lips. Oh, how he writhes in his bonds, so muscular yet so helpless. Tied down like a crazed, mad stallion, while two pretty handlers break his spirit; working a lather out of his chomping mouth; scorching his hide with crops and brands.

And she works her husband until the struggling and pulling and tugging and grunting slows down, until he hangs slumped on the rack with his arms stretched to their fullest extent. Cane, flail, then the long whip to nick between the red lines. 'See to him,' she says to me, when her work is done.

I throw a bucket of cold water across his smouldering back, tug the mask off his bright red head and then douse his face too with a sponge. All of his hair is wet against his scalp with sweat. His eyes are closed, but his hips move, gyrate ever so slowly. Madam has turned her back and is refastening two of her garter straps that pinged loose during her onslaught. I look down and see that Sir is pushing his truncheon of a cock against my stomach. Even now, this sweating beast cannot be tamed. I kneel down to adjust his ankle cuffs and stare at it. 'Madam. Come quickly. Look at this. Has it ever been so hard?'

It takes even her breath away. She also kneels before the quivering cock. 'It is for me?' she whispers.

'No one else. It was your firm hand that excited him so.'

'He is turning.'

'Soon all he will crave will be your touch, hard or soft.'

She smiles. 'I know it, Alice. I know this. I and only I will have the last of this. For the rest of its days and its usefulness I shall have it.' Then she stops smiling. 'And those who have been guilty of theft will pay. I have made so many of them pay, Alice.'

'Yes, Madam, you have.'

'But tomorrow night, Alice. At the party, it will be Lady Magenta's turn. She who claimed him so many times.'

My breath catches in my throat. 'At last, Madam. At last.'

Eyes wide, Madam wets her pretty lips and pushes her face forward. She opens her mouth wide. Her flicking tongue teases and tickles the thick strawberry head of her husband's cock. Lips embrace the tip and take it deep inside the dainty mouth. Her jaw almost locks, it is so big for her. Sir begins to push his groin, desperate for more of this rarely offered and precisely targeted pleasure, but Madam withdraws her mouth just as he is about to come. She stands up and slaps her husband's face twice and hard. 'Glove him tonight, Alice. And lock him down. He will not empty this vessel until I decide on its relief. And tomorrow, when we meet his beloved slut at the party, he will wear the tongue suppressant and the callipers, so Lady Magenta can see what has befallen the fine, handsome man she fucked so recklessly in my bed. She will feel pity, not desire. But we will not pity her. Not for a second when we separate her from the chattering herd.'

At the head of the table in the dining room, Sir sits in his wheelchair. I have undone the straps on his arms so that he may use his plastic cutlery to eat. Stiff and wincing in his seat, after the flogging endured before the wall of shame, even the motion of fork to mouth gives him discomfort somewhere on his back.

Across the table from my chair, Madam sits with her chin poised and spine straight. By candlelight she has an eerie, wraithlike beauty. And, as usual, after I have served Madam and Sir, Madam bids me to sit opposite her, within reach of her slender legs. The two of us talk throughout the meal, but Sir is forbidden to speak at the dining table.

'And what will you wear to the party tomorrow night, Madam?'

'Something simple and elegant in black, with something very tight underneath. I must look my best for Magenta.'

'And she will be astonished by your transformation.'

Madam smiles and shows her teeth. 'Thank you, dear. And you are right, she will soon discover I am not the woman I once was. And what delights do you have in store for us tomorrow night?'

'I thought my latex suit appropriate.'

'Indeed yes. It will show you are not to be trifled with. That vile Spencer-Smythe will not dare to touch your bottom again.'

'I hope not,' I say, my voice low. 'For his sake.'

Madam pouts her lips and her eyes develop an intensity I know so well. Beneath the table I feel her foot, high heel removed, snaking around my calf. Slowly, its silky presence moves between my knees. Adjusting my chair, I move forward. She lights a cigarette; her eyes not once moving from my own.

Sir looks at each of us and then continues to chew more slowly than before. Widening my knees, I invite her slippery foot further inside my skirt. Sighing, I close my eyes when her painted toes brush my inner thighs, above my stocking tops, before they tickle my sex. My panties are made from a fine gauze that is soon stuck to my lips.

Sir looks uncomfortable. He is aroused and frustrated; he knows what is going on under the table, but cannot see down there.

Both pushing my bottom forward and moving it around in my seat, I make her pretty toes rub my sex harder. Everything: lips, clit, stroke it all, Madam.

'Stop watching. Eat your food!' she snaps at her husband, who flinches, then recommences with pushing the remnants of his meal around the china plate.

'We can eat dessert later,' she whispers to me. 'In bed after I have finished with you.'

'Oh yes, Madam.

'I've felt your eyes on me all day, yearning.'

I blush.

'I liked it,' she says, her voice faint. 'And now I cannot wait. Right now, my dear, I must have you.'

'Let's go,' I murmur, with my head back, as her toes gently rub the little piece of me that electrifies the rest of me. I want to tear my uniform off, to thrust my legs so much wider apart so she can get to me, with anything she chooses.

After her foot is withdrawn from my skirt, it takes me a moment to gather myself. Madam replaces her shoe and then stands behind Sir. 'I'll take daddy up,' she says, smiling down at his red face.

Covered by his silk dressing gown, Sir's body is fully secured in the chair. Even the neck brace has been used to hold his head still. The black rubber ball gag stuffed between his jaws will prevent us from hearing anything but his exquisite panting. Along his arms,

59

around his middle and down to his feet, the leather cuffs are belted tight, keeping his hands and ankles apart and his posture straight. Only his eyes can move. They flit from side to side as he tries to see all of what Madam and I are doing to each other. Madam has positioned his chair at the foot of the canopy bed in the master bedroom, so he can view all that she wishes.

Our painted and shiny faces are buried between each other's thighs – our faces are prepared with the new method and we are never seen outside our rooms any other way now. Lying on our sides we pleasure each other with our lapping, smearing and sucking mouths, using our hands to stroke each other's bodies at the same time; stroking the back of seamed thighs and caressing pale buttocks with an intensity matched by the ardour of our feeding mouths. Our eyes are mostly closed in rapture, but occasionally I open my eyes and peer between Madam's legs to look at Sir, down there in his chair. His face is red. His staring at the bed is unblinking, unbroken. Fingers whiten on the armrests of the chair. Rising from the warm, pheromonal crevice between his thighs, his long and thick cock makes itself indiscreet by elevating his silk gown as if there is a clenching fist down there. Shame he cannot touch himself, for he knows we will take no pity on him, and he has not been relieved since early this morning in the park. He must learn to curb his appetite. He must suffer the pangs and sweats and frustrations of abstinence while he is rehabilitated. And this suffering – the constant cycle of arousal and punishment – is far from over. He has much to pay for, and much to change in himself.

Over the last three months, since we started his treatment, Madam and I have also visited each of the women in Madam's circle who have shared her husband's favours in the last twenty years. We flogged every name from his treacherous mouth, down in the cellar. And these ladies of leisure will never forget the day when Madam and I came to pay our respects. Just the thought of their tearful faces and shredded clothes makes me so shamefully wet that I make Madam's face especially glossy tonight. And tomorrow, Madam's revenge will be complete, when Lady Magenta will have the pleasure of our company.

Crying out, our long bodies shuddering from the contractions and tremors we have induced in each other with teeth, lips and tongues, we climax together, as we have done so many times. Madam's scarlet claws sink into the soft flesh at the back of my thighs, creasing my pure nylon stockings. I squeeze her bottom cheeks and press her sex hard against my mewling mouth to stifle the desperate profanities I utter.

Then, laughing wildly like schoolgirls who have sneaked a bottle of gin into our dormitory at boarding school, we fall together against the pillows and cushions. Kissing, sliding our tongues together and whispering dirty promises to each other, we have all but forgotten the trembling figure moored at the foot of the bed in that imprisoning chair.

'I have a surprise for you,' Madam says to me, smiling. 'A reward, if you like. Working so hard does not give you much of a life besides your service to us. And I know you are a girl with strong appetites.'

'You make me blush, Madam.'

'Well, I remember how you used to enjoy hunting down those young, sensitive things on your days off. And crushing them. But daddy's treatment of late has been so demanding, and I can't possibly cope on my own.'

'You needn't explain, Madam. My labours here offer many rewards I could never find elsewhere.'

'But still, every so often you must –' she presses her lips against my ear '– be penetrated. We all must, dear.'

I roll my eyes and sigh. 'Sometimes I crave it, Madam.'

'Then I have something for you.' She leans over the edge of the bed and rummages in her bedside cabinet, before retrieving a large fleshy, rubbery object. Under closer inspection, I can see it is a lifelike penis, and one that looks curiously familiar; long, with a generous girth.

I wet my lips and reach out with a finger to touch its pinky tip. I giggle. 'It even feels like one.'

Kneeling beside me, Madam straps the thick cock around her hips and then strokes its length with her cool, white fingers. 'I have cultivated something of an affectation for these beautiful things.' She briefly looks over her shoulder and stares accusingly at the immobile figure in the chair, before turning her attention back to me. 'This one may look familiar to you, my dear. I had it made from a plaster cast of my husband's cock especially for the final stage of my revenge.'

'So now it is you, and only you, who controls his cock and its replica too. Genius, Madam. Genius.' Pushing my bottom forward, I slip both of my legs around Madam's waist. Smiling at me, she nudges the fat head of her cock against my sex, but holds back from penetrating me. I begin to moan from the pleasing but infuriating sense of anticipation that blends with frustration. Increasing my pleasure and my need to be ruthlessly used, Madam leans over my body and seizes my breasts, so soft and slippery beneath their sheer cups. She then pinches and tweaks my nipples, knowing how I like her to be hard with them.

Rolling my head on the pillow, feeling myself rise again towards my peak, Madam finally, but slowly, pushes the cock through me. Choking on the pleasurable pain of being stretched so wide, and with the anticipation of being completely filled with this magnificent length – as I have seen it put to use in so many of the photos taken of Sir and his sluts – I claw the black silk sheets that make our fair skin seem so pale.

With three quarters of that frighteningly convincing replica stuffed inside me, Madam takes my feet and places them on her shoulders, kissing and licking my silky insteps. Sliding her hands down the outside of my legs, her hands grip behind my knees. Crying out, I await the deeper, faster thrusts.

And they come hard in an even rhythm, every stroke culminating in a circular grinding of her pubis against my clitoris. Making deep, grunting sounds from behind my sternum that seem to fill the entire room, I writhe and twist as my lady plumbs me. My every thought and feeling is focused on the sensation produced by that tremendous shaft that wets my eyes with tears. Above me, I see her haughty, cruel but beautiful face, so tight with concentration, as she impales her maid with such skill and enthusiasm.

'Fuck me! Fuck me!' I demand of her and begin to claw at her forearms until she is forced to trap my wrists against the bed.

'Are you a slut too?' she whispers through teeth clamped shut.

'Oh yes,' I declare proudly and unashamedly.

'A slut like the others. The others he did this to?'

'Yes, Madam. Yes.'

'Is it the cock that makes a woman a slut? That turns a wife from her husband? A mother from her children?'

'Yes! Yes! Yes!' And when I think of Sir's large cock in the palm of my hand this morning, and then Madam's ruby lips suckling its thick head in the cellar, I am overwhelmed by the most intense pleasure that seems to quake and thrill me to the very depths of my womb. And she keeps me in this state – twisting and crying out with delight – by pumping and grinding me, pumping and grinding me up against the headboard. It is as if she shares the actual physical sensation, the bestial exaltation and the momentary transcendence of a man thrusting himself deeply and wildly into his own pretty, young girl with a long, damp body so fragrant in sheer underwear and black seamed nylons. I nearly pass out.

I wrap my arms around her delicate shoulders as she collapses against me. Making a gentle lambish, coughing sound, and seeing her eyelids flutter, I realise that she too has climaxed. 'You came,' I whisper.

She nods. 'I had it designed to give me pleasure too. The harder I penetrated you, the greater my arousal.' She gives me an evil, irresistible smile and her green eyes open. Raising her voice, she says, 'And I can never remember experiencing so great a pleasure with a man, my dear.'

There is a perceptible stiffening of the body within its restraints in the asylum wheelchair.

'I wanted to test it on you, my dear. You, who have always been so loyal to me. Before I use it to master

Magenta tomorrow night. To remind her she is a slut and whore.'

'Darling! How long has it been?' cries Magenta, as she moves toward Madam with her arms open wide. Shimmering in red, from shoulder straps to ankles, her dress fits her body like snakeskin. As is her way, Magenta's tanned cleavage is both framed and exaggerated by the low-cut gown. She and Madam kiss each other on the cheeks and then Magenta steps back, flashing her Hollywood teeth and unnaturally thick red lips. 'You look wonderful, darling. Absolutely ravishing.'

Madam offers Magenta a tight, polite smile; little of her face even moves. 'Thank you. And it has been three months since last we met.'

Magenta struggles to maintain her preposterous smile. It has been three months since Madam's investigator photographed Magenta with Sir in a hotel room in Earl's Court. And although Magenta has never been sure whether Madam knew of the affair, she has been concerned about Sir after his sudden retreat from the world, three months ago, following a mysterious but debilitating illness. Calling, making inquiries, sending letters, undeterred by Madam's terse refusals to allow her to visit her sick husband, Magenta only invited us tonight as a pretext to either see Sir or to get some information about him. His old lovers are often determined to find him, but Madam has new methods that are more effective in deterring them.

'Well, it has been far too long. And we're too close to let things slide, dear.' Magenta still smiles, but it is strained now; she is desperate to ease the palpable tension that Madam's beautiful, though icy, presence has introduced to this lavish apartment. 'Let Arthur take your coats. I've had a fabulous Japanese chef, an absolute artist, make the –' Magenta falls silent. The smile sags, then drops. 'You still have Alice, I see.' But she is not looking at me, or Madam anymore. Her nervous, pained face looks past the superior expressions on the beautiful, smooth faces of Madam and her maid. She now confronts the stumbling, invalid spectacle that is her former lover: Sir.

Quickly, she recovers her composure and smiles at the figure that I lead into reception. Steel callipers are fixed to his legs. From ankle to thigh I have made sure they are worn outside his trousers. And because he cannot bend his legs he is forced to balance and move with the aid of two walking sticks. 'My, you are looking –' Magenta clears her throat '– as dapper as ever this evening.' The smile must be aching on her face now; her horror is barely submerged.

Sir nods and tries to greet her, but only a liquescent and unintelligible sound drips from his mouth. Before we left the house in Belgravia, the last addition I made to his appearance tonight was the rubber cheek implants that make talking difficult and slobbering a certainty if he even tries to speak. Madam wanted Sir to make a striking impression on his girlfriend and, to our delight, he has done so.

Eyes gleaming, chin raised in triumph, Madam leads our little party into the main throng of assembled guests. Following her, I hold Sir's elbow and guide him through. And, for a long and uncomfortable moment, there is complete silence among the beautiful people. The glamorous are in shock. They heard Sir was ill – something to do with his nerves – but to see him so infirm: no one was expecting that. And yet, his wife has never looked so good – where has the timid, pale and pretty waif gone that the handsome playboy married and deceived so many times? And how did she come to look so elegant, so untouchable, so flawless? How can a complexion become so smooth, so glossy and radiant? It is as if she has a new skin. A new face!

No one can take their envious, admiring, astonished eyes from us. Two society photographers take pictures of Madam and me. A dozen men are caught staring at me by their wives and partners, who immediately stiffen, tug at elbows, or hiss disapproval into their man's ears. The men are fascinated by my appearance: the tight latex suit; the jacket open to reveal a white rubber shirt and black tie; seamed nylons shining like polished glass from my exposed knees to my pretty feet, mounted on patent stilettos; under my pillbox hat with the short veil, my hair is shiny and pinned up; clinging to my carefully painted face, she shines. Throats are cleared as I walk past. Smiling male eyes are met by dark, ambiguous looks from beneath the smoke of my veil.

The women begin their usual whispering – a rustle of irritation that always spreads across the room from the mouths of the upstaged. Yet we walk past these pinched mouths and scornful eyes with our chins raised and our seams straight. Between us, we lead Sir past his old friends, acquaintances and lovers; we make sure everyone observes the demise of a once handsome, charming and eloquent man. Unable to talk, he grins – oafish, clownish. 'I did a wonderful job, Sir,' I whisper in his ear. 'This is the most humiliating experience of your life. This is what Madam felt like at parties when you were fucking her friends. But what I find most interesting is how, in your moment of total defeat, your cock is so hard.'

Sir swallows and perspires.

'Is it because you can still recall so clearly the sight of my face between your wife's thighs last night? Or is it more than that? Maybe because two cruel and dangerous bitches have taken honour, pride and dignity from a man who has been in control all his life?'

This terrible spectacle we have made of him, this ultimate demonstration of our power and influence over him, excites me so much that I become dizzy. It makes me want to reach out and slap one of these young waiters across the face. Or to guide one of them into a dark place where I can leave bruises on his tender parts and a longing in his heart that will never fade.

Madam is not insensitive either to the exquisite satisfactions of empowerment and revenge. Eyes bright with a sinister glint, and a curious half-smile creeping across her china-doll mouth, she watches and waits for an opportunity to separate Magenta from the chattering herd of these well-heeled exhibitionists. But Magenta avoids Sir and Madam and looks more and more harried, her enthusiasm forced, as the evening progresses.

And when Madam takes her elbow in the award-winning marble and steel kitchen, Magenta is given a fright by the sight of that ghostly, impossibly perfect face at her side, as if Madam had just manifested from out of thin air.

Wary of denying Madam, Magenta agrees to see Madam in private about a matter concerning Sir. Because, of course, Madam can only confide in Magenta, her oldest and dearest friend from school; could not trust another soul with this intimate matter.

Magenta smiles. Certainly. I should have come and seen you earlier tonight, but you know what it's like;

I've had my hands full with the other guests. Let's go up to my room. We won't be disturbed.

Excellent, Madam says. And then Madam gives me a quick look that communicates so much.

After they have climbed the stairs away from the increasingly noisy chatter and clatter in the large living room and on the balcony, and vanished into the upper reaches of the penthouse, I follow in Madam's teetering footsteps, leaving Sir alone by the refreshment table – the most visible spot I could find.

Second door down on the left, I know, is the master bedroom. I look about the landing to make sure no one sees me. Then I press my ear to the closed door of Magenta's bedroom to hear the mutter of lowered voices, before entering, swiftly. I close the door behind me. At last, we have her.

'Alice, lock the door,' Madam says to me, from where she sits on the vast bed, beside the puzzled and now nervous host of the party.

'You said you had something to tell me in private. Why is Alice here? Why does the door need to be locked?'

Smiling, Madam tucks a lock of hair behind the handsome socialite's ear. 'Alice, please show Magenta the gift we have for her.'

'A gift is not necessary, darling. I must return to my guests.' Magenta stands up.

'Stay where you are,' Madam commands in a voice that would have stopped the most delinquent school-girl in her tracks. 'I am not finished with you.'

Magenta sits back down on the bed, barely breathing.

Madam calms herself and then smiles again. 'You really shouldn't worry. We are merely returning something to you that, until recently, gave you so much pleasure.'

Magenta is pale; she looks a little sick. 'I really don't understand what it is you are trying to do.'

I pass the long rectangular box to Madam who places it neatly on her lap. It looks like a velvety jewellery box, only it is longer and deeper. 'Now, my dear old friend,' Madam says. 'This is something you took from me without asking.' Madam fingers the case with her slender fingers, the nails painted a dark indigo colour, her two thumbs about to snap open the lid. 'And it was something you used in the morning, the afternoon and in the evening. In fact, you could never get enough of it. You liked to put it in your mouth. Even rub it all over your face. That is, when you became really excited.' It is an effort for Magenta to swallow the lump in her throat. Madam speaks in a softer, sweeter tone. 'You were fond of taking it deep in your cunt.'

'Stop! Stop it! You're crazy. Both of you!'

Madam clutches Magenta's arm, just above the wrist. 'And eventually you even craved it in your arse, my dear.'

'Enough of this madness!'

'Hard and deep in a way that none of the other sluts could tolerate. I was impressed the first time I watched the film of the time you met my husband at the Ritz, after the fundraiser at the Dorchester Ballroom. However did you manage to take this –' Madam snaps open the case '– for one whole hour, so deep inside your tight arse, my dear old friend?'

Now Magenta's hands are on her face, fingers spread wide on her cheeks. Her mouth is open. She does not blink. Just stares down and into the box.

'And you haven't been able to stop thinking about it, have you, since those liaisons came to such a sudden halt? When my husband found himself af-

70

flicted with something quite severe that he never saw coming.'

Magenta shakes her head with disbelief, but she is still transfixed by the sight of the contents of the case in Madam's lap.

'But Alice and I have brought it back to you, because we want you to enjoy it again.' Madam turns her face to me and smiles. 'Alice, please help me out of my dress.'

Skirt around my waist and legs open, I relax on the bed, propped up by my elbows. Looking down with satisfaction, I feast on the sight of Magenta's expensively styled head rummaging between my thighs. Her heavily painted eyes are closed in concentration as she attends to another task we have set her. 'Mmm, that's good. Right there. I like that,' I say, to encourage this circular rubbing of her thick lips around my clit, as I replay in my memory the outright and outrageous submission of Lady Magenta that Madam and I have just accomplished.

Firstly, her shimmery red gown was torn away by Madam, ripped down and across her breasts. 'What are you doing? My dress!' Seized by the hair in Madam's hard little fist, the taller, fuller-figured woman was then forced to bend over, to stare at Madam's pencil-thin heels and nylon-sheer legs, while I tied the host's ankles and wrists together with tights I took from her own drawers. 'Stop this. Stop this now. This is ridiculous. I have guests. The party,' she said, in a low, tense voice, wary of raising an alarm.

'The party's over for you, slut,' Madam said.

'Stop pulling may hair,' she cried out. 'It hurts! You think I'm the only one he slept with behind your back? Stop scratching me!'

'I have seen to the others. But your betrayal was worst of all. I've saved my visit to you until last. And I intend to savour every single moment of it. I think you will too. Now lick my arse.'

'Never. Stop it. Get off!' But we got her down on her knees; her movement of arm and leg had become so restricted with those tight lycra and nylon restraints, so expertly tied by myself. 'I won't, I tell you. Are you mad? Just look at yourself in that mirror to see how ridiculous this is.' And Madam did pause for a moment to survey a full-length view of herself in the dress mirror – corset, seamed nylons, her body pushed up and on to her patent toes by the long, thin heels, and her arrogant face resplendent under this barely visible layer of latex skin. She tossed her head back and spoke through gritted teeth. 'I've never looked better, darling.'

'I think you're right, Madam,' I said, towering over our handsome captive.

'This is sick. Sick, I tell you!' Magenta cried out as Madam moved her white buttocks over the open mouth of her oldest and dearest friend. I held Magenta's head steady and angled her mouth upward.

'Oh come now, my friend. You are not among strangers. Don't be shy. We all know of your fixation with little, illicit back doors. My husband once serviced your tight arse, now you'll service mine. Eat, bitch!'

Magenta's eyes widened and her wide, full mouth was stuffed between pale, smooth buttocks. There was a muffled lapping sound from Magenta. Madam eye's narrowed with pleasure. 'Mmm. See, it's not so hard. And you're very good at it too.' And Madam used Magenta's face as a seat for her naked bottom, until Magenta left all of her lipstick on Madam's precious anus. 'Now the maid. Now you will suck the maid too.'

Magenta panted, 'Never. Never, you spiteful bitch.'

Madam's eyes filled with fury, the temperature of the room plummeting. 'Gag her filthy mouth, my dear,' she said to me. 'Gag it with your arse. Get your skirt up and make this Lady suck the arse of a maid.'

So I rolled my skirt up to my waist and, while Madam held Magenta's face still, I lowered my panties to my stocking tops, pulled my buttocks apart and then settled my most shapely rear on to this titled lady's beautiful face. And did her thick, cosmetically enhanced lips – that big, red, sexual mouth she had enhanced to attract new lovers – feel good pressed against my little rosebud? It was heavenly. And, if I was not mistaken, I do believe the task was performed with rather more enthusiasm than one would have expected, considering our captive's position: stripped down to her silkies in her own bedroom by her guests, bound and then made to suck their girly bottoms, and all as a mere preliminary for far greater indignities. Yes, despite her humiliating position, her thick tongue cleaned my tight skin from sex to tailbone. And she swirled her tongue tip about my little rosy until coldish shivers and stinging sparks ran up and down my spine from neck to coccyx. 'Oh, my,' I cried out. 'Oh my, my, my.'

And as if to make me even more dizzy with a pleasure so acute it almost became toothache, she forced her upper-class tongue right up this maid's bottom. Up into my tight tunnel until my eyes filled with tears.

It was then, after Lady Magenta's arse-eatery aperitif that Madam whipped her French panties off

73

and stuffed those damp silkies into our host's generous mouth. Silenced her with sheer, black, gossamer panties.

Hands in the small of her back, ankles hobbled with nylon, smudged mouth stuffed with underthings, Magenta was then strung across the velvet footstool we found under her dressing table and was held firm there by me as I knelt down and pressed her ankles against the floor. One hand on the back of Magenta's neck, Madam knelt at her side and raised her hand. 'Look at this slut. No panties.' This had surprised me too since we had torn her dress off. She was only wearing a transparent white bra and sheer tights under her gown – flesh tint pantyhose that were shiny from her painted toes to her big, smooth bottom. 'Disgraceful,' I said, frowning with disapproval.

'Slut!' Madam said, and then slapped Magenta's silky arse with her hand. Into the gag, Magenta cried out. Madam was not going to go easy with her: I could tell this by the determination and barely controlled rage all mixed up with sexy excitement on my Madam's shiny face. Slappy, slap, slap, slap! Over and over again, Madam beat that Lady's bottom like a drum until, through her sheer tights, we could see the big pinkish colour on her skin. Liking the way her bottom looked in that glossy nylon I slipped a hand between her thighs and started to rub at her sex. 'She likes it!' Madam said. 'Look, she's panting like a slut.' Getting spanked and being rubbed by my long white fingers through the thin skin of her tights was making Magenta so wet. Down to the base of my fingers, there was a warm and not unpleasant stickiness that I had a good taste of when Madam wasn't looking, in case she thought it was low class of me to lick my fingers. Seeping through her tights was the last of Magenta's resistance and dignity. Fragrant, treacherous juiciness from a slut's eager pussy: some women are just so incorrigible, despite all the airs and graces they put on.

When Madam sat back, breathing hard, her hand tingling from the force of so many slaps delivered against her nemesis's rump, she looked me in the eye and said, 'Wipe the slut's face down with a wet flannel. Then use her face to pleasure yourself, while I acquaint her with an old friend.'

'Yes, Madam,' I said, and so I have come to be resting on the bed with legs apart while my host from high society lavishes her attentive and, dare I say again, most eager mouth on my intimacy after I scrubbed her face with a damp cloth I found in the en-suite bathroom.

Standing behind the kneeling Lady Magenta, Madam fixes her huge, false, but ever so realistic cock around her waist. As I shudder and choke through a wonderfully wrought climax from our slut-captive's hot mouth, Madam smiles like an evil dictator and runs her slender, manicured fingers up and down her veiny prop. 'Alice. Turn her around,' she instructs.

'Yes, Madam.'

When Magenta kneels before Madam, and sees that preposterous, dangerous-looking appendage that roots out from her narrow hips, her eyes go wide with astonishment, shock, and recognition. 'Tonight you will break another of the commandments that preserve the reputation of well-bred ladies. After coveting your neighbour's husband and committing adultery, you will now worship before a false idol.'

'You are mad. You are quite mad,' Magenta whispers, her cheeks flushed with excitement, recklessness, humiliation. And then, to our surprise, she drops her head back on her shoulders, flashes her eyes up at Madam and provocatively wipes her tongue around her lips. 'I'm good with pussy, but you know I just love to suck cock. Especially this one.' And on to Madam's large shaft she attaches her mouth. There is a sharp inhalation from Madam, who is genuinely surprised at this change in Magenta. Madam's cruel eyes remain transfixed by the sight of that wanton face licking and sucking and kissing that great glistening phallus and solid pillar of latex cock-meat. Rocking back and forth on her knees, Magenta then starts to pump her face on and off the shaft, ever widening her jaw, breathing heavily through her nose, until she is swallowing three quarters of Madam's toy. We look at her, amazed. We knew she was a notorious society slut – we had heard such tales – but this flagrant flaunting of such indecent behaviour has taken us both by surprise.

'Alice, my dear. I fear we must go further with this slut.'

'I think you are right, Madam.'

'Alice, get her on her feet. Bind her wrists to her ankles. Make her face the mirror. Show me her arse.'

I comply with Madam's wishes, fetching more tights from Magenta's underwear drawer to bind her wrists to her ankles so she's bent double. And all the time I work, Magenta never ceases in her lavish oral praise of that rubber cock about my Madam's loins.

'Now hold her still, Alice. Hold her shoulders and make her face the mirror.'

Magenta's eyes become frantic. Her lips rise over gritted teeth. 'Go on, then. Do it. Do it. I can take it,' she hissy-whispers at us.

While standing beside Magenta and reaching across her back to hold her shoulders firm, I watch

Madam oil the penis with lubricant. Slowly, she peels Magenta's tights down to the mid-thigh area. One hand on Magenta's hip, one hand to guide that trunk between Magenta's buttocks, Madam presses the swollen head against the captive's tight anal bud.

Magenta inhales and then makes a groaning sound from deep within her chest.

'The slut is ready, Madam. Put it in her,' I say, excited and eager to encourage my mistress at her work.

Eyes wide, the stretched expression on her face that of the fanatic, Madam hisses through pursed lips, and pushes the great apple of phallus inside Magenta's bottom. 'Ah. Ah. Ah.' Pant, pant, pant. Deep breath. 'Ah. Ah. Go on. Go on,' are the sounds and words Magenta makes. And the long, pinkish shaft is seen by my very own eyes to slowly, centimetre by centimetre, disappear inside Magenta's stretched insides. She raises her face and in the mirror, we can see a woman unburdened and released from civilisation. Gargling at the back of her throat, she takes more and more of the baton until Madam's pelvis is squashed into her buttocks.

'How is that, slut? Is that good, bitch? Is this what he did to you in my bed, friend?'

But Magenta cannot speak; her eyes are white moons and her whole body has become rigid to withstand the colossal intrusion in her bottom. She goes on to tiptoes and, as I grip her shoulders to keep her upright, I think how nice her red polished toes look under her tights.

'At school, Magenta: do you remember when we were at school and the teachers used to say that we were inseparable? Joined at the hip?' Madam issues a long and cruel laugh that has ice chimes in it. 'And here we are, so many years later, and nothing has changed besides the roles, my dear. They're reversed, my darling Magenta, who I always looked up to, and forgave. Who walked on me and took, took, took from me, year after year. Bitch! But whose arse is plugged now? And whose once-proud husband is nothing but a battered doll under my heels?'

And as she laughs, Madam begins to withdraw the cock all the way out to the head, and then slide it back in, all the way down to the thick root. And it is as if Magenta is blowing on hot soup, then blowing into her hands to keep them warm on a frosty morning, until she eventually looks as if she is tossing a hot roast potato from one side of her mouth to the other. And when I feel between her legs, and begin to tickle and slide my fingers about her sex-lips, I have never, ever known a woman to be so wet.

If you are ever walking in Hyde Park during the autumn and winter months, you may see an unusual but very elegant group of people walking beside the Serpentine: two women, dressed in chic black suits with matching hose, gloves and high, high heels, and little hats perched upon their sleek hair – as if they are going to a funeral with those sombre, pale, beautiful doll faces beneath their fine veils – and a distinguished-looking gentleman being pushed before them in a wheelchair. Hair going silver, well-groomed moustache, tweed jacket, shirt and tie, a red tartan blanket tucked around his waist to keep his legs warm, this gentleman looks into the middle distance, or at his feet, as if he is wary about meeting anyone's eye, or afraid of drawing attention to himself: a handsome, but sad figure, flanked by two beautiful guardians. Even able-bodied men envy him those companions. And when the two ladies leave him alone for a while, to reflect as he faces the water, they stroll off with arms linked and are often heard whispering and smiling to each other as they walk away with tiny steps in tight skirts. And from the other side of the lake, as their heels strike the path, the sound carries like distant gunfire, all the way across the flat, dark water to the other shore, where the gentleman in the wheelchair waits, patiently, for them to come back to him.

4

Archivist 2

On the red latex sheets of my bed, I arranged my purchases. Everything had been bought compulsively, in a frenzy of excitement. While my credit card was zipping through the tills of the boutiques in Soho, I told myself these purchases were essential – vital to gaining a greater understanding of the collection I had been chosen to curate. This was fieldwork more than a perverse delight in buying erotic clothing.

Ordinarily, I am a woman who finds the output of the entire fashion and beauty industry both expensive and superficial. Until recently I would have considered these garments and accessories something alien, even sinister, belonging to squalid lives and puerile interests. But when my room was thick with the smell of the beach balls, wellington boots and balloons of my youth, while my eyes were transfixed by the lustre of the fabric and the powerful imagery of the garments, even when lying inert and empty upon the bed, my thinking changed. I was beginning to find the scent and texture of rubber superior to that of fur and silk. The night before I ventured out of my apartment to purchase a new wardrobe, in order to better empathise with the narrators I had read in the Neretva archive, I spent sleeping on latex sheets.

Luxuriating in my own heat, and in the illicit smells, my sleep had been filled with dream fragments in which I was beautiful, empowered and sexually daring. I awoke late the following morning, sticky and languid and fragrant. A wholly irrational experience that I must not make a habit of. I would, I decided, in a more sober frame of mind, feeling a trifle foolish, have to ration my use of the new clinging bed-linen. But, at least, I had learnt by first-hand experience something of the allure of latex and of the strange tastes involved with the collection.

And these clothes I had bought would have to be worn in private also, with the curtains closed and the phone off the hook. The ordinary world would only find such things absurd. But I felt tremors in my stomach and delightful icy pinpricks goosing my arms and neck at the very thought of transforming my body through their colours and contours and daring cuts. A deeper understanding of the props of domination and submission that I curated at work would almost certainly result.

So, before my first month at the collection concluded, I found myself owning the kind of clothing I associated with prostitution, or worse: knee- and thigh-boots of rubber with spike heels, two latex dress coats, two strangling miniskirts, a corset that could be worn as outer wear, gloves, authentic nylon stockings, retro lingerie and panty girdles. And as I made these purchases I imagined how slick, streamlined and sexual I would be, all at once. And there was no point in not doing things properly; my habit of wearing little or only natural make-up would not do the outfits justice, so I also indulged in a complete regime of beauty treatments from a pretty young girl in a white smock at an Estée Lauder counter in a

Kensington department store, who instructed me how to create a more dramatic look. For surely this is the point of the Neretva treasure – to transform the flesh of women so they are able to transcend the roles they occupy in real life; to escape routine, drudgery and tradition and to discover in themselves some secret sensuality, some uncharacteristic, unexpected role and deviant purpose, that has the potential to lead a woman into intensity and euphoria and power.

Unable to contain my excitement and curiosity any longer, I stripped out of my trouser suit and plain underwear and carefully applied a lavish makeover to my face, lengthening my eyelashes, thickening the lips and making them glossy, emphasising my cheekbones. Then I slipped my long body into some of the new lingerie and stockings. Black – everything black against my pale flesh. Shimmery under the electric lights. Slippery against my skin. And once the knee-boots had increased my height and re-sculpted the contours of my body, I barely recognised myself in the dress mirror. Immediately I felt the benefits – feminine, sexual, striking. I became giddy with nerves. My sense of recklessness increased as I added another fine skin of black latex over my tight nylon underthings.

And then a moment of panic overwhelmed me and I could hardly breathe while my pulse thumped, making me dizzy. I suddenly wanted to tear the clothes off my body and scrub my face clean, before plunging everything I had just bought deep into a dustbin. The alteration was too great. Would it undermine my intelligence and reason? How would one behave in such outfits? Could I even trust myself under the powerful influence of such garments? It was as if some part of me was issuing a stern warning against imminent self-destruction.

Even though I was alone in my flat so there would be no witnesses, I felt as though the foolish impulse to wear such garments was similar to flicking lit matches at an open box of dry fireworks. After all, what was I to make of the confessions in the archive? They were written by women who wore these same things of latex and nylon and leather. Women obsessed by a sexual will-to-power through transformation of the body and the very face by these shiny materials. Was it all madness? Had I encountered and fallen under the spell of some secretive, sinister cult of fanatics? Perverts? Inventing sophisticated fantasies about transgressive female desire?

This was the academic in me struggling to rationalise. And I was trying too hard, I told myself. Taking on too much all at once. It would take a team of anthropologists and psychoanalysts even to begin to make sense of this secret culture with its props and symbols and brutal rituals. But my doubts and fears were soon eased, then surpassed again, by the stronger and more enduring excitement at having been transformed, at feeling different, and at the prevailing sense of future possibilities while being someone else.

For the remainder of that first evening, I paraded around my apartment in my new clothes, encouraged by the sound of my heels on the floorboards, seduced by the brush and slither of nylon between my thighs, enjoying every one of the gentle discomforts that came from wearing tight boots on my feet and an imprisoning, body-hugging dress of latex.

Soon it became a habit of mine to dress straight after my evening meal in one of my outfits, completed by an ensemble of accessories. I'd never imagined that such pleasures could be experienced from both wearing rubber and sleeping between its clinging grasp. These hot, stifling nights became so addictive. But they lulled me into a false sense of security when I was, in effect, courting great danger. Eventually, I possessed the poorest defences against what would soon befall me. The little became a little bit more until . . .

In my defence, the presence in my working life of so many strangely beautiful but sinister devices of correction, and costumes designed and worn by the empowered and the cruel, not to mention the endless reading of so many illicit confessions in the archive, was bound to make me, or any woman, susceptible to acquiring my own wardrobe so that I too could experience at least something of their thrills. Mysterious women whose love lives were chronicled in the Neretva rooms like ancient queens. But I had unwittingly made myself vulnerable to a greater involvement in the lives of the women I studied. I will admit that. And it was not as though I hadn't been warned by the Director about the power of the collection.

Another warning was not long in coming either – this time from a stranger in the street.

As I left the building on the Tuesday evening of my third week as curator, I noticed the unusual figure of a woman standing, half blended into the iron railings of a building, opposite the Neretva collection. Dressed from head to toe in a black coat, her legs covered by patent boots, wearing dark glasses and a chiffon headscarf, she scrutinised the building, and then me, in a manner I found unnerving. And when she began to follow me through the wintry streets of Farringdon, my fear grew. As I approached the underground station the ominous rapping of her tipped heels on the pavement grew louder. I turned to face her just as a gloved hand seized my elbow.

'Don't put it on your face,' she whispered, her mouth a bright red slit in a delicate, pale face. 'For the love of all that is decent and sane, do not wear her. She's clever. She'll trick you. Don't do her bidding.'

But before I gathered my wits and was able to confront her, the glamorous lunatic was gone, across the road at a clattering canter on high heels, ducking behind a bus before folding away through the rush-hour crowd. Only her powerful musk and the vivid memory of her intense face, too pale in tone and complexion, remained behind with me in the darkening street. And soon, the remnants of her perfume too had faded.

I found the incident alarming and intrusive, but could not bring myself to tell the Director. It left me shaken. Perhaps, I began to think, my association with the museum had put me in danger. Who could say what squalid, depraved and even dangerous individuals might be associated with such a place?

And from the beginning at work, had not the Director been evasive whenever I asked him specific questions about aspects of the collection? Where were the masks manufactured? How did the female confessors acquire them? Were they sold commercially, or made to order? How did they exert such an influence over the wearer? And for whom were these devious recollections and memoirs ultimately collected? What purpose did it all serve?

Surely, the collection could not produce anything but a purely mental stimulation for the Director, as he was paralysed from the waist down. My questions annoyed him. Smiling, he would deftly change the subject of discussion. Or say, 'All in good time, my dear.' If I persisted, he would become irritated and would make himself scarce in his study until his chauffeur arrived in the evening to take him ... where? I don't know where. I never found out where he lived. I knew very little about him. Or, for that matter, any of the people he had so many whispered conversations with on the phone at his desk.

But I needed the job; I was already spending the salary in advance of my first pay cheque. And I had never found myself so intrigued by any material it had been my duty to archive, curate, preserve and display.

My alarm about this place did not stop with the woman in the street and the Director's reticence to share the truth, either. Over the first few weeks, my senses regularly alerted me to the possibility of a hidden presence in the archive that I'd first sensed during the interview. At times, when alone with the collection, I felt as if I was being watched. And maybe it was nothing more than my imagination, but I suspected that the scrutiny originated from an impure and eager source. It was not just the sudden, insistent and untraceable subterranean draughts, down in the basement, that had me starting from my chair, or covering my breasts or buttocks with my arms and hands. I heard voices too. Down there, alone, I heard whispers issuing from nearby. And laughter. It forced me to question my own sanity. 'Who's there? Show yourself!' I even called out, when a twittering or giggling voice slipped out from behind a packing crate, or an open aisle of the library. But my cries were ignored.

Mentioning my fears to the obfuscating Director would have made me sound foolish. I feared he would laugh, or worse, annul my contract. The thought of being jobless in this merciless, expensive city was a far more appalling prospect than enduring the elaborate prank someone appeared to be playing upon me in the basement. So I decided to steel myself against the powerful influences of the collection that were making me susceptible to strange imaginings, suspicions and impulsive purchases of clothes I could never wear outside my apartment.

But, in hindsight, I was already too far gone down the slippery slope. My growing predilection for latex clothing and bed-linen was more cause for alarm than I could ever have imagined. It was the first step towards putting that mask upon my face. And with her in place, I was never the same again.

Like the subjects whose experiences I collated by day, it was only after I fitted one of those eyeless masks to my face that my life changed beyond anything recognisable in my entire experience. It was no longer about just dressing up. I was taken to a new level. A different place. My very character altered. I am not sure how, but my judgement, my natural reticence and caution, my sense of propriety all seemed to become impaired at once.

Can I now defer responsibility like some hoodlum and take no blame for my own actions? Blame an outside influence? Or was the impulse to transgress in such a deviant and cruel manner inside me anyway? Will I ever know for sure?

5

Mother

Written Statement. Submitted January 2003. Archive number 8970. Following items also submitted: one pair of thigh-length leather boots; one black corset; three used pairs of fully fashioned, seamed stockings; one pair leather gloves; one leather pencil skirt; one pair sling-back shoes with six-inch heel; collar and leash; whip; cane; ball gag; rectal plug; cuffs; thirty feet of white rope; fifty Polaroid photographs of two figures bound and arranged with ropes; one Ottoman trunk. Latex mask missing.

Below my bedroom window, my daughter, Miranda, and her boyfriend, Wilbur, were lying in the garden, basking in the afternoon sun. Through the open window I listened to them talk.

'At the risk of sounding ungrateful, I don't think your mother likes me.'

Miranda raised one eyebrow but didn't alter her position on the sun-lounger.

Her boyfriend was clearly uncomfortable, but was compelled to talk about me. I had made it thus. 'I mean, don't get me wrong. I don't want to sound like a jerk. She's been really good putting me up for the weekend.'

'But?' Miranda said, her eyes half-closed in the sunlight.

'I dunno. It's the way she looks at me, or something.'

'Don't sweat it. She doesn't like anyone these days.'

'Why?'

'She's changed. Everyone is scared of her. Especially Dad. People change. I think maybe they get tired of who they were before. It happened a while ago with Mum. She totally changed her wardrobe and everything.'

Wilbur nodded his head. 'She's very glamorous.'

Miranda turned on her side and squinted at Wilbur. 'Are you saying you fancy my mum?'

'No way!' Too quick.

'You do. Yes you do. I've seen you watching her in the kitchen. Always staring at her legs. And you blush whenever she talks to you.'

'Hey. Knock it off. That's not fair. I just wondered what I've done wrong. That's all. What I've done to displease her.' There was pity in his voice – and it was not the first time I'd overheard this tone of his, intent to win my daughter's sympathy. A natural pleader. I pressed my fingernails into the palms of my hands until they hurt.

Miranda turned her face away from Wilbur, who sat cross-legged on the grass beside her feet. As it should be. He slipped buttercups and daisies between her toes. 'Maybe you're worried I might turn out like her,' Miranda said, taking charge. 'Be really cold and uppity and sharp.'

Wilbur smiled and then laughed that charming laugh of his that made me think of twisting things whenever I heard it. 'If you look that beautiful at . . . what, forty-five?'

'Fifty-five.'

'No way.'

'Yes, way.'

'Well, if you're that hot in your fifties, you'll still be seeing plenty of me. Even if you are a ball-breaker.'

A not altogether pleasant smile appeared on Miranda's face. I was reminded of myself; the glimpses I caught of my face as I toyed with something on the floor, in front of bedroom mirrors. 'That's it. I'm telling Dad,' she said and sat up on the sun-lounger. 'He'll throw you out.'

'Hey!' Wilbur caught her by the wrist and pulled her down to the lawn. Wrestled her beneath him and made her giggle by burrowing his mouth into the side of her neck. Muscles defined themselves on his smooth, brown back and tight waist. I sensed a swelling between his legs. But of whom did he think? Having seen and heard enough, I stepped away from the bedroom window. It was time.

'Diane, no. No, I say. We can't do this.'

'Silence!' I said, in a hissy voice. My husband's pathetic cries did nothing but drive me further into a dizzying state of anger and arousal. If he stayed quiet and complied, I often wondered if I would be so tough.

When he tried to pull his wrists away from the cuffs that I held poised and open before his hands, I slapped his face, hard. Tears welled up in his eyes. Emotion moved his facial muscles; anger, self-pity, injured pride. In my stomach, something wonderful happened. Oh, why do you feed me with such exquisite food, I wanted to ask him.

With a snap, the steel cuffs clamped his hairy wrists together. 'Get on your feet.' Not liking my cold eyes and tight, mean mouth one bit, he obeyed at once. Of late, I had proved with a growing frequency that there were many ways I could make him hurt. And I used to be such a good wife.

'No. Please, Diane. Miranda could walk in,' he said in a choked voice.

Shaking my head, I smiled. 'She knows better, Malcolm.' Our daughter knew more than her father could guess. Like her mother, she excelled at manipulation and understood how to tap into her innate power over men. I knew why she had chosen another soft young man as a boyfriend. A handsome, malleable boy with a special kind of weakness that even he barely understood. Every one of her young paramours had been the same. Already, she was practising. Sharpening her claws. And, last month, when I returned from the cruise Malcolm treated me to, I found signs that our daughter had come in here, into my chamber, to try on her mother's beautiful things, to touch her mother's tools. 'Poor Daddy. Poor, poor Daddy,' she would often say, while smiling to herself after I had issued a command and sent Daddy on an errand, or put him to work. Poor Daddy indeed. This simple wretch I married, the father of my own special girl, the provider of this lovely house and fabulous lifestyle, had only just begun to feel the painful sleet of my new icy passions. These changes came to me late in life, but I thank strange gods they came at all.

It was nearly time for dinner so I had to work fast up there in our room that afternoon. I had no patience with dithering. Our young guest was hungry for something food could never satisfy.

Kneeling down, I hobbled my husband's ankles together with leather braces that were connected by a chain. Something I ordered through the mail from an unusual place, because I liked the look of strong, binding leather on his muscular legs. Washing-line cord and then my stockings used to do the trick in the early days, but they lacked the aesthetic I was seeking. And artists must always go through a process of refinement to achieve their vision. Now I had the correct accessories, he was my galley slave. How I once dreamt of being some ruthless bitch queen of the ancient world. Mistress of a long, sleek galley where so much hard man flesh sweated and rippled in the hot sun. Chained to wood below my pretty toes and looking up at my royal, white limbs as they lay composed among the silks and cushions of the bridge. Faces full of longing, of adoration, of terror, afraid to look up, but unable to look away.

This charming, handsome and very rich shit I married would have to do for now. But there would be others. Right before his eyes, I would collect and discard, collect and discard. The pain he felt that afternoon as I clamped his hairy nipples with silver teeth, and the humiliation he suffered as I pushed the greased steel plug into his affluent arse, was nothing compared to the exquisite pain of his impending betrayal.

'Not the gag. No, Diane. When you put it in my mouth, I can't breathe properly.' Is that why your rather delicious cock is pressing against my shin as I unknot its leathery straps, darling? I was tempted to ask, but the time to talk was over; I had plans for the evening. So that was the very last complaint he would make until the following morning when I would let him out.

Tighter than usual I buckled the straps behind his head and pushed the ball into his mouth. I didn't want to hear much more than a whimper that night. The eyes still pleaded, so I sedated him with a stick that made little noise but left plenty of marks.

'Get inside.' I knicked his thighs and buttocks with the cane until he was standing upright in the Ottoman trunk we kept at the foot of the bed. It was one of the gifts he'd bought me in Egypt on our 25th anniversary. But as his gold card had flashed in the eastern sunlight, he'd had no idea his wife intended to use the large container for a purpose other than storing bed-linen. That day in a Cairo market, he had bought his own prison cell.

I placed my hand on top of his head and pushed him down into his box, into the darkness. Smiling, I closed and then padlocked the lid. Immediately, I heard him shuffling about inside, trying to peer through the little chinks in the wicker. It had taken some time to prepare him for this moment.

After withdrawing my favours two months ago, whether I stored him in the trunk at night or permitted him to sleep alongside me, Malcolm suffered the added indignity of watching his attractive wife undress each night. And every morning he would watch me slip my face on before dressing in corsets, nylon stockings and high heels.

'It's not for you. Not now. Not today,' I had told him that very morning, as he again tried to initiate relations by stroking my silky thigh. 'So keep your hands to yourself.' Tortuously, I then slipped my long feet into high-heeled sling-backs and spent an age adjusting the seams of my stockings right before his puppy-dog eyes. He wanted me so desperately; he did everything in his power to keep his hands from his erection.

In the early days after my 'change', as he would always refer to it, he had been so understanding, never daring to criticise or pass snide remarks or harsh words in case he blew it with me for good. No, instead he sympathised, became romantic again. 'It's no big deal. Whenever you're ready, darling,' he would say, while always eyeing the alterations in his 'new' wife's wardrobe – the sheer black underwear, shoes with higher heels, the tight leather pencil skirts, silky blouses, suits, the new hair, the make-up, or whatever it was she was doing with her face. He desired me more than he had for years, possibly even since we'd met, and finding me tantalisingly unobtainable at the same time drove him mad; he was aroused, baffled, frustrated, mine, in training to be servile and he never knew it. Hypnotised by dark seams on shapely calves and taut suspender straps on pale thighs, he acquiesced to my every whim; disempowered himself, gave away his kingdom like some libidinous King Lear. But it could only go on for so long before he erupted, before he could no longer contain his feelings. And in due course, he raised his voice at me and petulant accusations were made about fidelity. It was wonderful. It was then I initiated the next stage and began to punish him. Broke him down with gags and trunks and canes and restraints and harsh, harsh, dirty words. And this morning, when I announced for the first time that he was no longer capable of delivering satisfaction in the marital bed, and that my patience was at an end, he stood wordless before me, trembling and mute, his cock hard at this hint of his seductive wife's powers. He had seen those good friends of his watching me at the golf club, and how there was a marked change in attitude among the younger men at his rugby club whenever I pulled up at the training ground in my new Mercedes. A fast car for a woman only picking up speed with age. He knew how those boys felt. He understood longing.

And this morning, fitting my last suspender clip to my stocking top, I issued him with a list of my requirements for the day – his only day off work.

'Forget it,' he had said in a tense whisper. But there was no other resistance after I calmly slipped my pedicured feet into my new Manolo Blahniks and then took the belt from his jeans and applied it directly to his own back. My word was final; the list was completed in due course, and now he was inside a box. Bitch.

And from inside his little hutch, he peered through the slats and knew I was taking our marriage to another level; that there was going to be yet another change in our relationship that he despised but desired at the same time. And so, in silence, he just watched his wife's shapely bottom and silken legs walk away and go out of the bedroom door. Which she closed behind her on her way down to dinner with Miranda and the guest.

And, shortly after midnight, Wilbur tiptoed right into Mother's trap. Like a trapdoor spider, I pounced in the dark of the hallway on the first floor, so close to his planned destination – my daughter's room. No, young fool, you will not lie with my daughter tonight.

Earlier, he had eaten my food at my dining table. Mother at the head of the table, daughter seated at the side and our guest of honour opposite me, trapped at the bottom of the table by my scrutiny and by the tension and restraint of a formal meal in the house of his girlfriend's mother.

'Where is Daddy?' Miranda had asked.

'Not eating with us tonight,' I replied with a smile that confused young Wilbur. 'He's tied up with one of his hobbies.'

'Not again,' Miranda said, innocently, eating the Mediterranean salad.

And the remainder of the meal passed in relative silence, though I sensed Wilbur tense when I leant over him to collect his dishes. Twice, he dropped his napkin to get a closer look at my shoes: sharp-heeled sandals with spaghetti straps, revealing cherry toenails; flesh nylons thin as cobwebs. And afterwards, while we sipped chilled wine on the patio and watched the purple and gold of the sunset, I felt his eyes on my legs again, on my hard breasts, my cinched waist, my indifferent face. Such liberties he was taking – leering at the hostess while her husband was otherwise engaged, and planning a night of passion with her daughter under her roof. Behind my glossy lips, I had to clench my teeth to restrain my feelings. He would suffer for his indiscipline, be tamed like a prowling animal at the height of its fertility and looking to mate, be corrected like an urchin and thief caught trespassing in a queen's palace.

So I waited for him, up there in the dark. Against a wall in the hallway. Enshrouded by shadow, I waited for battle. And I had dressed for combat: boots with spike heels that clung to my legs all the way up to my stocking tops; a black corset with four suspender straps to each leg; gloves of latex to the elbow; a fresh coating of war paint on a face already made as shiny as the complexion of a porcelain doll by a thin latex mask. I waited among the quiet exhalations of the sleeping house. Concealed by a moonless night. Still as a statue in a hidden museum. Barely breathing. My limbs tensing to pounce on my prey. Eager for the preparation of man-meat. Ready for the kill.

And along the hallway it came. Pausing for a moment by my room, its nostrils flaring once they picked up the scent of the huntress, for I never hunt without perfume. But then this is her territory, the eager beast thought. That is why her fragrance is so strong on this darkened path I sneak along. Nothing more. Proceed to where the princess lies sleeping; her flesh so warm, so white beneath the sheets. I will surprise her, it thought. Will creep to her side and wake the beauty with a kiss before asserting my baser urges. Almost there, past the bathroom door, my trembling paw upon the handle of her chamber; my cock already astir within the cotton folds of my shorts, the only raiment I have worn for this night of seduction.

But the handle was never turned. For a guard had been posted outside the princess's room. A guard who stepped from the shadows and was upon her prey with a swiftness that stopped the breath from leaving his sweet, young lips. Latex hand across his mouth. Shiny fingers bending a thumb into the palm of his left hand, paralysing him with pain. Long, white bitch teeth sunk into his throat. And backwards he was dragged, away from where the princess lay dreaming of long black gowns and adoring eyes. Back down the hallway and into Mother's lair. Door shut.

Silence returned to the hallway outside. His muffled yelp, his scuffling hooves disturbed nothing out there in my kingdom.

'Silence, boy. Stop struggling. Don't make this any harder than it has to be.'

'Mrs Chandler?'

'Who else, boy? Who else can be trusted to protect her daughter's virtue and the sanctity of this home?'

'I, I, I was going to the bathroom. I swear –'

'Liar!' About his wrists the steel cuffs locked with a click. A click that carried into the confines of the Ottoman trunk to wake the resting slave. Canework creaked as my husband adjusted his position to stare from his cage into the moving darkness. 'Turn around. Face me if you dare,' I commanded the young poacher.

My wet lips moved to show stainless teeth no more than a hair's breadth from his own young mouth. He tasted my breath, my lipstick, my scent in his mouth. His tight body trembled against mine. From the cold, or something else? Dropping one hand, my latex fingers closed around his rock-hard shaft as it tented out the cotton of his teenage shorts. 'What's this, boy? Eh? Where was this going? Mmm? What is your game? To abuse my hospitality? To bring your disgusting habits to my clean home?' I squeezed and pulled at that long, thick manhood to extract confession; every drop of remorse and guilt and humiliation.

'Mrs Chandler . . .' Poor Wilbur swallowed. 'Your . . . I mean, what about Miranda's father?'

'Taken care of. No one will disturb us. No one would dare.'

'I can't. I'm your daughter's boyfriend.'

'You're my boy now. You'll follow my rules. In my home my word is final. You have disgraced us all.'

'Sorry. I'm sorry.'

'A word. An empty sentiment. Too late for sorry.'

'What do you want from me?'

'Penance. Respect. Obedience.'

Guiding his hands, I placed them upon my corseted bosom. 'You have been watching these closely. You are obvious. It's embarrassing. Even Miranda has noticed.'

'No.' He stroked my breasts.

'Yes.' His hands slipped down, stretching the chain of the cuffs taut, and stroked my waist.

'We'll get caught.' His voice was barely audible. He swallowed again. Eyelids fluttered against the tips of my long lashes like a butterfly beating its wings in the palm of a hand.

'Doing what, boy?'

And those impatient fingers could not help themselves. They stroked at the front of my panties; that little triangle of see-through gauze that whispered across my shaven sex. I had to close my eyes and steady myself for a moment. Then a finger curled around a suspender strap. Three more fingers slipped inside the top of my left boot and stroked between leather and nylon. A shiver ran up my spine. A cold frost prickled over my scalp. His mouth tried to engage my own for a kiss. Enough.

I pulled away and tugged him behind me by the cock. I led the boy-slut by his disgrace, across the room to the Ottoman trunk. His bare feet found themselves sticking to the rubber sheet I had placed there, in preparation for his slaughter. He looked down at my hand working his cock into the consistency of varnished maple. Twisting his ear, I made him whimper then forced a gag between his lips. Muzzled his dog mouth and pulled the straps tight in his soft hair. He snorted like a pig through the nose so I put him down on all fours, guiding him slowly by the ear and by the hair scrunched in my fist. It felt as if it could tear from the roots at any moment. 'I'll teach you to walk through this house with your bestial meat sticking out. Are you a dog? Some dumb, baffled animal that mounts the female of the species to spread its vile seed? You think I want my heir soiled by such a wretch and its foul excretions?'

But the boy just grunted and snuffled and snorted through his muzzle, no more than a few inches from where my husband lay in the great stillness of horror and suspense, inside a box made for blankets. I kept my livestock close to each other; the old stud and the young stud in their separate pens.

Pushing Wilbur's face into the rubber sheeting, I raised my hand. Then I paused for just a moment to enjoy the cool night air that bathed my pale skin, and I luxuriated in the power that engorged and electrified my whole body. It was the happiest I could ever remember being; the most fulfilled, the most complete.

But this boy-flesh beneath me would have to be skinned and salted and tenderised; there was work to do. So many wicked things I wanted to do all at once before dawn. But I had to steady myself, pace myself, sustain the brevity of this very rare pleasure. One step at a time.

I shoved a boot under his face, so he could smell new rubber. Then I pushed a knee into his ribs to hold his position steady: legs apart, arse uppermost, face down, arms splayed for balance.

My hand fell from a great height. Fingers slightly bent over the palm, the joints and muscles relaxed in my arm, flexible. A swish of glove and then the echo of a wet slap filled the room with sound. Wilbur moaned. I slapped his buttocks harder. He choked back a scream. I slapped him again, and again, and again. I went to a red space inside myself where I wanted to hurt and be hurt and shake about on a giant cock. I came hard. I became wild. I flayed and branded my cattle with a rubber fist. And inside his wooden cage, my husband's breathing was hard and noisy: the heavy air of a captive but excited animal.

'Disgusting little slut. Filthy little pig. Time you were trained. This is not a house of ill repute.' Once my hand tired, I flayed his back and ribs with a leather whip. Burned by a bitch's black hail of stinging leather, his torso turned red and tender and oh so hot in under five minutes. Then I mounted his back and rode him around the bedroom. Using my spike heels for spurs against his thighs I made that bovine-boy salivate on to the rubber sheeting. 'Still hard?' I would whisper down to him, while reaching underneath to find that hard and hairy beastliness suspended in the gloom between his strong thighs. 'Pretty pony want some sugar?' I should have ridden him all the way down to the train station and left his naked body shivering on the platform in payment for his vile and unseemly behaviour under my roof, but I wanted to sustain my own exquisite pleasure by observing the changes in him the next day before Miranda drove him to the station in the evening. 'Time to tether my horsy,' I said, and spiked him flat, face down on the rubber sheets. From one of my secret drawers, I fished out my thin ropes and then arranged then in lengths along the lid of the Ottoman Trunk.

Turning a solitary bedside lamp on, I stood over Wilbur's streaky-bacon back and admired my handi-work. His chest worked heavily as he tried to breath through the muzzle after so much exertion and discomfort. He looked to the side and saw his prostrate body reflected in the long wardrobe mirrors. He closed his eyes and tried to shut out the sight of his humiliation, but found himself unable to resist a look at me in thigh boots, risen to my slender, contoured, magnificence above him. The leather cor-set, gloves, wild hair and cold, damningly beautiful face, and the hands – those gloved hands twisting rope.

He tried to talk, to plead with me, but he could verbally communicate no more effectively than a dog with its master. 'Bad doggies have to be tied up, Wilbur. Naughty doggies with big cocks that sneak around women's bedrooms cannot be trusted. No house is safe with one of them on the loose. They must be collared and put on leashes. They must be trained.'

Right before the Ottoman trunk – with so many apertures in the wicker slats – I practised my knots and rope-work on poor Wilbur. He never knew his feet could touch his fingers behind his back. Or that his wrists could effectively be bound to his ankles while he balanced on his shoulders. And even such a young man creaked and groaned and winced as his limbs were stretched and contorted by evil strings. I exhausted him and then I rested. Peeled my panties off while sitting on the Ottoman trunk. Giggled to myself when I felt the gentle abrasion of a nose sniffing at my buttocks through the wicker – the closest my husband had got to my flesh for months. But I allowed him to inhale me through the bars of his cage and to press against my moist sex from inside his kennel, because he had been so patient, so compliant this evening. And inside the trunk, inside the darkness, he must have known that his torments were only going to increase. Dawn was still a long way off.

Peeling my boots off my legs, I decided to appear more sensual, more feminine for my next usage of Wilbur's body. Bound so tightly, trussed up like a sail on a mast, he could move his fingers but nothing else. But his obvious, strangling discomfort did not lessen his ardour. When I rubbed my hot, silky feet all over his body and face, the top of his magnificent penis glistened with a saline I longed to taste. So I reapplied my cherry lipstick and then moved his immobile body against the trunk. It must have been agony with the ropes cutting into his flesh like that, itching agony. My husband knew that – I had practised through the spring on his larger and more muscular frame. He knew exactly how Wilbur was feeling. But perhaps he had forgotten how soft lips and an eager tongue could feel on his hard cock. So I showed him how good it could be, by taking Wilbur's sex in my mouth. By really working it in and out of my lips, moaning to myself, rubbing it all over my latexy chin, around my heavily painted eyes and lapping up any juice that beaded the tip of his strawberry. And when Wilbur erupted and all of his limbs and muscles strained against the inflexible ropes, I turned my head on its side so that my caged husband could watch me collect and swallow every last dollop of young, virile cream. I sucked him soft; I sucked him dry; I sucked him into stillness. Then I kissed the side of the trunk in the spot where I could see one of my slave-husband's moist eyes.

But I also had other more biological needs.

Once Wilbur had recovered sufficiently to display another hard-on, I staked him out. Tied his feet to the iron legs of the bed and wrists to a cabinet. A perfect star-shape with his ankles on either side of the trunk so my husband could look up between the valley of the younger man's legs and see his bitch-wife's sex lower itself upon the erect root of youth. And so I took my pleasure; rising and falling on that thick meat. Moaning and throwing my head around on my shoulders. Biting my fingers and grinding myself on the first cock other than my husband's that I had enjoyed since before we were married. And neither

Wilbur nor I paid much attention to the rhythmic shaking of the Ottoman trunk, nor to the muffled cries that came out of that padlocked container as I rode Wilbur's groin and raked his belly with my red claws. And the second time, Wilbur lasted a good forty-five minutes inside me. He lasted even longer the third time when I lay beneath him, on the lid of the trunk, directly above my husband's unblinking eyes. I had decided some time before that Malcolm would only truly accept his new status and the change of power in our marriage when he saw a younger man between his wife's legs in their marital chamber. A young man with a collar around his neck, and with a pretty face that I licked and kissed with delight as he came deep in my womb. And I would never have deprived my captive husband of the wonderful sounds Wilbur and I made together. All the 'Fuck me. Fuck me' stuff. All that 'Fuck me with your young, hard cock' stuff. All that 'This is the biggest cock I've ever had inside me' stuff. I didn't pay much attention to the trunk while Wilbur pounded between my legs, but I can remember it becoming curiously silent. Filled with the silence and calm of utter defeat. A tranquillity that lasted until dawn as I slept with the boy-meat chained under the covers, down by my feet where he suckled my toes for the remainder of the night, like a greedy lamb at a teat.

Breakfast the following morning was a quiet, solemn affair. We all ate on the patio. Malcolm and Wilbur needed fresh air; they both seemed so listless and drained, forever yawning. And they took little part in the conversation. Miranda and I talked, gaily. And it was refreshing for the women to talk while the men sat beside us and listened.

6

Archivist 3

'Miss Lisle, allow me to compliment you on your outfit this morning. Very chic.'

I blushed. 'Thank you, director.'

Smiling, he reluctantly removed his eyes from my new boots and wheeled himself away toward his study. These were the boots I had purchased in Soho, and it had been a month before I had the courage to wear them outside of my apartment. At home, I had spent hours getting accustomed to the new height of the thin, sharp heels and the grip of the patent leather on my ankles and feet. Striding up and down before the full-length mirror in my bedroom, I had long adored the startling transformation they worked on my body. Elevated by the spike heels, I noticed the accentuated curves of my lean figure. They also contributed to a refreshing assertiveness in my walk and promoted an irresistible aloofness to my manner.

Seamed black stockings were worn that day, to match the boots as if they would not accept anything less. Cut shorter with a straight fringe, my new hair style complimented both the boots and my recently acquired predilection for heavier make-up. I went for the effect of dark red lips and black eyes in a pale face that seemed to have the effect of momentarily stunning men when they looked at me.

These last two months, for the first time since my teens, I relished the ritual of dressing up in private. This exhilarating loan of another woman's guise. For I always felt, at the start, as if I were in disguise during some curious gender experiment. I was wearing a dangerous woman's clothes and luxuriating in her identity too. And even though I had covered my nylons and most of the boots with a long, silky, black skirt for fear of eliciting unwelcome attention on the journey to work, I was actually wearing my new clothes outside the apartment for the first time. I can't deny it was a thrill when the director noticed.

But the next time he spoke to me that day, he left me confused and irritable. He made me do a foolish thing.

'Oh, Miss Lisle, I almost forgot to tell you that you are free to go home at noon today.'

'That's is very kind, director.' I frowned to prompt him for a reason, but none was forthcoming. At eleven o'clock, however, I took delivery of a case of champagne bottles and several trays of canapés.

Unable to look me in the eye, as I delivered the goods to his office, the director said, in a nonchalant tone, 'The refreshments are for the directors of the board. You may meet them in due course, but today's meeting is not the right time.'

'Oh. I see.'

'Do not feel excluded, my dear. Take advantage of the early finish and enjoy yourself. It's not often the weekend starts so early.'

'Why yes. Thank you. Of course. I only wondered if I could be of some assistance with the refreshments.'

The director cleared his throat. I suspected he looked a trifle uncomfortable. 'No, no, no. That won't be necessary. Next time, perhaps. Even though you are a valuable part of our family, and I will be saying as much at the A.G.M, it will be some time before certain members of the board can reveal themselves to you. I apologise for the subterfuge, but there are matters of privacy to be observed. As well you know.'

But I did not want to go home early. I wanted the meet the most important patrons of this perverse museum. And I had set the afternoon aside to create a display for a new bondage exhibit – recreating the knots, trusses and severe lines I had seen in the Polaroid photos that accompanied one of our latest submissions. I planned a three-dimensional installation encased in a large glass cube. The confession, the photos and the artefact had arrived together the previous day by courier delivery. At once, I had found the story and its props to be unsettling, but compelling stuff. These cruel fibres had recently been used to restrain and contort the living, writhing body of a young man by his girlfriend's mother – a formidable character who had omitted to return her latex mask. Something that had gotten the director excited after we opened the package; he left the basement immediately to 'make some calls,' as he put it.

But now I was being sent home early like a child. It made me angry with the director. How could I not feel excluded? I was the archivist. All of this secrecy was making me impatient. I mean, we were hardly dealing with secrets that affected national security. This was not cold war espionage; it was merely a perverse collection of artefacts and letters donated by the deviant. Could I not be trusted to meet the board?

107

Petulant, sulky, irrational, I stomped down the stairs of the basement to take my petty revenge. And to satisfy my most long-standing curiosity about the Neretva collection.

Laid out on the palms of my hands, I raised the mask to my face, my head tilted down. While flaccid it was weightless, but I felt a tingling sensation where it touched the base of my fingers. When I had the mask an inch from my face, I imagined that it moved and tried to rise from my hands to cling to my face. Feeling foolish, I lowered my hands to the desk. Glancing around the basement, I again experienced an acute sense of being watched. Convinced I had heard someone breathing behind me, I placed the mask back inside its box and quickly checked the basement over again. No one down there with me. As I had left it, the fire-door to the basement steps was shut and the service elevator was still idle on the ground floor. The director was in his study and there were no security cameras in the basement. Just my nerves.

I shook the feeling off and returned to my desk. Sitting down, I bit my bottom lip and was forced to acknowledge that this was something I was not supposed to be doing. Each mask had to be handled with rubber gloves and could only be worn by one user. On arrival at the museum, they had to be stored inside a sealed, dust-free glass case to await display upstairs in one of the hermetically sealed cabinets. Otherwise they ran the risk of contamination. The director had been very specific about this. I had only put this mask to one side because of its irregularity. It had arrived that morning without any of the usual accompanying paraphernalia: clothing, equipment, a typed or written confession. Alone, in its protective box, I had put it to one side with the intention of later referring it to the director. But soon, I had it in my gloved hands again and found myself staring down at the transparent, glossy underside of the mask. Compelled by curiosity and excited by the thrill of misbehaviour, I just had to try it on. What harm could it do? I was not part of this latex cult, but a scholar attempting to understand its culture. And it appeared to be nothing more than a clear, water-based rubber compound. Like a soft contact lens, but marginally thicker and resistant to tearing. I had little idea of its specific composition and doubted whether it could contain any suspect chemical properties. No, I decided, it was merely a prop; a kind of facial placebo designed to manipulate a change in a woman's behaviour, by virtue of it being worn in a ritualistic manner. Such a change in mood I had already experienced with my fetish wardrobe and erotic underthings; I had felt more seductive, daring, confident when dressed up. This mask was of the same family. Part of the game. An accessory to encourage a woman to adopt a dominant sexual role. Something I was entirely safe from.

Holding my breath, I fitted the mask over my face, aligning by the eye-holes and indentation for the nose. It was extraordinary. The clear film of rubber immediately adhered to my features without a wrinkle. Across my hairline, behind my ears and down my throat, I then smoothed the edges out until they disappeared against my flesh. It's cosmetic qualities were instantly apparent. Peering into my compact, I was astonished to observe that every freckle, blemish and line had vanished. My skin was smooth, shiny, tighter, younger. When I opened my mouth, a tautness spread over my entire face and neck. It's elastic properties would rapidly contract after the flex of any facial muscle in order to draw my face back into a perfect, doll-like mask. Then, under a closer scrutiny, with the aid of my desk lamp, I became aware of the sheen the semi-visible layer of rubber created on my face; similar to the way the skin shines wetly right after the application of moisture, or if a portion of human skin is wrapped in cling-film.

I liked it: the lustre, the tight smoothness of my skin. And I enjoyed the way it made me feel while walking around the basement. Any residual self-consciousness at wearing the boots and heavy make-up vanished. Such thoughts were trifling, ridiculous. I could wear anything and stare any critic down. Even the acquisition of wealth, status, luxury, all the trappings of power was no longer a mystery either. Why, it was all so simple. Life and people were not so mystifying or complicated. Things were much simpler than I had ever suspected. The vagaries of mood, mind and emotion were the real enemies to one's progression, to one's finding purpose, power. For the first time in my life I felt like I understood the true significance of all those seize-the-day clichés, the will-to-power, and every other philosophical and popular jingoism about discovering your potential. Why, it was so easy. Confident, beautiful, assertive, impatient with fools and obstacles, one simply had to stride forward in life. Keep the mind clear and still, and the right thoughts would compose. I could stay one step ahead of the competition – quickly intuit types of intelligence, levels of vulnerability, specific weakness. Then exploit, manipulate and usurp accordingly. Life had never seemed so whole; I had never felt so strong, complete, uncomplicated. Overpowering, dominating, humiliating, trampling – all of these wonderful, fruitful pursuits had never seemed so . . . arousing before.

The very suggestion of fully realising my beauty and strength at the expense of others – the raw materials to facilitate my ascendancy – spread a heat beneath my pale skin. A glowing, sensual energy filled my body. I sighed and then laughed aloud at the thought of handsome male faces and strong, muscular backs submitting to my shiny, dangerous feet. I imagined dozens of illicit scenarios all at once. My head filled with a delightful chaos of erotic images: I saw the face of a young man – once proud and confident – blindfolded and kissing the sharp toes of my patent shoes; I saw my gloved hands holding thin canes and black crops and beaded flails, rising and then cutting down across the backs of respectable men; I imagined a dozen grey-haired men trailing me – their ice-queen – like they were a pack of broken wolves, steel chains stretched from their collars to my hands, their naked legs made pretty patterns in the snow; from all directions I then saw long, rigid cocks stretching toward my marble, superior flesh; in my mind strong, grown men cried, they begged to penetrate me; I broke them all.

Enough!

Reaching for my throat, my fingers then scrabbled to find and peel the edge of the rubber from the base of my neck. My heart thumped. Panic raised the tiny hairs on my back and neck. I felt dizzy, faint. Too much stimulation. Something blocked my throat. I desperately needed fresh air. No, cold water. Exercise. I must strip naked until my body and mind sweated this psychotic fever from my brain.

Dropping the latex face into its box, I slumped into my chair, breathing heavily. The acute anxiety

111

passed. As the last sparks of the strange electricity drained from my body, my thoughts slowed. The perverse visions were gone and hard to recall. My pulse quietened. As if I had been momentarily possessed, the evil spirit had now left me. Left me as I was before. Myself. Was this me: indecisive, anxious, irritable, paranoid, emotional?

Already, part of me missed the woman in the mask who had watched me with cold eyes from my make-up mirror. I had gotten carried away, that was all. Did not know how to regulate the stimulation, to savour the tremendous energy and clarity and strength contained in that thin face. Instinctively, my fingers reached out for the box containing the discarded mask.

I stopped myself. No, not here. This place was too exposed. I needed a safer environment. Sealing the mask inside its box, I then slipped the container inside my bag and tidied my desk. It was nearly noon. I rushed from the basement, ran through the museum to the front door and only paused to call out a hasty farewell in the direction of the director's study before leaving that accursed place.

7

Doctor

Written Statement. Submitted January 2003. Archive number 8971. Following items also submitted: four latex masks; four pairs of high-heeled sandals; four corsets; four used pairs of fully-fashioned, seamed stockings; one nurse's uniform; one school mistresse's uniform; one female riding outfit; chariot bridles and reins; cane; steel cuffs; leather collars; one chastity sheath, universal size.

1. Consultation

'Step on the scales, Mr Pillo ... Ah, exactly what I thought. At least fifteen kilos overweight. Smoke?'

'Er, trying to give up, actually.'

'How many per day?'

'Mmm. Five-ish. Maybe a few more at the weekend.'

'Now, now, Mr Pillo. All smokers are liars. I asked how many.'

'I don't count.'

'How many, Mr Pillo? I have a long list of patients to see today and I do not have time to play games. How many?'

'Twenty. Sometimes more.'

'Good. Please stop perspiring. Exercise?'

'Well, I've been a bit slack lately, because –'

'Nothing at all. I see.'

'Well, that's not strictly true. But I've been very busy lately.'

'Do you exercise vigorously for one hour, five times per week?'

'Good lord, no.'

'Nothing, then. No exercise and a twenty-a-day man. Drink?'

'Socially.'

'How social are you? Units, please.'

'Hard to say.'

'No it is not hard to say. But it is hard to acknowledge indiscipline, grossness, poor grooming. Bad habits, Mr Pillo. You are a big fleshy bag of bad habits. Step behind the screen and remove your clothes. I can see we will have to be thorough today.'

'Yes, doctor.'

'Your resting pulse is one hundred and twenty. When was the last time you ate a raw vegetable, Mr Pillo?'

Mr Pillo clears his throat uncomfortably.

'How does your wife feel about your weight? Your smoking? The drinking? The breathlessness? Lack of energy? The lethargy? The inertia? The inability to perform?'

'Pardon?'

'Come, come now, Mr Pillo. Do you expect me to believe you are able to conduct an adequate physical relationship with a healthy woman with healthy needs?'

'My wife left me, if you must know. She, she . . . left me.'

'Understandable, given your decline.'

'Now, look here! I am not prepared to discuss –'

'No! You look here. Never raise your voice in my surgery or you will have to find yourself another doctor. I am not in the habit of repeating myself, nor do I tell people what they want to hear. I will not tolerate dishonest people. I expect total candour from my patients and in return they must be prepared to receive the same.'

'I'm sorry. But you have a most unfortunate manner.'

'I am a specialist, Mr Pillo. A specialist to whom you were referred by your GP because of your chest pains, breathlessness, depression, despair, the break-up of your miserable marriage, and your pitiful life in general. I will not temper my attitude nor my words when I encounter such a serious case.'

'Serious? What do you mean? Am I going to –'

'Enough, Mr Pillo. You are not beyond all hope.'

'Thank God. Thank you, doctor.'

'I do have a specific expertise in matters of most concern for the male in mid-life. For his mental health and physical constitution. I have an excellent record for reversing the characteristic decline which you suffer. My practices are considered unconventional, but effective. Relatively new in this country, but in Switzerland and Austria my methods are commonplace because they are highly effective. I do, however, have my doubts about your suitability for the treatment. The programme involves total commitment. Complete discretion. It is a long and exhausting course of treatment, Mr Pillo. In the short term the cure is considered worse than the decline it is designed to correct.'

'No pain, no gain.'

'Mr Pillo, this is not just about bowls of bran, or running your fat body around the park in a tracksuit with the price tag still attached. It is not simply a matter of reducing your smoking and drinking. It is not about reduction. There are no half measures, Mr Pillo. No packet of crisps and a smoke after a salad. No delusions are permissible. Personal correction is addressed in a more severe matter than you could imagine. The treatment relies on considerable levels of discomfort. We accept nothing but total rehabilitation.'

'I'm willing to give it a go, doctor.'

'There is no question of giving it a go, Mr Pillo. There is no question of trying. Because merely trying suggests that there is a chance of failure. There is no possibility of failure, Mr Pillo. Failure will leave you in a worse condition than the pathetic state you are currently in. No one fails, Mr Pillo. No one is allowed to fail. You begin the treatment and you complete the course with full marks. You will never be the same again.'

'Guaranteed?'

'Absolutely.'

'I want to be better doctor. I've forgotten what it is like to feel well. To be happy. I'll try anything.'

'So you are prepared for humiliation?'

'I, I don't understand.'

'Are you ready to relinquish all control and independence of thought and will? To be utterly reduced? To start again, Mr Pillo? Physically, emotionally, mentally? Most men would find that humiliating. To succumb, Mr Pillo, to a woman who knows what is best for you. A doctor who can make you a new man. Sober, fit, clean, disciplined, orderly. Who can give you standards again. Meticulous, rigid standards.'

'Yes. I can, yes.'

'Can you be humble, Mr Pillo? Can you regain control by first losing all control, Mr Pillo?'

'I'll try.'

'Not good enough. Get dressed. Get out.'

'Yes, I can. Whatever you want. I can and I will. Please. I want to show my wife I have changed.'

'All right. You start now. Put your cigarettes on my desk on your way out. Ask the nurse for the starter pack before you leave the building. Sign the contract and surrender your credit card. We will be in touch.'

2. Assessment

'On Tuesday afternoon at exactly eleven p.m., you smoked a Benson and Hedges middle tar cigarette. Before you went to bed that day, also at a later time than specified in your manual, you smoked another seven.'

'How, how did you know?'

'Since then you have smoked regularly in secret and also strayed from the prescribed diet. You have lost no weight and your blood is full of carbon monoxide.'

'How –'

'Do not interrupt me. You have only taken two walks through the park that were terminated prematurely with visits to public houses. You have failed to visit the swimming baths and your gym membership has not been used once.'

'You're spying on me.'

'Four late nights, four late starts. Sixteen hours on the Internet looking at a Japanese "upskirt" web page in only seven days.'

'This is preposterous. There is a matter of privacy!'

'Read the contract. Section five, paragraph three. You have failed the first week of your treatment. The easiest week. The very beginning, Mr Pillo. You are a disgrace. You lack commitment, application, motivation and any modicum of self discipline. We cannot waste another minute, Mr Pillo. We must act immediately. On your behalf we have taken the liberty of signing you off work for one month's compassionate leave.'

'What!'

'All of your engagements have been cancelled. A bag has been prepared for you. Though, where we're sending you, you will need little but the will to survive. Nurse Belteen, please come in and collect Mr Pillo.'

3. Vigorous Exercise

'I can't. I can't go any further. I feel sick. I'm dizzy. Oh God, I think I'm having a heart attack.'

The leather straps of the harness cut into his fleshy shoulders whenever he takes up the slack of the reigns. We've barely moved half a mile through the forest. He has fallen on to his hands and knees to pant and wheeze in the mud. He is pathetic and I tell him so. I give him a minute to catch his breath. Then I raise the horse whip and crack it close to his left ear. Mr Pillo shrieks and staggers to his feet. Blinded by blinkers and by panic and exhaustion, he tries to tear at the blindfold with his podgy fingers. Another crack of the whip against the knuckles of his right hand makes him wail and clutch the burning hand against his stomach. The carriage begins to move along the dirt track; a few creaking inches at first and then I lash him into a trot to get us back to the stable.

He is hungry and tired and weak. For twelve days he has eaten nothing but oatmeal from a metal pail, and an occasional orange that the stable girl delivers to his pen each morning at five a.m., and then again at six p.m. If he is alive on Sunday, I may move him indoors.

When we near the stables beside the manor house, he breaks into a canter; desperate to dip his hot, pink, shiny head in the water trough. The first sign of progress I have seen this week; Mr Pillo can now pull a grown woman in a buggy for exactly one mile on rough terrain.

While he slurps and gulps at the water in the trough, Sabrina, the stable girl, takes off his harness and blinkers. Then she wipes his naked, wet back down with a cloth. She pulls his head out of the trough by his hair to wash his face and to clean the mud from his fat legs. I admire the way her short, muscular body handles the livestock here: efficient, businesslike, indifferent. The men see no pity in her eyes, no love, no compassion, but I believe they see admiration in her eyes when they begin to respond, instinctively, to her commands and to the very sound of her boots striking the cobbles of the stable yard. Mr Pillo is particularly responsive to her boots. Tight leather riding boots that hug her legs to the knee. Boots he cleans and polishes after being retired to his pen for the night. Each evening, he is permitted to remove them from her hot, athletic legs. A strictly controlled act of intimacy. Kneeling, naked in the straw, his body warm and soporific from exhaustion and the effects of fresh air, while she sits on a small wooden stool and extends a leg, ending in a soiled boot, towards his lap. Gently, he works the tight leather sheath from her calf, ankle, foot. Removes the sock and then rubs the pale feet with the red toenails. When the foot is removed from his shaky hands, it will be another twenty-four hours until he is permitted to touch a member of staff. He is locked in for the night with his oatmeal and a pair of boots he must attentively restore to their gleaming splendour. And in his stable he must rest his body and mind for the ardours of the following day.

At night, some of them disturb us. They rage from nicotine and alcohol withdrawal. Some of them weep, some demand lawyers or policemen. We do not like to be disturbed at night. We are hard with them after the sun goes down. Only once so far have we been forced to discipline Mr Pillo after lights-out. On his first night here, I went to him wearing a long black dress and high heels. I went to him with a beautiful face that shone with an unnatural lustre. I went to him with a riding crop and his buttocks still bear the marks. I silenced him.

There are rules here at the Manor. Simple, strict rules for men to follow. All of our boys learn to carry the weight of a woman; learn to worship at their feet; learn complete respect and total subservience to their betters. When they leave us, they love us and they fear us. Desire and terror – this is what boys need.

4. Morning Constitutional

Each morning of the first week in the stables, the men are milked. Like cattle who need a farmer to nurture and care for them, they are relieved of tension by a trained female handler. Self pleasure is monitored. All of our pupils must learn to curb their appetites. Beastliness is strictly forbidden at the Manor.

At five a.m., Sabrina enters Mr Pillo's pen and uses her long crop to poke at the bulk of his body under the straw. He wakes with a shriek and sits up. Blinking his eyes, it is as if he has awoken from a nightmare only to enter another, far worse than the first.

Sabrina towers over Mr Pillo. He looks at her shiny boots that go all the way up to her knees. She wears tight black riding trousers that give her bottom an appealing shape. Her white shirt is open at the sternum and he can see a glimpse of her white brassiere. It is very important that all of our entrants are made continually aware of the power of female beauty. But they must learn that touching is prohibited, and leering and all unseemly traits of their gender are unacceptable. They learn the rules of abstinence and courtship all over again.

Sabrina places her milking stool on the cement floor before the heaps of straw that Mr Pillo sleeps under. 'Assume the position, Mr Pillo.'

On all fours, eyes staring straight ahead, Mr Pillo crouches beside the milking stool. Sabrina pulls the latex gloves over her small, pretty hands. She sits down and reaches between Mr Pillo's thighs from the side. Embracing the stiff organ with one hand she begins to gently massage and then squeeze the muscle. 'That's it. Don't hold back.' She places a ceramic bowl under the genitals and points the phallus at the centre of the bowl. Mr Pillo moans and begins to weep too. Not an uncharacteristic reaction, we find. Gratitude, blended with an overwhelming stimulation from a warm, rubbery hand that only the day before functioned as a tool of restraint and pain. They learn to feel pleasure on our terms. When we desire it.

Mr Pillo is not long in climaxing. Sabrina's small knees press against his ribs. He can smell her perfume; the most wonderful and overpowering scent of a woman in this place of straw and dung and tears and sweat and wet cement. And that skilled hand with the scarlet nails is pulling and pumping and then tickling the end of his teat, looking to draw and extract the cream. She purrs and whispers to the naked fat man on hands and knees. 'That's it, baby. That is good, no? Give me your milk, baby. Give your milk to Sabrina.' And Mr Pillo calls out, he moans and his skin shivers. 'Yes, ma'am. Yes, ma'am,' he cries, and releases so much of the pressure inside him. Out it comes in long, warm dollops into the little bowl.

Then the stool is put away and the bowl is cleaned under a farmyard tap and Mr Pillo is washed. Smashed by the cold water from the high pressure hose. Jumping and spluttering, he is doused, drenched and drowned in freezing water that gets warmer by increments, until it is hot and steaming and lathering his body with hot liquid loveliness in the stable yard. Sabrina dries him with a towel and powders his body too. Then he sits quietly and silently, as he must, while she shaves him with her pretty hands. Milked, washed, powdered, shaved and fed from a bucket by a beautiful French stable girl – Mr Pillo will never forget his time in the stable. When he leaves the Manor, he will have learnt to start each day with the regime dictated to him by Sabrina. He will rise early and make himself fresh and clean. And he will save all of his vigour and vitality for the woman he will serve and protect and honour. Save himself for when she has a need for that part of him.

5. Classroom Dummy

'I would like the whole class to turn around and look at the dummy in the corner.'

Madam Kraka instructs her pupils to look at the lone figure facing the wall at the rear of the classroom. They have all stood in that place too and felt a dozen eyes burn into their backs. Each of them has worn the dummy hat after failing the rigorous daily tests on grooming, hygiene, domestic skills and etiquette. It usually takes two weeks of intensive study and vigorous correction until all of these fundamentals become instinctive.

'Now, boys, I would like you to tell me why the dummy is standing in the corner. Yes, Mr Spindle?'

Mr Spindle stands up and bows to Madam Kraka. 'Madam, Mr Pillo forgot to say that the ears and nose must be groomed of hair every morning following the shave and preceding the application of the skincare regime.'

'Correct, Mr Spindle. You may come to the front of the classroom and kiss my shoes.'

Mr Spindle walks to where Madam Kraka sits on the high stool. He kneels before her feet and gently kisses the pointy toe of her stiletto. 'Good boy,' she says. 'Return to your seat. Who else can tell the class about the errors the dummy made during the spoken test?' Every hand in the class is raised. 'Yes, Mr Simper?'

Mr Simper stands behind his desk and bows to Madam Kraka. 'Madam, Mr Pillo forgot to mention his underwear and socks must be changed every day. And that he must floss and use mouthwash. Gargle too.'

'That is correct, Mr Simper. Come and kiss my shoe. Mr Pillo is a big, fat, smelly dummy. He cannot look after himself, or feed himself. He has no self-respect. Mr Cavendish, give me four of the essential reasons why Mr Pillo is so useless.'

Mr Cavendish stands and bows to Madam Kraka. 'Madam, Mr Pillo is guilty of self-pity. Mr Pillo is guilty of deferring responsibility. Mr Pillo is guilty of uncleanliness in body and mind. Mr Pillo is undisciplined, Madam.'

'Good boy. Come down here and kiss my shoe. You may also stroke my leg once.' All around the classroom, there are sharp intakes of breath. Mr Cavendish is top of the class; he completes the course in three days. His rewards are increasing; his punishments are lessening. After kissing Madam Kraka's pointy shoe, he slowly strokes the streamlined calf of her right leg, tracing his fingers down the seam at the back of her leg. His face goes red and he swallows.

Whereas Mr Pillo has a long way to go. 'Mr Pillo, approach the front of the classroom. Now, slide your trousers and underwear down to your knees. Bend over my desk with your feet approximately twelve inches apart. Look at your classmates and make your confession.'

Red-faced Mr Pillo clears his throat while bent over Madam Kraka's desk. 'Classmates, I have failed again. I am a dirty man. I am slow to learn. I have bad habits. But I want to improve, classmates. I would be very grateful, Madam, if you would help to correct my slovenliness and ignorance.' This is the middle of Mr Pillo's third week at the Manor with us. And he has been a dummy and spoken this mantra every day so far in the classroom. At night, in his solitary cell, he sleeps on his stomach with ointment shining on his buttocks.

'My pleasure, Mr Pillo the dummy.' Madam Kraka selects a cane from the rack beside the blackboard. All of her pupils tense when she selects the long walnut stick. Graceful, her smooth face raised, she stands beside Mr Pillo's buttocks and raises the cane. 'Ten strokes for the dummy. Boys, please count me in.'

'One!' The cane slices the air and cuts into Mr Pillo's buttocks. His mouth opens and his eyes go white. Both of his hands rub against the desk.

'Two!' One of his legs rises from the ground and pedals at the air. Madam Kraka's face is whiter than usual; her eyes wide and fierce; she pauses to flatten a stray lock of hair against her bun.

'Three!' All the boys hear the sound of garden shears cutting through a rose stem. Tears make Mr Pillo's face wet.

'Four!'

6. Swedish Enema

Stretched along the surgical gurney, his wrists and ankles cuffed tight to the four corners, Mr Pillo lies face down and listens to the sound of Consultant Kristianson's shoes on the green, tiled floor. He catches glimpses of her long legs as she teeters about the clinic to prepare his daily cleansing. He can see the tight hem of her white uniform, shiny white stockings and the white high heels. He wets his lips and is afraid to look for too long in case she turns around and catches him.

Cleansing occurs every day during the third week of his stay at the Manor. This morning he was severely caned by Madam Kraka. So much so, Consultant Kristianson was forced to collect him from the schoolroom and to wheel him down to the clinic in a bath-chair. All the other boys were giggling.

Whirring, the pump on the steel trolley beside the gurney is activated. Consultant Kristianson unravels the length of rubber hosing and prepares the evacuation chamber. She snaps rubber gloves over her hands. Although blonde and very beautiful, the bespectacled Consultant Kristianson is perhaps the most feared woman at the Manor. And not without good reason. Her work has a penetrative quality that is most clinical.

First, there is the chilly smear of salve around the rim of the rectum. This brings forth the customary sigh from Mr Pillo. Then steel surgical forceps part his buttocks. All of his muscles in his thighs and stomach tense and he pulls against the gurney cuffs. Consultant Kristianson moves a chair with a high back to the side of the gurney. Crossing her legs she allows the hem of her uniform to rise to the top of her stockings. They shimmer under the surgical ceiling lamps. Peering through his armpit, his head on one side, Mr Pillo comforts himself in this moment of tremendous vulnerability with a marvellous view up her skirt. When she leans forward and adjusts her position, in order to insert the funnel, he can see that she is wearing only stockings under her uniform. Her skin is brown and her sex is closely trimmed. Mr Pillo cannot contain his excitement – it grows along his belly. But then there is a rush of saline through the inner chambers of his bowels. Gurgling and scouring through his innards, the pressure of the fluid produces a great discomfort. Stroking his back, Consultant Kristianson, asks him to be quiet and to relax as best he can. She does not want to use a gag but she will if he makes more of this unnecessary fuss.

Once the saline is extracted, the natural yoghurt with live bio-cultures is pumped deep to restore balance to his unpleasant canals. Though on the verge of a scream, Mr Pillo manages to restrain himself, so the gag is not applied. Progress. Rinsed with another dose of saline, Mr Pillo's enema session is concluded. He is released from the gurney. Leading him by the hand, Consultant Kristianson takes Mr Pillo to the wall rack, where the Svenke Leather Posture Regime is to be conducted.

Lashed secure so he hangs from the steel bars, the consultant begins to turn the levers to stretch Mr Pillo's spine. As he is pulled to his natural height, as every muscle and tendon in his limbs is slowly stretched to its furthest extreme, the consultant casually unbuttons her uniform dress coat, peels her stockings down her legs and then ties her hair back in preparation for the water cure. Pointing at its object of desire, Mr Pillo's full erection directs its blind gaze at the consultant as she slips into her white swim suit. He apologises for his indiscretion, for his disgraceful conduct.

'Did I not milk you this morning?' Consultant Kristianson asks.

'Yes, ma'am.'

'I see. The rigours of exercise, diet and fresh air are already vorking vonders on your constitution. No nicotine, alcohol, caffeine or refined sugars in your system any more, Mr Pillo. See how vell you can do vithout the artificial stimulants?'

'Yes, ma'am.'

'You have responded vell to the course of your treatment vith me. You have learnt not to scream also.' The consultant snaps a fresh glove over her right hand and then secures a medical waste bag over the erect penis of Mr Pillo. 'But I vould prefer it if you vould concentrate on the vater treatment. Ve cannot have this in the ice pool and sauna, Mr Pillo.'

'No, ma'am.'

Looking into his eyes, her painted lips parted no more than a centimetre from his mouth, Consultant Kristianson holds Pillo's penis and, as is her style, applies a vigorous and effective force. When she places the tip of her tongue on the edge of her front teeth and rubs the thickest part of Mr Pillo's erection with two fingers and a thumb, he fills the bag.

7. Bedtime Story

Mr Pillo is exhausted. Eyelids are heavy. Muscles hurt more than he can ever remember them hurting. From his buttocks to his shoulders he is striped like a tiger with welts from Madam Kraka's cane. His insides are fatigued by Consultant Kristianson's rigorous alimentary hygiene.

Today he graduated from the classroom with full marks in both oral and written examinations. His uniform has been exchanged for a plain, black three-piece suit. Nude like a baby in the stable, then uniformed like a schoolboy for his education, and now dressed like an adult in preparation for his impending release after the 'finishing' process, we were forced to completely reform Mr Pillo. We have purified his body with exercise, enema, stretching, basic food stuffs, fresh air, pain and discipline. Losing weight, shedding addictions and developing a new shape even after three weeks, Mr Pillo's preliminary treatment is on schedule for a successful completion. But, of course, this is only the start. His mental and physical education will continue long after he leaves the Manor. He does not know this yet, so I have come to inform him.

The door to his bare room opens and I enter. While I am in residence at the Manor, the pupils refer to me as the 'Governess'. In the past they have known me as a consultant, but at the Manor they soon realise that I adopt a more fitting role. 'Congratulations, Mr Pillo. I hear you passed the theoretical course with full marks.'

Without moving his body, Mr Pillo looks at me. He remains silent, too tired to be confused at this unexpected visitation. Nothing would surprise him any more, but his respect for the staff and his unquestioning obedience has become instinctive. Whatever we do is for his benefit; no matter how much it hurts. He understands this now.

'You are about to enter your final week, Mr Pillo. I am pleased with you despite your slow progress in the classroom. But I never doubted Madam Kraka's ability to instruct. No one has ever failed her class. In your final week, I may make visits to your room in order to prepare you for what will follow your stay at the Manor. You may have guessed now that your treatment at the Manor is but the start.'

His eyes widen, moving from my spike-heeled boots, up my tight, black gown to my face, so ghostly, so pale, so cruel in the dim light. 'The start?' he says.

I nod. 'You will be monitored each week for three months. Providing our assessments at the clinic are encouraging, assessment will move to a monthly basis, then to a quarterly arrangement, until, finally, there will be rigorous annual checks on your health and lifestyle and behaviour.' I laugh at the expression on his face. 'Do not look so alarmed, Mr Pillo. As long as you never smoke again, never venture beyond your ideal weight, never drink more than twenty units of alcohol a week, manage to maintain the clinic's regime of grooming and cleanliness, and refrain from self-pleasure, you have nothing to worry about.'

He swallows. 'If I don't? If I weaken?'

I smile. 'You will be visited.'

His whole body seems to deflate on the bed. 'I see.'

'But there are benefits, Mr Pillo. You will live longer and enjoy better health. You will be well groomed and courteous at all times. You will be sober. You will enjoy a more orderly and civilised existence. Women will find you more attractive, more . . . how can I say this? Enthusiastic, and appreciative when you supplement their interests. You will become a closer approximation to what they want.'

Mr Pillo closes his eyes. From my little black case I take the restraint and unfold the straps and buckles. The sound of tinkling steel makes Mr Pillo open his eyes quickly. He flinches. He stares at the device in my hands. 'Yes, Mr Pillo. We cannot risk the possibility of self-pleasure. Besides supervised urination and cleansing, you will not be permitted to touch your genitals for the remainder of your stay at the Manor. And only during these necessary periods will the device be removed. You were milked on a daily basis in the stables, then evacuated by our nurse during school. But, for the last week, there will be no further relief of your unfortunate biological impulse for self-relief, despite the temptations. And there will be many. Lie on your side, please. Hands above your head, feet together.'

Slowly, my cool white fingers raise his balls and cock. Then I fit the black surgical restrainer to his genital area. Immediately, his penis begins to harden, but there is ample space inside the restrainer to glove even an extraordinary erection. 'It will fit comfortably inside your underwear and can be worn against either leg.' I run the straps over the top of his thighs and then lock the device in the small of his back. Then I unbutton my gown down my left leg to the knee.

Mr Pillo watches my boots and legs with fear. My footwear is tight, made from leather, worn to the knee and finished with long, silver heels. Sheer, seamed and pulled tight to the top of my thighs by six garter clips to each leg, my stockings never fail to introduce tension in a room. He looks up at my face. His expression pleads.

'Our culture is ridden with temptation, Mr Pillo. And you must learn to resist its temptations, to live with frustration, to save yourself for the women who decide to pleasure themselves, or procreate, with you. For them you will always be at your best.'

Now, as is often the case, being in the presence of a debased, naked, chastised and utterly submissive creature of my own devising has begun to stimulate me. I remove my gown and untie my hair. Perhaps it is this tangible evidence of my own superiority and power that arouses me so. Through the sheer cups of my brassiere, I begin to pinch at my nipples. Mr Pillo expands into the restrainer with a groan.

Slipping one hand down and inside my French knickers, I flick and tease my own sex, already dampened from the caresses of the clothes I have worn this evening. Rolling my head around on my shoulders, I begin to sigh with delight. 'Sometimes my own touch is not enough. I am a woman with strong appetites, Mr Pillo. Sometimes I like to be filled. Stretched. Penetrated.'

He swallows again. His face is red and his brow is wet. 'Yes, Governess.'

'Do you find me attractive, Mr Pillo?'

'Oh, yes, Madam. You have a beautiful body. You dress so well. Your face is so . . . perfect.'

'Yes. It is, isn't it? Would you like to have me?'

'Yes. You know it.'

'Put your hands above your head.' Mr Pillo instantly complies. 'Lie on your back. Feet together like before.' When he is in position, I take the wrist cuffs and ankle restraints from my case and lock his arms and legs to the ends of the bed. As I secure him, he looks up at me, surprised, helpless, then confused. I smile. 'No, no, you cannot touch the Governess. None of my clients can touch the Governess. But, occasionally, if I deem them suitable, I may pleasure myself in the final week of their induction. All of the staff have this privilege.' I sit astride Mr Pillo and angle his restrained erection towards my sex. He will feel nothing inside the rubber shaft. None of the tension of entry, no friction from the thrusting. Nothing. The physical pleasure is to be all mine. He must learn that his satisfaction is secondary to that of a woman's. In the final week, our candidates are relentlessly tormented, teased and deprived while the staff may indulge themselves at whim.

I lubricate the shaft with salve. Slipping the thick rubber shaft inside me, I slowly ease my weight down toward Mr Pillo. I slap a hand over his eyes and take away the sight of my long body in black lingerie and boots, riding his sealed cock.

8. Formal Gathering

In our rooms we women get ready while the men wait downstairs for us to make our appearance. On our faces we smooth out the invisible masks. We are painted, fragrant, soft; we are tall, pale, severe. High heeled, bare shouldered, corseted beneath our gowns, shiny of face and hard of eye, we leave the staff wing together in an uncanny synchronicity and descend the stairs. I lead the procession of cold beauty; Madam Kraka follows; Consultant Kristianson is next and Sabrina takes the rear. We walk in step, we do not speak, we think terrible things.

And in the long room, the men stand solemnly in their dinner suits. They await our lead. Every air molecule seems to cease in its incessant vibration when we enter the room. They have never seen us looking so beautiful, so terrifying. Each and every man lowers his eyes and gently bows. We spread out and stand in the middle of the room, beneath the chandelier. We wait. Nervously, they approach with platters of food and crystal flutes filled with chilled champagne. We take nothing to eat, but accept drinks with gentle nods of the head.

Throats are cleared. Each man comes to us and pays his respects. 'You look very elegant tonight, Madam.' 'May I say how well red silk suits you, Governess?' We smile, stiffly, politely, our faces barely move. Our sculpted features are ever compelled to return to their haughty, uncompromising masks of perfection. We drink many glasses of champagne and indulge them with some light banter, but only to make sure the men never drop their eyes to admire our trussed breasts or shimmering legs that slink through our long, silken gowns.

We grow tipsy and find it harder to restrain the fury inside us, the red, spinning desires we have learnt to control, but are hard-pressed to when drunk. To their credit the men's behaviour is impeccable. When Sabrina decides to start smashing glasses against the marble floor, Mr Dowd is on his knees with a damp cloth and dustpan. Madam Kraka begins to kick her strong legs high as she performs the steps she once learnt as a dancer in her youth. Stiff-necked, I scan the crowd looking for those wayward eyes that may drop to peer at her garters and rustly under-things so recklessly put on display. But the men applaud, anxious, forcing smiles and eventually helping her to a chair with a glass of water. Good: everything is as it should be. They are unfailingly polite and attentive.

Inside their suits, they are strapped down and restrained.

We drink more and Consultant Kristianson unleashes her silken tresses of blonde hair down her backless dress to her waist. She is so hot after all that dancing on the table with her gown hiked up to her stocking tops, so she removes her dress and looks marvellous in her blue corset. And it is then, and only then, that Mr Snape pushes his luck, fooled by these uncharacteristic displays of informality and fraternisation by the staff. Too enthusiastic, he laughs with her. Sips from a champagne glass when he thinks no one is watching. Devours her with his eyes, as she lies on the table and raises her legs in the air. Hands hovering out in front of his body, he immediately pretends to support her in case she rolls off the table when no support is required. He touches her leg!

'Dear Lord, no,' Mr Whittle says, with a wince. And all the other men who stand nearby exchange woeful glances.

'Madam Kraka! Sabrina!' I call out, and stride to where our Consultant writhes on the table. 'A member of staff has just been interfered with by Mr Snape.'

Snape turns to face me with a nervous smile. 'Now, now, Governess, I was worried she might fall. She's had a lot to drink. There's no need. No need at all to lose your temper.' I slap the grin from his face. 'Inspect him!' At once, Sabrina and Madam Kraka seize the hapless Snape and drag him to the floor. It pleases me to see two stern-faced beauties in haute couture, handling a man whose behaviour has become unacceptable. 'Strip him!' I command.

Consultant Kristianson has stopped smiling. 'Yes. I did feel something. On my leg.'

'You are a disgrace,' Madam Kraka cries out, and tugs Snape's jacket down his back. Sabrina tears the trousers and underwear from his feet. One of his shoes falls to the floor without a sound. 'Get him on his stomach,' I order, and my three giddy members of staff wrestle Snape on to his belly.

'Please. It was an accident,' he pleads. The tone of his voice makes all of us shiver with delight.

'Silence!' I say. 'It was no accident, it was a grave mistake, Mr Snape.'

The other men are subdued and look at their polished shoes.

I enter the fray and unbuckle Mr Snape's penile restrainer. 'On your back.' I turn my head away as if surveying the remnants of a road crash. 'Ah, I knew it. I knew it.'

'No!' Mr Snape cries out and clasps both hands over his exposed erection. 'You cannot be serious. Enough of this.' We are all shocked at his tone and pause, momentarily, at our business with this half-naked wretch on the floor of the long room. 'I am but flesh and blood. And look at you all. Dressed like tarts and behaving like drunken sluts.' Then he falls silent, his capacity for speech crushed by the gravity of the terrible words that have just left his mouth.

Madam Kraka looks me in the eye. 'Governess, it has been a long time since such misbehaviour has been witnessed at the Manor.'

'Indeed, Madam.'

Consultant Kristianson shakes her blonde head. 'If only you had kept your fingers to yourself. None of this would be necessary.'

'What are you going to do? Enough, I say.'

'No. Mr Snape,' I add. 'It is only enough when I

135

say so.' I nod to Madam Kraka, Consultant Kristianson and Sabrina. And the crushing begins.

Standing around the naked, struggling man, we begin to trample him with our cruel shoes. Press his face into the floor, spike his fleshy buttocks with tipped heals, squash his back, his hands, his legs with our expensive shoes, we go at him. We call him names, we smash food into his body and pour wine over his spluttery face. From the stained and slippery floor, he looks up at our beautiful painted faces, our long silken legs and hard breasts that rise from the excitement and exertion of his humiliation.

Madam Kraka then extends her fan into a short cane and all the men gasp. Bemired with caviar and cream, with a cracker stuck to his forehead, Mr Snape tries to escape on all fours but Madam Kraka is fast and agile on those dancer's legs. By the time he has crawled, yipping, beneath the table, she has lashed his backside half a dozen times. Scattering the chairs left and right, she makes room to whip at him under the table. When he flounders out the other side, I am waiting with the shackles and mountaineer's rope.

And up he goes to the ceiling, pulled high, the ropes squeaking through the pulleys by the giggling Consultant Kristianson. And as he moves up through the atmosphere, his arms and legs bound to his body by my tight, expert knots, all the men can see that he has an apple jammed into his salivating mouth. And as he hangs above us, we drink long deep draughts from champagne bottles and hurl food at his pathetic carcass. I strip down to my leather corset and Madam Kraka follows my lead. Soon all of us stand resplendent in corsets, stockings and high-heeled sandals. 'Listen to me, all of you! Mr Snape has let you all down. When one of you fails to control himself, you all fail. Now strip. All of you! Now!'

Madam Kraka lashes them into a long single line and shrieks at those who pause in unbuttoning and untying.

And it is then we go to the mad place at the very centre of the Manor's soul. When they stand naked and subdued and trembling, nervous and guilty, with their erections on display, unable to help themselves and unable to fool us, it is time to show them the future. The consequences of failing to meet our expectations must be punished. These men will leave the Manor and go out into the world forever changed. So different from their peers, they will become examples. They have had their turn, their unfettered freedoms. This is the dawn of our time.

The cock restraints lie empty at their feet. They huddle together when the staff break out the canes, the chains, the gags, the hoods and plugs.

8

Archivist 4

Who could imagine that in the old and derelict places
under this city such cultures exist?

When I emerged onto the long platform of the
abandoned underground station, the women had
already gathered and were just beginning to assert
themselves over the naked wretches in the cages.

A Place for Assertive Ladies and their Pets to Play
was written on the invitation I found on my bed after
returning from another shopping spree. It must have
fallen out of the plastic bag containing my new retro
garter belt from the boutique in north London. The
sales assistant – the tall girl with the purple-black hair
and the pretty eyes – must have slipped it inside the
bag along with my purchase, for I had not seen this
card among the other flyers on the counter of the
shop advertising the capital's fetish clubs. Entrance to
this place was by invitation only. And I could see
why.

There could be no first names here, no cameras, no
films, no evidence.

As I appeared on the end of the platform, two men
crawled past me to enter the long tiled corridor that
led to the abandoned wooden escalator I had just
descended. Naked, moving rapidly on all fours,

salivating over ball gags between their teeth, they pulled on their leads like untrained dogs. Their heads concealed by black rubber hoods as thin as swimming caps, they crawled before a beautiful woman clad in a tight-fitting latex two-piece suit. Her hair was black and styled like a 1950s bitch-wife from Park Avenue: a Manhattan ice queen, who used and discarded men like toiletries, mere consumables. There was a fetching streak of white that ran from her fringe to the back of her head and, as she drew closer to me, I tried to guess her age. Immediately, I saw that her broad, handsome features were unnaturally flawless. To my surprise, I saw a perfect, painted face sealed under a clear film of latex.

In the coming months would I receive her evidence and her flimsy doll mask in a special delivery, to curate and then exhibit at the Neretva Museum? This uncanny coincidence made me wary. How was it possible that two of us should be here at the same time?

As she teetered alongside me, the black eyes of this magnificent bitch turned to me. I stepped out of her way, but experienced a delicious shiver in her presence. Smitten with admiration, I could not restrain myself from looking her over more closely while she was so near. Between the open lapels of her jacket, her breasts were displayed in a see-through brassiere. Her stomach was flat, the navel pierced. Sheathed in black nylons, her legs were muscular and gleaming like highly polished perspex. From one gloved hand, two leads stretched to the studded collars around the throats of her man-pets. In her other hand she held a glass of champagne. Tucked into her belt was a whip and, as the doggy-men crawled near the spiky toes of my boots, I saw the lines it had already cut into their backs and buttocks. Then, as I turned to watch her go, the mist parted, and I could see blood on the steel heel of one shoe.

Looking over her shoulder, sensing my admiration, she smiled invitingly at me. I saw something dangerous in her mouth. Behind glossy red lips, her white canines had been sharpened. Before she vanished into the dry ice that seemed to pour and swirl from the very tunnel, I returned her smile but did not follow as she wished; I wanted to see more, everything.

I walked further along the platform and peered into the glowing distance. Half-lit from the strings of temporary electric lights, coloured red and purple and blue and fixed to the oval ceiling, dark figures moved and twisted through the heavy white fog. Such a hellish sight would have disturbed my sleep for a long time had I not prepared my face in the special method this evening. With her so tight on my face, I felt no nerves, no reticence, only excitement and a narcotic curiosity.

Into the warm and foggy air, I strutted on my long and pointy boots, so tight over my fully fashioned stockings, with my corseted upper body mummified by a red dress – buttoned to the throat like some plasticated version of a Mary Quant model. Long gloves concealed my arms. On my face she clung and gave me that look – a mixture of the arrogant, the indifferent and the seductive. I felt more alive and keener for new experience than I could ever remember; the dreaded inertia and boredom and routine of my past was gone the moment I fitted her to my features earlier in the evening. That night, I looked through her eyes.

Industrial music assaulted my senses from the old public address system. Concussion drums and shredding guitars at full volume. At various points along the platform, in between the old benches, naked men peered out from the iron cages. Their eyes were restless. Dozens of captives, that suddenly jostled together and pressed against the bars as the women strolled past, indifferent to the slaves, content, for the most part, to talk to each other and drink champagne.

But some of these pitiful specimens had been taken out of their iron pens and put to use. Over the misty, disused rails, a series of silent figures, their bodies, heads and identities entirely zipped away inside black rubber suits, hung inside harnesses attached to the ceiling by chains and wires. I paused and counted eight. Did they breathe through those tiny mouth-pipes? Who cared? Angled to stare at the platform and the studded bitch-princesses who stalked there, these figures were unable to move their legs, so tightly strapped together – or their arms, folded into a shiny single glove behind their backs. I briefly wondered how long these rubber chrysalises had hung there, before deciding it was of no consequence.

Another four figures had their wrists bound flat to the wooden slats of one of the old benches, bolted to the floor of the platform. With their ankles shackled together, they were forced to face the cold, municipal tiles of the wall. A passing beauty wearing a tight latex gown, idly, though viciously, struck each of their buttocks with a hard stick, for no reason that I could deduce.

Further along, in a tunnel that branched off from the platform, I observed another pathetic wretch, tied up and lying on a single mattress covered by rubber sheeting. Wrists and ankles bound, and arms restrained against his body by white rope, he had been forced to wear a great pink cock on his face, strapped behind his head. Only his eyes and forehead were visible under the fleshy latex of that absurd and tremendous shaft-nose that no living thing here could match. And was he forced to breathe through it, and through her? The plump Japanese woman with the long black hair, wearing PVC boots, who moved her sex up and down the length of this servile fool's penis nose? And as I walked closer and then passed, I noticed she held his ears and began pulling his head off the mattress to push that nasty thing further inside her. And inside me, as I watched, a vast space seemed to open and invite intrusion until it too was filled. I shuddered and walked on, into the fog, where more of the long, shapely silhouettes teetered through the hellish smoke and red light.

Next, I came across an upright armoury filled with canes of varying lengths and densities. There were flails, crops and whips on silver pegs too. Cuffs, shackles, cock restraints, silver plugs, electrodes, clamps and masks also hung from the next tier down; enough to equip every woman here or to supplement the personal tools she brought with her. Fascinated by these evil things dangling together, calling out to me with their secret tinkling music, I approached the rack and began to stroke the implements. Slipping it away from the rack, I held a long black cane in my gloved hand and began to slap it against my long boot just to hear it sing. For the first time in my life, I was armed in a place full of unarmed, vulnerable men. Closing my eyes, I leant one hand against the curved wall, determined to control myself despite these powerful urges that demanded I throw myself at the naked, fleshy pets with this evil stick in my fist.

A makeshift bar had been set against the wall in the middle of the platform – a collapsible metal table covered in black cloth. Behind the table, a thin man in a gasmask poured drinks. To add to this incredible detachment, this separation I felt from my former self, with her on my face and this wonderful, hellish music pounding against me like an invisible psychic surf, I glared at the thing in the gasmask and took two drinks from the table.

'Darling, you look fabulous!' Someone shouted into my ear, as I drained a third glass which made my rapacity grow even worse. I turned and looked into the deepest eyes of emerald I had ever seen, exquisitely framed by long eyelashes. 'I thought there were only to be twelve of us here. But you make it thirteen,' she said, before looking over at the naked figures in the cage nearest the bar. She shook her head. 'Unlucky for some.' The laugh that followed was long, cruel, piercing. I found it as delightful as the music. She too was wearing a mask; I could see the flashing red and blue lights reflecting off her perfect complexion like emergency lights on the face of a shop mannequin behind glass. This alarmed me further; had the Neretva collection had a hand in organising this gathering? I inspected two more of the well-heeled beauties who strutted about the stone floor nearby. To my horror, they too wore a latex film over their faces. And there were only supposed to be twelve, my friend at the bar had said. 'Do you know the other girls?' I asked her, inhaling the wonderful fragrance of her black hair.

'No. I have never seen them before. This is my first time. All I know is that we are the married ones.'

'Where are the husbands?' I asked.

She turned and looked at me as if I had said something ridiculous. 'On a night like this, who can think of husbands?'

'Of course. I just wondered if any of them had been brought along.'

She smiled. 'Mmm. Humiliating them with another woman? I like your thinking.'

'Maybe they get enough at home.'

'They do.'

'They are spoiled,' I said.

'They are, but tonight we tidied them all away. Yours?'

'Pardon?'

'Where did you put yours tonight?'

I thought quickly. 'I slipped him into something uncomfortable he'll never untie on his own.'

'Darling, how wonderful.'

'Thank you.' I wanted to ask her more, find out who she was and how she came to be here. But she had become distracted. 'You will have to excuse me. That young one on his knees in the corner is trying to ingratiate himself with me again. He hasn't stopped looking at me since I arrived.' I followed her stare and saw a pretty man, barely out of his teens, crouched into the corner of the cage. He smiled at us, then blushed and lowered his eyes when we stared back at him. My companion gritted her teeth. 'Darling, I have to teach these little shits all day. But I must not touch them. Then my son brings them into the house. Lots of pretty little rats. I cannot bear their sluttish flirting, their pouting, their ridiculous self-importance. They are worse than the girls, I can tell you. But I will not tolerate it here!' Away she marched on her spiky boots and unlocked the gate of the cage. The expression on her face alone caused the other men in the cage to back away, stumbling against each other. She reached into the cage and seized the hair of the young, bashful man. Dragging

144

him out, she forced him to sit on all fours. Grinning at me like a mad thing seen through the window of a haunted doll's house, she cried out to me, 'The young ones don't last so long. Don't hang about or the sluts will all be gone.'

I was not fooled by the youthful face or the slender, innocent-looking body of the young male she had selected. I knew how he dreamed about women like us. What foul imaginings he put us through in his dirty mind, in his foetid room. I hoped she would make him pay.

Seizing a bigger handful of his hair she pulled his head back and made him face the shaven and pierced sex she proudly displayed between her booted thighs. Then she slapped a collar and leash about his throat and shouted, 'Go find me a bed, you little shit!' With a short horse crop, she began to lash his backside. Whimpering, he stumbled through another tunnel that led to either an adjacent platform or a central concourse leading back to the escalator, where more of the makeshift beds must have been stored. But why to the beds? Would she let one of these things actually penetrate her?

I turned my attention back to the many eyes that were now watching me from between iron bars. This cage full of naked men – the pets – I could just have my pick? Just take as many as I wanted, to do with them as I pleased? It had been so long since I had taken a lover. Years since I had indulged in sex on a first meeting with a man. It had never really suited me, though I liked the idea. Over the last two years, beside the occasional hot, aching pang of physical lust for a man, I had grown weary of them. Their egoism irritated me. Their desperate boasts or manipulating indifference bored me. The games they played or didn't play frustrated me. Being submissive to their pride had long infuriated me. I felt ashamed to recall my diffidence and patience and weakness before them, and my dishonesty with myself and what I really wanted for so many years. What had I been thinking? All I ever had to do was please myself, like these women, these sisters under latex. And tonight I wanted to take revenge and to take my pleasure too.

As I walked before the cage, this feeling made me dizzy; a desire to be pleasured conflicted with an urge to punish. Their eyes devoured the glossy lines of my booted legs; their ears strained to hear a whisper of nylon between the thigh, or the crack of tipped heel against concrete. 'Madam, you look beautiful,' a voice cried out, its tone obsequious, the intention obvious and loathsome. 'So fine, my lady,' a fat man said, his cock hard and purple between his short thick legs. 'Bitch. Pretty bitch in lovely boots,' another goading voice added. 'No. Don't push her. You'll make it worse for all of us,' someone said, eagerly, hoping I would indeed conduct a thrashing massacre inside that enclosed space. Taking them all by surprise, I turned on my heel and lashed the cane across the bars, glancing a set of knuckles. 'Silence!' I cried out. 'Have you no respect? Were you never taught how to behave?' They all fell against each other and then moved away from the bars. All except one – a young man with long, shaggy ink-black hair and tattoos on his shoulders and stomach – who surreptitiously stroked his long penis while staring with a fierce passion at my legs.

Unlocked, the cage door swung open. Jabbing the cane into the writhing flesh, I parted the squealing livestock until I had separated and cornered the young fool with the disrespectful genitalia. Drunk, not sure what I was doing, but not really thinking about it either, I hauled him from the cage and dragged him on to the platform. Driven by emotion, all I knew was that an example had to be set. I could not risk being seen as a woman whom they could take advantage of. Never again. They would fear and respect me in every way they feared and respected the other women here. Locking the door, I then turned and, before all of his cell-mates, I brought the cane down across the back of his knees. Dropping, with a shriek, the filthy cock-handler knelt before me. Pushing his head down, I then placed the sole of my left boot on the back of his head and ground his face into the cold ground. An audience of voyeurs pressed against the bars, all wishing they could take his place down there in the dirt. Striking him too softly at first, I noticed the puzzled looks on those faces squashed between the bars of the cage. I corrected my amateurish reticence with longer, firmer strokes, and redesigned the pert arse with patterns to my liking. Both of his hands slapped at the floor and I felt cries vibrate through my foot. By the tenth stroke, I could feel my panties clinging to my sex and I fancied it would not be long before I found myself impaled on something large. Must have been the drink, the clothes I was wearing, the music, the mask; it was not like me even to contemplate such things and yet here I was dressed in thigh-boots, stockings and rubber, caning a young male stranger on the platform of a tube station.

'Good work, darling,' a sly voice said beside me. I turned and looked at a beautiful, white-faced creature with long raven hair, wearing a black military uniform – tight-fitting jacket, shirt, tie, Italian insignia. 'We don't know how he got in here. He has no idea how to behave. He was shouting at me earlier. Touching himself too. Several other girls have marked him for later. He will be fucking destroyed tonight.'

'He was pointing his cock at me,' I said, my face trembling with emotion.

She nodded and looked at the wretch under my boot with undisguised loathing. Her eyes were a reddish-orange, and her fingernails were long, curved, claret, shiny. They clacked together with impatience. 'He kept crawling to the back of the cage when I tried to fish him out earlier. And then the others would just push forward, get in the way, hoping I would take them instead. I just couldn't be bothered when I had so many of the others to string up there –' she pointed toward the domed ceiling above the tracks '– so I decided to bide my time.'

'You put them up there?'

Under the peak of that cap, she smiled and then pouted her beautiful mouth. 'A speciality, darling. I started doing it during a stag party, when the bride was nervous about strippers or something. She was a friend of mine. She knew about my reputation for hurting men. So she paid me to intercept. And I was only too happy to oblige. I put nine rugby players in a tree. Now I get more corporate clients than I can handle. At the underground meetings, we always put the worst of them up there.' She blew a kiss at the leather chrysalises hanging above the rails. 'They won't be coming down tonight. Two of the girls who work in the city like to come down during their lunch hour to play. They'll all be reported as missing persons before those girls are satisfied.'

Calming down, I took a moment to admire her shapely hips in the black pencil skirt and the seamed stockings of her uniform. Relaxing my grip on the handle of the cane, I giggled at what she said. 'I want you to make this one suffer.' I took my foot from the back of his head. The moment my boot was gone from his skull, the young shaggy-headed man clutched at his stripy backside. He then turned his face to me. Tears stained his cheeks, but he was still grinning and his cock was hard and moist at the tip. 'Shocking,' I said, and prodded his tight belly with the point of my boot. 'Look at it.' Chasing my boot with his face he tried to suck and then kiss my heels, until the uniformed girl grabbed his hair and held him still.

She smiled, her thick red lips peeling across long white teeth, her face smooth as freshly cast wax. 'I can see now how you just lost it with him. This happens to us all in the beginning. You haven't had her long, have you?'

'My first night out.'

The uniformed girl smiled. 'I guessed you were a late addition looking to lose your cherry. You wouldn't mind if I took a turn with him?'

'By all means,' I said, eager to watch a more experienced girl go to work.

'Don't worry. You'll soon learn how to deal with the worst of them,' my new friend in the uniform said knowingly, and began to detach things from her utility belt. 'Never let them show their face to you. And shut their mouths down tight before you even begin. I know how easy it is to just lose your temper and flay one alive, but if you control them and their environment you'll find the experience far more satisfying. I realised this after a pilot on one of my flights pushed his luck once too often. He would never have believed I could get all of him inside a hotel linen buggy. And then when my best friend's father misbehaved at a party, I dealt with him in his garage. His wife even thanked me. She wasn't bothered about having to cut him down from the rafters. Watch.'

Hands and fingers moving with swift assurance, she slapped the youth's face and pinched pressure points in his neck until the delinquent was sitting at heel before her spiky sandals. Tugging his head about, she fastened straps behind it and then plunged the gag deep into his mouth. A constricting rubber hood was tugged over his head and snapped under his chin. 'Lack of air will restrict his ability to play you up.' After belting his arms together behind his back, she pushed his torso forward, so his slick black face was eating the concrete floor. Producing a silver egg-shaped object in the palm of her hand, she deftly and efficiently inserted it between his buttocks. It was as if his whole body had been electrified. But before he could scrape and kick with his feet, she'd also snapped his ankles together and secured them inside a thick leather cuff. Stuffing him under a bench and chaining him to the metal legs, she then stood back and smiled. 'This is the simplest and most basic containment I've learnt. I use it in the car all the time. If a man ever misbehaves when you're driving, get the bastard strapped down like this and stuff him in the rear footwell or in the boot. He'll never bother you again. I often pick up hitchhikers for just that reason. Soon as they start looking at my thighs – I like to get my skirt hiked up when I drive and I always wear stockings – I get them locked down and choked in about three minutes flat. Now I never drive on the motorway without having something struggling in the boot. Just wouldn't be the same.'

I smiled. 'I don't have a car, but I have never heard of a greater incentive to acquire one.'

'You should come out with me some time. I'll give you lessons in vehicle interior restraint. Take my number before you go.'

'I'd like that.'

'More and more of us are playing together now.'

'Really? But you seem too young to be married?'

She laughed. 'Served is more like it. It is an arrangement that is convenient for me.'

I nodded.

'Remember control,' she said, and then strutted back to the cage to get another pet out. Under the bench on the platform, the youth with the shaggy head had stopped moving.

After watching a woman pass holding reins attached to the collars of the two men whose shoulders she stood upon as they crawled across the floor, I walked to the far end of the platform where it was quieter, so I could rest my feet. As I sat down and sipped at another drink, I watched the woman perched on the next bench along. She had also retired for a short while.

Wrapped in a floor-length fur coat, she reapplied mascara, holding a compact mirror before her porcelain face – her beauty was accentuated and exaggerated nearly to the point of parody by her operatic make-up. But my attention was drawn to where her body emerged from the folds of dark brown fur. Tight skirted in latex to the knee, she had crossed her legs and offered the front foot to a small bald man who knelt before her long shins. Chained to the leg of the bench, he had been waiting patiently until the spiky foot was offered. Slowly, he unzipped the first of her long, tight boots with the spiked heels. Unable to blink, lest he missed a second of this wondrous sight he feasted his senses upon, he peeled the leather from her warm calves down to the ankle. Nose quivering, eyes bulging with adoration, he slipped the boot from her heel and then her toes. At once he lowered his lips to her long feet, so pale beneath their nylon coverings, and kissed her painted toes. Then, with attentive, insistent hands, he softly kneaded her sole and instep, while she continued to fix her make-up, as if unaware of the presence of the servant before her. He was merely a function to her, not an identity. He then attended to her other foot. When she had packed the make-up away into her chic little handbag, she raised a foot and smothered his face. Gripping his forehead with her toes, she pulled his head to the ground and issued a short, curt command that I failed to hear. Immediately, the little man slid on to his back and lay facing the ceiling, so that she could support her feet on his chest. Sipping her drink and then wiping her cane down with a silken hand-kerchief, she kneaded the foot-slave's body with the balls of her feet, either to massage more circulation back into her long feet, which had been so tightly bound, or to enjoy the sensation of pressing her slippery soles across the little man's hairy chest. As she idly pressed and massaged her feet on the man's body, he placed one of her open boots over his face and began to breathe through it as if it were an aqualung. Finally, when her feet had been restored and were ready to renew relations with her boots, she ordered the little man to redress her legs. Without any hesitation, he scrabbled to his knees and proceeded to zip her long legs back inside tight leather. When the boots were secure, she spiked him away with a high heel and then walked off. During the entire exchange,

I realised she had hardly looked at him. He had served his purpose and now he was forgotten. Smitten by the pangs of rejection, and thrilled by the pleasure of being used as a foot product by the imperious woman in furs, the little man crawled under the bench to lie on his little blanket, where he sucked his fingers and stroked his cock.

'Madam. May I assist you? I am very skilled.'

I looked down into the alert and sensitive face of a man approaching middle age. In his eyes, I could see the excitement at being so close to my thigh boots and dagger heels, but I also intuited an acute caution in him, in case he displeased me and provoked my wrath. This one knew respect; it would be unlikely that he would push his luck like the young fool now entombed under a station bench. And not only did I want my feet soothed, but I was again intrigued by the extent of a man's subjugation before us.

'Lick the spilled champagne off my boots,' I ordered. 'Restore the shine.'

'It will be my pleasure, Madam.' Lowering his face, his eyes half-closed, the slave attended to the stains about my boots. Amused, I watched his little tongue darting back and forth to carefully and thoroughly cleanse the soiled latex. When he was done I asked him to open his mouth so I could throw the dregs of my drink in there. Spluttering, he thanked me and then waited for my next command. 'My legs are hot. My feet too. Tired as well. See to them.'

He bowed his head in acknowledgement of my command and then reached into my lap to find the zipper. Had he used this as an excuse to touch my soft inner thigh, he would have been sitting on his bandaged fingers for a week. But this creature was experienced, his manner professional, his touch

153

skilled. Without so much as a faint caress of my nylons, he managed to unzip and remove both of my thigh-boots. Placing both of my hot, slippery feet in his lap, just to watch his cock grow and then strain itself, I bade him comfort my feet. And he revived them with such skill that I was thrice forced to groan out loud with pleasure. These sounds I made gave him the sweats, but such was my satisfaction with his work that I allowed him to place his nose under my back-stretched toes so that he would know the narcotic scent of his superior. I even overlooked the gentle kiss he planted on my right instep as he lowered them to the ground. Once he had zipped my boots all the way back to my stocking tops, I stood up, refreshed and feeling as if I was in possession of two new feet. Now that I had received exactly what I wanted, I lost all interest in the man with the slender face and gentle eyes. Without a word of thanks, I strutted away from him, looking for another toy.

And in the darker, murkier regions of the underground station, in the tunnels connected to the platform, I found a distraction that gave me great pleasure.

Away from the stronger lights, it was as if I had stumbled into one of the very dimensions of hell where the sinning souls of men were being tormented by painted demons. Wrists and ankles tied to small steel hooks fixed into the tiles, I watched one man stretched into the shape of a star, face pressed into the wall, as he took a long shiny cock between his buttocks – a shaft strapped to the waist of the tall, raven-haired beauty whose laughter barely failed to drown out his cries of discomfort, his pleas for clemency. Littered about the floor, suspended from the ceilings, chained into arches and fastened to the walls, dozens of restrained and bound men, bearing the marks of cane and flail, waited in silence, in dread, or in thrilling anticipation of being visited again by another petulant, impatient, sadistic bitch with a dollish face. I wondered if those restricted by elaborate bonds of white rope were the victims of the uniformed girl.

Before the open door of a cage, a frightening but utterly exquisite creature in a rubber police uniform belted two younger men with such force I could hear the slaps of leather over the beats of the music. Impressed by her rough handling of them, I watched her drag each figure across the tiles by an ankle before going at them again, this time with a rubber billy club, in order to force them inside her jail. Her face was possessed, her teeth snarling, and out she went again, into the moving darkness, to capture and thrash more of the strays that had defied her curfew, or merely offended her eye. The next time I passed that way, the cage was full of squirming man flesh, and she stood outside, wearing a gas mask, throwing smoking canisters into the spluttering crowd of prisoners who may have attempted a breakout.

Chained by the neck to each other, a long queue of naked men shuffled forward around a corner and through a tunnel to the next platform. Further along the corridor, another column of men emerged holding their backsides or tip-toeing delicately along, wincing and looking over their shoulders at the marks on their buttocks. Curious, I walked alongside the first column of subdued figures to where the procession stopped on the platform. At the head of the queue, a man with grey hair was being strapped over a black leather stool by two naked men who collaborated with the haughty woman with the white streak in her fringe, whom I had seen walking her dogs when I first entered the station. Once he was tied in place, the smiling mistress in the black PVC suit stepped away from the stool and drew her arm back. Wielding a long whip with a silver handle, she lashed the subservient wretch six times and laughed, exalted, at his cries. After nodding at her accomplices, she stood back, hands on hips, and watched them untie the slumped figure. After pushing him away to join the departing column, they seized her next victim under the arms, from the column entering the platform, and strapped him over the stool to take his turn. Kneeling at her ankles, her two dog-men wearing the rubber hoods barked with delight after each stroke of her whip was delivered to the fresh backside.

I stopped to enjoy this spectacle for a while, wondering how many men she would punish this night, before she went home and peeled her alter ego from her face. And as I watched this almost industrialised whipping of the submissive, I became aware of being watched from nearby. Inside the shadows, not far from my right foot, something was hiding and watching me; longing, adoring, but afraid. With a smile, I turned and pretended to walk past the figure crouching against the wall. When I drew level with it, I reached out and seized a handful of soft, blond hair.

Pulling the young male out from where he spied on me, I dragged him under one of the white lights in the centre of the tunnel. Tall and slim, with a tight musculature, the young thing was very easy on the eye. But I stared at him with an antipathy that made his lips tremble. 'Who do you think you are? What is the meaning of this?' With the end of my cane I pointed at the slowly softening erection he had been toying with while staring at me from the sidelines of this subterranean nightmare.

'Forgive me, Madam. I never meant any harm. I was just –'

'Just what?'

'Nothing. Really, it's nothing.'

Pulling him around by his arm, as if he were an errant child in a supermarket. I whipped the cane in and out against his thighs and buttocks until he sang soprano for me. 'What were you doing down there?'

'I'm sorry, Madam. I couldn't help myself. I know it's forbidden. But ever since I saw you come in, I couldn't stop –'

'You followed me,' I hissed at his face, holding his jaw with squeezing rubber fingers and looking deeply into his pale blue eyes.

'Sorry.'

'Sorry doesn't cut it. How dare you assert your intentions. This is no place for that.'

'Yes, I know. I was wrong. I'll take any consequences.'

'Damn right you will.'

His voice dropped to a desperate whisper; every word quivered with emotion as if he were about to cry. 'As long as they are from you, Madam.'

My eyes narrowed. 'Do you fool yourself that I could care a thing for you?'

'No. Never.'

'Then why do you waste your time pursuing me?'

His face screwed up and he began to choke back his tears. 'Because I adore you, Madam. I can't help it.'

I released his jaw and stood back, amazed at this creature's complete devotion to a woman he had never even spoken to, nor seen before tonight. 'Enough! Stop that crying. Don't snivel. Stop rubbing your eyes. Now, to cure you of this foolish infatuation for a woman so far out of your league that it's just absurd, I may have to take measures.'

157

Reluctantly, he nodded and cupped his hands over his genitals, as if suddenly ashamed of his nakedness.

'Go and fetch a lead from the rack in there and then return here without delay.'

Eyes bright and wide, he nodded and then ran away in the direction of the equipment rack. When he was gone, I smoothed back my hair and began to take deep breaths, but I felt giddy. How long had it been since such a good-looking and virile younger man had found me attractive? I was at least fifteen years his senior and yet here was a pretty youth, with a lean, broad-shouldered physique and not an ounce of wasted flesh on him, tearfully confessing his feelings for me. It was the mask: she had transformed me into the kind of woman a certain man, no matter what his age or background, cannot resist. As an archivist, and a PhD student before my professional life, I could recall no man like him – the kind who never even had to try with women – feeling this way about me. Drunk with power and drugged with a thrilling conceit, I doubted if I could control my behaviour if this pretty thing came back to me. I was not myself; had not been since I first arrived here. I had flogged a youth, allowed a stranger to massage my feet, enjoyed the sights and sounds of men suffering the severest corrective treatment. And yet, I could not remember ever feeling so comfortable, or so inspired, so exhilarated in any club or bar or party before. This was my world. I would return. I doubted if I would ever have patience again with anyplace in which I was not so empowered.

The young man returned to me and I attached the leash to his collar. Smiling and sniffing, he thanked me sincerely and then said something not at all to my liking. 'My mistress does not mind me being walked or corrected by the others here.'

'Your mistress?' I said with a sneer.

Alarmed at the obvious irritation in my voice, he nodded. 'I wear her collar. She brings me to all of the gatherings down here. Nothing too harsh can be done to me, though, without her permission. You have to ask if you want to pierce or penetrate me, or mummify me. Otherwise she gets mad. Please don't tell her about my crush, or I really will be crushed. She gets jealous. You should have seen what she did to the girlfriend I had when she first saw me in one of her lectures.'

'Who is she?'

'Doctor Sylvia Kloster.'

I frown. 'Who?'

He looked surprised. 'The Doctor. You know? The leader.'

'And what does she look like?'

Confused, he shrugged. 'The woman with the white streak in her hair. Everyone knows her.'

'Some of us are impatient with reputations and status,' I said to him. 'Now go and get your clothes. This place is not suitable for what I have in mind for you.'

Swallowing, he stared at me with a combination of disbelief, intrigue and arousal. 'But we cannot, Madam. She would kill me.'

'That'll be your problem tomorrow when I throw you out. All I'm interested in is my pleasure tonight.'

'And she'll kill you. I've seen her fight other mistresses. They never had a chance. It's why none of them dare to play with me here. They know how possessive she is about her property. She owns me. I belong to her.'

Furious that I might have this slut-boy and his impressive cock taken from me before I'd even sampled it, I said, 'Fuck her. Now get your clothes. I will not repeat myself.'

He nodded. 'They're up there. At the top of the escalators. We'll have to hurry. She's always looking around to see what I'm doing.'

'Move then!' Angry at the risk this flirtatious slut was forcing me to take, I struck his buttocks so hard he howled and then took the steps on the escalator three at a time.

The youth was stretched out on my black silk sheets, his wrists and ankles cuffed to the bedposts. I stood beside the bed and sipped my cold red wine, admiring his long, athletic body and thick cock whose erection had refused to abate since I ordered his departure from the underground station.

'Are you going to whip me?' he asked in a tremulous voice, drawing my attention to his sensual lips, the sight of which were just about to make me scream with frustration.

'Maybe. Does she whip you?'

'At least twice a week.'

'You live with her?'

'At weekends and when she needs an escort.'

'Is she your girlfriend?' I ask, with a petulant snigger, unable to restrain my caustic jealousy that seemed so much worse with the mask on my face.

He frowned, puzzled, as if I had asked the most ridiculous question. 'No. How could she be? I am just one of her possessions. There are four of us. Always four. The number never changes, but the members do.'

'She loses the odd one to other girls, I bet,' I say, trying to keep the hope out of my voice.

'Never. Maybe she gets bored with us. I don't know really. She never explains herself to us. Doesn't have to. My friend Damien was the last to go. Haven't heard from him since.'

'Enough about her. I didn't bring you her to talk about your old mistress.'

'Be careful, Madam. I am a slave. I cannot defy one of you. But I will always belong to her until she decides otherwise. Once you have used me, you'll have to drop me back and hope she hasn't noticed. Coming back here was a bad idea.'

My eyes narrowed. 'Thought you adored me?'

He reddens. 'I do. But it makes no difference. You know I want to be with you. But she is in charge.'

'Not of me, she's not,' I said, feeling more confident, intent to enjoy this hard body in my lair. Sitting beside him on the bed, I peeled both of my latex gloves off my arms and dropped them to the floor. With a naked hand I reached out and touched his thick cock.

The young man gasped. 'Madam, I am an untouchable. Worthless. Your glove. Don't soil your hands. You must put your glove back on.' Instead, I stuffed a glove into his mouth, tired of hearing about the rules that streaky-haired freak had indoctrinated him with. With the boyish slave silenced, I then began to stroke and handle and pull at his thick meat. Feeling light-headed, saliva pooling in my mouth, I needed to feel its living firmness inside me and to taste its salt between my cheeks. Moving my smooth doll-face between his legs, I swallowed the head of his cock and began a vigorous, desperate sucking. Paying the price of being a highly sexed but ever-abstaining fool, I ended up devouring this stranger's meat in the early hours of a weekday morning – and making the most sluttish sounds as I ate. Lapping, smearing red lipstick, licking the stem, nuzzling the yeasty balls,

161

swallowing every greyish drop of pre-come that tear-dropped from his pinkish nib, I mauled him, luxuriating in my tartish attire and wanton behaviour. Why not? He was nothing but a pretty plaything and I had gone without for far too long. When I looked at his eyes, I could see he was deeply shocked that one of 'us' – and by that I believe he was referring to one of the 'masked' – was actually engaged in direct contact with his naked genitals. Perhaps he was only used to being touched by the end of a whip or blade of a cane; at the very least, he probably expected a layer of latex to exist between his cock and a mistress's body. But tonight, I had other, long-neglected needs to take care of.

Sitting astride his midriff, my red latex dress unbuttoned, I pulled my thong to the side and then pushed his long naked cock inside my hot, tight, hungry sex. And, with wide eyes and an open dollish mouth, I looked up at the mirror I had recently fitted to the ceiling. Groaning from the pit of my stomach, I felt as if this young cock had filled my entire abdomen and was now in danger of entering my torso. Clawing his shoulders, I slipped my hips up and down, fucking his stem, getting wetter and wetter, stretching my sex wider so his entire girth could slip to the back of me. Eager to kiss his pouting, damp lips, I tore the glove from between his teeth and swallowed his mouth within mine. Stabbing my tongue into his hot cheeks while pumping my buttocks on and off his shaft, I stopped thinking about everything as my entire consciousness ascended towards a peak I was sure would make me faint. Oh, to just select and then abduct another woman's young slave from a private party! To line his buttocks with my stick. To selfishly use his body and sex for my own pleasure. Such piracy! The power! With a triumphant scream, I continued to pump his lap through my orgasm. Bouncing up and down, slapping his face, pulling his hair, clawing his chest, I made him cry out and release himself from the agony of infatuation. 'Come. Come in. Come in me,' I commanded. His back arched off the bed and, thighs straining, he threw his buttocks toward the mirrored ceiling, packing and compressing his meat inside my latex-wrapped girly-pocket. Long hot ropes of cream streamed upward into my womb. I held his cock at the base and squeezed every last drop inside before I let him catch his breath. Rubbing at my own nipples, I rotated my sex around the bones of his groin, tickling my clit to sustain the high.

'That was good, no?'

'Oh, Madam.'

'Mmm? What do you say to that, boy?'

'Oh, Madam. It was wonderful. I have never known such pleasure.' He began to laugh with a pure, unrestrained joy and I knew he belonged to me now. 'It has always been forbidden me. To penetrate one such as you. I have not been released inside a woman since my mistress took me from my girlfriend. It has been two years. Only last month did she take off the chastity belt.'

'Well, there will be no more of that. When I see fit, I will pleasure myself on your naked cock.'

He smiled and thanked me, but my enjoyment of him was slightly marred by the fact that I could see he never truly believed what I was promising. It was as if I had committed such a dreadful transgression that this arrangement could not possibly go on.

I took him again into my mouth while grinding my wet sex all over his face. Stripping off my boots, I uncuffed his hands and feet and allowed him to penetrate me from above, while my feet rested on his shoulders. I drained his balls, exhausted the muscles of his cock until five in the morning. And when I was sated, I cuffed him again, so he would lie beside me until the morning, bound.

After removing her from my face and carefully stowing her away with a kiss to her rubbery forehead, I climbed back into the bed and suppressed a giggle at what I had seen and done that night. I could not remember experiencing such a sense of achievement, such illicit thrills, such adventure.

As he rested – so still, so quiet – beside me, I drifted into a deep but haunted sleep. And in the dark and vague places I visited, in the early hours of that morning, I dreamed of dogs hunting me. Big black dogs with the eyes of men, sniffing and snorting as their paws pattered after my scent. And they led something old, clever and cruel to me in the dream. Something evil and unrepentant that never fully defined itself, despite the flashes of lightning all about me; something with black eyes and needle teeth I knew I could never escape. And then I thought of chains. Tinkling, sliding chains, and of a loss as if something important had been taken from me.

When I awoke in the morning with a thick, aching head and a dry mouth, I quickly realised I was alone in bed. After opening the curtains, I turned and saw, to my horror, that the chains of my lover's cuffs had been cut during the night. With a strangled cry, I raced to the bathroom.

My relief at finding her still sealed and safe within her box, on top of the bathroom cabinet, was short lived. Written in red lipstick on the cabinet mirror were the words, 'What was lost has been found.' And then, no longer able to reason or to fully comprehend this insane situation, I saw the Polaroid photograph my visitor had left behind in the sink. It was of my young lover from the night before: in my bed with his head at rest on a pillow, his eyes closed, his mouth full of rubber ball, and around his smooth throat, a black silk scarf had been tied far too tightly.

9

Manager

Written Statement. Submitted February 2003. Archive number 8972. The following items also submitted: one latex mask; one pair of high-heeled sling-back shoes; one pair sheer black panties plus matching brassiere; one two-piece pinstriped suit; one two-piece latex suit; two used pairs of fully fashioned, seamed stockings; one pair latex gloves; one black cane; ball gag; cuffs; one five-metre length of electrical flex cord; one steel wire waste-paper bin; three audio cassette recordings of office subjugations.

'Not so fast. There is one more thing I would like to discuss with you,' I said to the most headstrong of my two young employees. His name was Creech and for the last thirty minutes he had been sitting before the desk in my office while I criticised most aspects of his work, attitude and performance during his staff assessment.

Both of his fists were clenched against the side of his chair. Hot blood filled his cheeks and forehead. Never before had I been so scathing to a member of staff. At the side of his jaw I noticed the tendons stand out as he clamped his teeth together to hold back the impotent anger, this frustration at his powerlessness, and a growing despair at being unable to please me no matter how hard he tried.

I straightened my skirt and then moved around to the front of my desk. Perching my tight backside on top, I looked down at him. Slowly, I crossed my legs. Nylon whispers slithered through the conditioned air. Pointy and sharp, the toe of the high-heeled shoe on my front foot hovered between his knees, a little distance from his crotch.

Perspiration broke out on his forehead. Not once removing my eyes from his damp face, and pleased at how quickly so much colour could drain away and leave behind the sickly-white tint of nerves, I lit a cigarette and inhaled. Confusion settled on his face: this was a no-smoking building. From between my lips, painted the colour of a waxed fire engine, I blew a plume of smoke at his face and said, 'Creech, do my legs bother you?'

He tried to swallow with a dry throat. Hands no longer fisted, he tried to adjust his tie that needed, in my opinion, replacing rather than this unnecessary fiddling. Creech stayed mute.

Raising my voice and making the tone sterner I repeated the question. 'Well, do you have a problem with my legs?'

He fidgeted in his chair and his eyes darted about the office as if he were looking for a hiding place. He coughed, then whispered, 'No.' Cleared his throat, said, 'No,' louder than the first time.

'I see. Well, then perhaps you can explain to me why you stare at them all day.'

Chest rising and falling as if he had unexpectedly been forced to run hard, dark patches of sweat began to appear under both arms. In the office the air felt warm and thick. 'Excuse me?' he said, then coughed.

'My legs.' I raised the front foot slightly and rotated it between his open thighs, touching nothing. With my free hand I stroked my shin. The sheer fabric of my stocking slid over the delicate skin beneath and produced a little tingle inside my stomach. 'You stare at my legs whenever I walk through the department. I can feel it. Your eyes follow me. Why is this? Did you think I would never notice?'

Panic joined the other emotions twitching his facial muscles. The blood of humiliation irrigated his skin once more. It never failed to surprise me how mere words could torment a man when I was dressed a certain way. I knew what he was thinking; if I, his boss, was aware of his nasty habit then maybe other women had noticed too, discussed him, spread the word. 'And I am not the only woman in this company to notice your unfortunate compulsion.'

He stayed mute, was white with fear.

'Oh, yes. It has been brought to my attention a number of times by several female members of staff who work in this building.'

'Who?' he blurted out.

'That is confidential,' I snapped back. 'Two of them are considering a formal complaint to human resources. Another has asked my advice on whether she should confront you, in public, to teach you a lesson. You now have a reputation. Some of the girls call you "pervy Creech." Did you know that?'

Using a forearm, he wiped his brow and looked at the floor. Of course I was lying, but a man in his position with such a particular weakness is unable to use his reason when confronted.

'I advised them all not to pursue the matter.'

'You did?'

I nodded.

'Thanks. Thank you, Miss Torse.'

'I only interceded so you could not bring further disgrace upon my department. And I am a firm believer that matters of this nature, of this sensitivity, should be handled here, by me.'

'Yes, yes, of course.' Relief made his muscles relax, collapsing his body into the chair. He covered his face with his hands. 'Oh, God,' he murmured to himself.

'Do not start feeling sorry for yourself. You only have yourself to blame. It's not enough that I have to correct your tardiness and inefficiency on a daily basis in your professional life, but now I must also concern myself with your squalid personal defects. You should be ashamed of yourself.'

Clasping his hands behind his head and threading his fingers through his hair, Creech stared at the floor between his feet. 'I am so embarrassed. I never knew. I should resign.'

'An option to be sure. Unless, pretty damn quickly, you are able to turn both your performance and conduct around, I would be within my rights to take steps against you.'

He nodded, leant back in his chair, his posture one of exhaustion, submission even. My preparations were nearly complete. The meat was almost tender. I glanced across his shoulders and chest; they were well developed. Perhaps it was his physical presence that had endowed him with the swagger, the self-confidence I had just demolished, and the ease with which he charmed his colleague, Brown, who always followed his lead; a surreptitious resistance to my will he had led in my domain. Now it had to end. The resistance was over; the revolution had begun. He would be brought to heel; I would not tolerate any of these self-styled A-list males in my department. Since preparing my face each morning with this new method, I no longer had any patience with competition from anyone. It would be rooted out and destroyed.

'Of course. I will stop, er ... doing it. My behaviour is unacceptable, Miss Torse.'

'Acknowledgement is a start, I'm sure.' Stubbing out my cigarette, I said, 'But tell me, what makes you stare so much?'

'Please, this is very difficult for me. Let's drop it. I get the message. You'll never catch me at it again.'

'Is that so?' Slowly, I re-crossed my long legs, allowing the hem of my skirt to ride up my thighs. At once, as if obeying some primitive instinct, he dropped his eyes to stare up and into the shadows of my skirt as I completed this simple manoeuvre.

Shrilly, I laughed into his face. 'You will never change of your own volition. Never. You are pathetic. So we must find a way of correcting your disorder through discipline. It's a matter of realignment.' Using a sarcastic tone of voice I baited this dog further. 'Is it the shoes you like? Mmm? Spike heels flashing under the lights? Soft patent leather on our soft feet?'

'Please, Miss Torse. Please –'

I continued to rotate my foot inches from his trouser leg. 'Or is it the stockings? The sheer things we wear on our shaven legs that get you so excited? Tell me?'

'I, I, I –'

'Get your sneaky, dirty, leering eyes from up my skirt!'

'Sorry. Sorry, miss. I –'

'Tell me.' I pinch some black nylon off my calf with glossy fingernails. 'You like these? With the shoes? Or am I missing something?'

As if hypnotised by a dangerous serpent ready to strike, Creech stared at my shiny leg as it moved closer to his shin-bone. He looked dizzy.

'See what I mean? I only have to draw your attention to my legs and you're in a state of total mental disrepair. You are ridiculous. Look at yourself. Down there. At your trousers. Disgraceful.' His cock poled itself down the thigh closest to my foot. 'You can't stop yourself. Do you think professional, intelligent, capable women want to see that wretched little creature pointing at them in the office?'

'No.'

'No what?'

'No, Miss Torse.'

'So perhaps you also suffer the delusion that we wear high heels and stockings and tight, tight skirts to get your attention? We teeter around the offices to arouse you? In your dreams, you squalid little man. You are incapable of controlling your urges. You are worse than a delinquent teenage boy. You will be treated accordingly until you have learnt to respect your betters. Get on your knees.'

Afraid, humiliated, puzzled, he looked up at me, his handsome face shining with sweat. 'I don't understand.'

'On your knees!'

Embarrassed, uncomfortable, but eager to placate me in any way possible, Creech slid from the chair to the floor. The tip of my shoe touched the end of his nose. Eyes half-lidded and full of an uncontrollable mania, he inhaled the scent of my patent leather sling-backs.

'Open your mouth, pervy Creech,' I instructed him.

Dutifully he opened his mouth. Wide with panic and excitement, his eyes became transfixed with the beautifully presented foot before his lips. Into that hot dry place, I slipped the spike of my heel. 'Suck it. Go on. Like a foul-mouthed boy who needs soap in his mouth. Go on, all of it, you dirty, disgusting little boy, suck it,' I demanded in a voice that sounded too deep for any woman. A tone reminiscent of something forbidden by angels to show its eager face in sunlight.

Following the simple command, Creech moved his head backwards and forwards while his eyes strained to see up my skirt. A hand rose, feeble and trembling to touch my ankle but I spiked it down hard with my other foot. A muffled, wounded cry escaped his mouth, but he would not release the heel.

'Now lick the soles, bitch boy. Lick my soles. I want you to taste these nasty shoes. Lick them clean, dog boy.' He whimpered and then began to draw his tongue all over the sole of the shoe; the whole tongue pressed flat against pale, new leather until it was shiny. He struggled to keep his hands still at his side.

'Now lie on your stomach, bitch boy. Creepy, crawly, dirty bastard. If you can't control yourself and behave like a grown man, I'll treat you like vermin. Go on, you office creep, get down on the floor. Lie down. Hands at your sides, you cock-hard baboon. When I said I had the authority to take steps against you, I meant it literally.'

And onto his buttocks I stepped, and down his back I walked with small, careful steps, allowing my weight to sink through each spear, into his muscles and bones. His body hardened and then softened and then tensed again. He did the 'Ha, ha, ho, ha, ho,' sounds with his mouth, as though there was a hot potato in there burning up his tongue. Upon those broad shoulders I stood and casually lit another cigarette.

Then I tried to calm my impulse for further transgression; such urges so recently given free rein in my working life. Oh yes, everything was going to change around here for these boys. Soon, the halcyon days of late lunches, the trips to the bookies during the world cup, the laughter that followed their errors that created inconvenience elsewhere in the building, the shrugging off of their forgetfulness and incompetence, my struggle to be heard above their laughter: soon, all of this would be nothing but a distant memory. They would see this new shiny face more often, and with it would come a whole new set of working practices, with time and motion studies following late nights, following retraining and endless trips to my office to make confessions and to seek absolution. Praise would be seldom, discomfort plentiful.

I looked into the ceiling and grinned like a madwoman with blood around her mouth. Down into his broad, proud shoulders I sunk the long, black nails of my shoes. His face ate carpet tiles. His nose ran and his mouth gaped like a fish on the deck of some bitch-queen's yacht. My voice dropped to a sibilant whisper, a hypodermic needle to puncture his ape pride. 'You terrible, dirty little shit. If I ever have occasion to see or hear of you so much as glancing below eye-level, I will crush you. I will totally fuck you over. You will be finished both in this company and as a man in your life out there. Do you understand?'

'Yes,' he murmured, his voice thick with emotion. 'Yes, Miss Torse.'

I stepped off his shoulders and stood with my feet either side of his head, making sure my cruel spikes marked his cheeks. 'Turn over and look at me.'

Young Mr Creech obeyed.

'Not up there! Don't you dare let your eyes roam up there. That's not for you. Keep your eyes up here. Look into my eyes, doggy boy. Good. Now I have your attention I must tell you that I do not trust you, do not believe that you have even begun to change your strange ways. But I am prepared to give my own time to retrain you. To teach you the right levels of respect. Each day we shall meet and you will be taught a lesson. You will start at the very bottom. Down there on the floor. Down by my feet. Do you understand?'

'Yes, miss. It's very good of you.'

'Good. Now look at that hard thing poking up at me. That thing between your legs.' It looked large; I could almost taste it, wanted to draw its aroma inside my mouth and throat. 'We will have to train that. Soon it will rise on my command and fall on my command. This means a great deal of commitment on your behalf. For the immediate future, in this office, it will belong to me. Can you understand that? On no account is it to seek any kind of wayward stimulant until you can be trusted to behave in a suitable manner.'

Creech cleared his throat. 'Yes, miss. I promise.' His voice was hoarse, his words quick with excitement.

'You are not to touch it at home. None of the pathetic slut girlfriends you fraternise with are allowed access to it either. All cock privileges are henceforth revoked until I give further notice. Discipline. You need discipline in your life.'

'Yes, miss.'

'And I will know if you have so much as stroked that disgusting ape cock.'

'I understand.'

'Because you will empty it in my office, into a suitable receptacle. And if the correct volume is not achieved I will know you have been guilty of indiscipline. Now stand up.' Creech regained his feet and looked sheepishly at the sizeable tumescence between his thighs. 'Now, you will be under a strict surveillance at work until the foreseeable future. Certain female members of staff, unknown to you, have been instructed by me to watch you and report back to me. If you are seen to continue with selfish, unseemly behaviour, you will face dire consequences.'

'Yes, miss.'

'It is both unfortunate and an unpleasant situation you have forced me into. Now, take off your clothes.'

'Miss?'

'All of it. Shirt, pants, socks. Get rid of it. We'll start right away. Give you a preparatory taste of the treatment necessary in this matter. It is not going to be easy. I make that plain right from the start.'

When he stood naked, blushing and self-conscious before me, hands folded across his cock, I sat on the desk and crossed my legs. Leaning back, I pulled the black cane from my top drawer. 'Kneel down before me.'

Creech knelt before my shoes. 'Take your hands away from there this minute.' Then I softened my tone. 'Now, I want you to look at my feet, my legs, my thighs in this tight skirt. Go on – all the little details you adore. That's it, take in the suspender clasps that you can see when my skirt is tight across my thighs. Now, I want you to imagine how silky these legs would feel in your hands. How fragrant these shoes would be under your nose. Picture how red my toenails you cannot see. Even how a pair of legs like these might feel around your waist, or stretched up your body.'

'Oh, miss.' His thick, veiny meat seemed to clench and pant and struggle to grow a further inch in length so that it could touch my shoes.

'Can you imagine that?'

'Yes, miss. They look so good. They would feel so good. You have the most beautiful legs. It's the main reason I come to work. I can't help myself.'

'Enough! So you would like to touch them?'

'So much. You don't know how much.'

'You think about them all the time. Adore them?'

'Yes. Yes.'

'They make you this hard whenever you see them?'

'Yes. When you wear boots too. Those knee boots with the sharp heels. Sometimes . . . Sometimes I have to . . .'

Against the side of his buttocks, the cane smacked with a wet sound. Writhing on his knees, Creech rubbed at the red welt that immediately appeared following the lightning strike of my arm. Then I struck the other, vulnerable side. He yelped and tried to crawl away.

But there was nowhere to go. No escape beside a streak through the department where so many eyes were ready to mock. 'Stay where you are!' I stood up, towered above him and struck him across the back. He fell flat but still crawled. About him I went with the stick, beating my big-cocked mule into the dirt. Biting his knuckles, he contained his desire to shriek and weep. Shoe on face, I ground him into the dust and dross. Over his writhing limbs and torso, I leant into each subsequent stroke. Whatever he saw in my mad green eyes reduced him further. Confronted by the angel of discipline, he wept and salivated through the branding of his skin. Tight skirty whispers, streamlined calf muscles in a web of slick nylon, bitch heels silver-tipped for maximum, clinical penetration, opera paint on the grimacing face of a deranged princess – his big eyes surveyed the total co-ordination of my heart-thumping beauty. Paralysed by the poison of my slick, black aesthetics, hypnotised by the rubbery sheen of my complexion, his trembling body submitted. It offered no resistance. His cock – his thick cock meat – saluted me.

I stood back from the flayed wretch and pointed the cane at his face. 'This is the only way you're going to learn respect and self control. I'll beat your cock soft if I have to.'

'Yes, miss.'

'If it gets hard, I get hard. Understand?'

'Yes, miss.'

'From now on, you will enter my office before and after work and I will be waiting for you. I will be wearing slut-black stockings with seams. The heels on my boots and shoes will be long, evil needles. Underneath my skirt I will wear open panties of the sheerest gossamer. All of me will smell so good your head will spin, but you will never remove your eyes from my face. Never, you hear me?'

'Yes, miss.'

'And I will inspect you. Dressed up like this, I will inspect you. And if I find you to be anything but respectfully flaccid in my presence, until I give the order, I will go at you with this stick in such a way that you will be forced to seek medical help on your way to the job centre. Is that clear?'

'Yes, miss.'

'And then, if I find your balls to be too dry, I will cut them off.'

'Yes, miss.'

I caught my breath and steadied myself against the desk. 'Good. We have an understanding. In time you will learn to make a valuable contribution to my department without experiencing a single wretched thought about another woman. You will not fraternise with any other female colleague. You will be civil and nothing else. You will only think of me during working hours. I expect you in my office at eight sharp every morning until further notice. And then again at six in the evening after the others have gone. I don't care if the trains are running late, or if you have plans for the night. You will report to me at these times and you will be scrupulously clean. This matter of the inspection is unpleasant enough for me. Do not make it any worse.'

'Yes, miss.'

'Remember. Any unauthorised rigidity at all in my presence, regardless of how I am dressed, and you will feel a pain so great you'll wish you were a eunuch.'

'Yes, Miss Torse.'

'And –' I soften my voice so he can hear strong cigarettes and cherry lipstick in my words '– if you can comply with such a regime, you may be rewarded.' His eyes widened. 'Your weakness may be indulged in a limited and strictly controlled manner. I can make no promises, but there is a slim chance, if you fulfil my expectations, that you may be permitted to touch me in a designated area.'

'Thank you.'

'Now cover yourself. And get that ghastly thing out of my sight.'

'Yes, miss.' As he dressed, I smoothed my stockings back up my calves in front of his face and then returned to my leather executive chair. Only this time,

I stretched my legs out and placed my heels on the desk so he could see his spit drying on the soles.

'I'll see you at six sharp, miss.'

'Get out.'

When Brown looked over his shoulder he saw me unburdened of the politeness, the indecision and the diffidence he had been so used to taking advantage of in the past. Naked except for his socks, his wrists tied fast by the flex cord of my desk lamp, his ankles manacled by a ruffle of underwear, his long body lay collapsed across my desk – the sacrificial altar for all the naughty lambs in my flock.

'No, Miss Torse,' he whispered in alarm to the tall woman in black who stood above his buttocks. He may have been thinking, how have I come to be like this, face down on the bitch's table? For it had all happened so fast. So rapidly had my will achieved its malign designs on this one. After the belittlement of Creech, Brown was next on my list for this special brand of re-education. And I took him the very next day. Perhaps he stripped on command in my office because he thought that eager young cock was going to stretch my tight, manicured sex. An arm-lock and forceful hair-grip had alerted him otherwise and now it was too late: the fly buzzed in my web.

Ignoring his pleas for clemency, for decency, for all of those privileges suddenly removed, I continued to slide my pale fingers into a pair of soft leather gloves. And in my painted, haughty features he saw a woman transformed; a woman possessed by this new purpose that had already diminished one of his colleagues to a perfect example of timidity and complete obedience. The bitch is mad. She's lost it. I read his thoughts and dropped them in a paper shredder.

On my face she was slick and wet. Her lustre was matched by the two-piece suit I wore: black, tight-fitting, tailored latex; oil you could see your face in. It had been recently commissioned by a very special craftsman for my working life and brought to the office inside my briefcase, itself a confining box of expensive leather that soon filled up with her rubbery breath. Sometimes, during the working day, I felt compelled to place my new and immaculate face inside the case just to inhale. Cocaine is dead; latex is the new executive's drug.

Before this scheduled appraisal with young sweet-boy Brown, I had changed out of my pinstripe jacket and skirt and then squeezed my body into this designer loveliness. Over my sheer black underwear and fully fashioned stockings, the latex now squeaked as it compacted my figure into something that looked as hard and inflexible as a mannequin cast from fine plastics. Cuban-heeled shoes that pushed me up and onto my toes clung to my slippery feet. Glossy and smooth from head to toe; tight-bodied with pushed-out breasts; sexual, powerful, cruel – who could blame the poor boy for thinking his ship had docked?

Fear and desire combined forces in his eventual surrender. Capitulation was what I needed. That is what I achieved. I could see it in his eyes the moment he entered my chamber.

'Had you read your contract of employment you would be aware that misuse of company communications will result in immediate dismissal. I have here an itemised list of all your personal calls made in the last three months. Plus, copies of all the pornographic emails you have been sending and receiving from a slut in the accounts department.'

'I can explain. It was just a bit of fun.'

'Do you want me to notify personnel and then security?'

'No.'

'Do you wish to be escorted from the company premises with your personal effects stored inside a plastic bag?'

Brown shook his head.

'You may or may not be aware that you have a choice.'

'I'm all ears.'

'It is permissible that an immediate superior can confidentially discipline an employee's unacceptable and negligent behaviour.'

'What did you do to Creech?'

'That is confidential. So what is your decision? My time is precious. My patience is finite.'

'Yes. Yes. All right. Do your worst.'

'Self-pity is an ugly trait.'

'I'm not scared of you.'

Choked by rage at this outburst, I closed my eyes and drew a deep breath. Like his girlfriend in accounts whom, in the car park that morning, I had forced to ingest her own pantyhose, I was compelled to wonder why they must make it worse for themselves, worse than they could ever imagine. He carried on with the bravado while I made sure the gloves formed an airtight fit over my hands.

'You did a real good job on Creech, but don't think for a minute that I'm scared of you. I'll show you my cock and balls. We all know you like that. But you'll never get me to kiss your arse.'

I stifled the first tremors of a scream. These were the last words he would ever speak against me. Calmly, following this outburst, I walked around my desk and opened the top drawer. 'It is most

181

unfortunate. I did not anticipate being so severe with you. Creech was a ringleader, but I thought you had more sense.'

'What do you mean?'

'I hoped this wouldn't be necessary.' I placed the ball gag and cane on the desk before his pallid face. 'I had hoped that a quick shock – a mere taste, if you like, of what I am truly capable of doing to you – would have been sufficient. But we must begin from the start. This I can see now.' I fought to stay calm, to control my breathing, but the taste of latex was rich in my mouth and the constriction of my clothes had taken me beyond the beginnings of arousal.

'You're mad. Fucking crazy. You had your little thrill. Played your little game. Now get this shit off my wrists. I'm getting changed if you don't want . . . If you don't want to fuck any more.'

Belligerence is the first part of denial. It is most fortunate I can intuit such things in young men. In truth, he wanted to hurt. I only had to look at the disgraceful condition of his genitalia, so self-absorbed and ripe now, to realise he was hopelessly smitten by these examples of his manager's secret life, these bad things in my top drawer that did not belong in offices. Evil things that women are forbidden to touch for very good reasons.

Grinding his face into my mouse mat to minimise bruising, I pulled his hair at the same time with my leather fist. This started the tenor moans that would have flourished to offer a symphony of male submission in my honour. But I had to be discreet. The music of his cries would have to wait until another time. For there would be another time. I liked the way this caged birdy sang. Gagging his mouth with rubber, I transformed him from a naked man into a dog-boy. Straight away, he salivated like a puppy with a thick fur coat and no tree to shade himself under. Working fast, I secured his wrists in a more robust fashion with surgical steel and re-used the lamp cord to tie him against the leg of the desk; if he wanted to run he'd have to take the desk with him. Doggy was muzzled and leashed. Time to groom him.

Under my second clinging skin of rubber my white flesh made the smoke of my lingerie damp. Between my legs the electricity of arousal increased its current. Breathing quickly from excitement, I teetered around the desk and took up position to the left of his prepared buttock meat. Not so close as to limit the swing of my strokes, but not so far away that I might cut him in two.

Yanking at his bonds and stamping his feet about, he made a token gesture of resistance. From around the gag he made idiot sounds. Gibbery, jabbery sounds into a nightmare pillow he could not get off his face. So I brought discipline to this muted woodwind by introducing rhythm with my conductor's baton.

The first ten strokes I delivered in perfect time, barely restraining my urge to ride this big-cocked pony all the way to hell. I wanted to saddle and suckle the strong man-beast all at once, but my appetite had to be contained. I had to find his limits of discomfort with the nasty stick, really give him a taste of the fire-wand in my hand. Build up the intensity, guide his surrender, reduce his remaining pride, hurt him, hurt him, hurt him so cleanly.

Panting through the surgical perfume of my new face, I fixated on the sight of his firm clenching buttocks and lashed out and down with the cane. By the seventh stroke his limbs were still. By the tenth his body only twitched after the delightful wettish sounds of my cane on his flesh.

Head tilted to one side on the desk, he watched me through watery eyes. I acknowledged his subdued stare with ten shorter strokes – five to each thigh – and experienced a sense of tremendous fulfilment that left me dazed and drunk. Resentment fell from his face like a pair of badly fitting spectacles. This obstinate and cheeky young pup had been mastered. There was little point in his carrying on with a charade of resistance to my new presence in his life; my figure contoured by severe heels and tight garments of the most luxurious waterproof fabric; my creamy flesh utterly feminised by fine silks and flimsy nylons; my claws glinting like the bonnets of sports cars; the cold beauty of my face capable of producing an exhilarating ice of desire around the heart. He adored me; the tip of his cock sweated pearls. He feared me – physical, emotional and mental anguish could be meted out at whim from my hands, heels or voice.

Mistreatment was becoming narcotic so early in my campaign; I satiated my need to supply and they could not resist their need to receive. The serpent had swallowed its tail. Only beauty can produce such a reaction in a man; only the beauty she has wrapped around my face.

Brown's rump was lined with red stripes. It was as if he had mistaken a hot grill for a stool. I pulled back on the gag straps and widened his mouth. I pinched his muzzle and made him dribble through the mouth cavity. 'You will learn, my sweet boy. Darling boy, my rules are simple. Easy to follow. But there is no place here for those who cannot learn and obey.'

Moving his face up and down on the mouse mat, he nodded his assent.

'Look at you, bitch-boy. Taking stick on office furniture.' I slipped a hand between his legs and handled his balls. When I touched his cock with my leather fingers, the rigidity that had recently been interrupted by pain returned at once. Closing his eyes, he moaned aloud for more of his mistress's favours.

'You have a good cock,' I told him. 'For a slut in accounts, of course. Some scrubber in cheap tights and pink lipstick. But it will never be worthy of me.' Again, I tenderised him with the stick. Curled up on the desk and eerily silent, he clenched his disgraceful erection and welcomed the lash. When I leant across him to unbuckle the gag, I deliberately brushed his face with my warm breasts. I anaesthetised him with the gas of hot rubber from a pretty girl's skin.

Tracing the stripes on his back with a fingertip, I asked him whom he adored. 'You,' he said. Then I told him that if I put him in a big rubber sack and beat his body through the sides with a flat paddle, I would expect him to thank me. He promised me that this would be so. 'And you said, you would never kiss my arse,' I taunted. 'But I have news for you, sweet boy. There is no better proof of your devotion to your leader than such an act. So get on the floor, bitch.'

Standing over him so his face was pressed into my gauzy knees, I unzipped my skirt and peeled it down to my feet. Stepping out of that shiny puddle of rubber, I turned and showed his astonished eyes my buttocks, the very cream of them filtered through a black triangle of gossamer. At once, he rose up against the back of my thighs so his nakedness was stroked by the seams of my stockings. 'Eat. I want to feel your puppy dog tongue inside. Show your love for me. Do it now.'

Washing me from sex to tailbone with a wide, ticklish, lapping tongue, he ate his meal with relish. Listening to his moans and gulps and noisy breath, I swooned from the pleasure of complete dominance. And when, down there where dogs should not poke their noses, his darting, pinky tongue parted my puckered lips and explored upward to the secret chamber of his queen, so rich with its unique, bitter flavour, both of his hands began to tug at his wood. Pleased with his change of heart – this proof of his promise to reform and serve – I forgave the hot dollops of dog seed that he pumped over my pretty feet and shiny heels. It was nothing but a tribute.

And before he left my office, so sore and humble, he knelt before me and kissed the red nails of my right hand.

'Merry Christmas, sir!' I said and then cracked his plump buttocks with my long cane.

And around and around in wounded circles, on the floor of my department, went Mr Strom Reynolds, Chief Executive Officer of our illustrious company. And what a silly thing he was with that wastepaper bin stuffed on his head, and with the electrical cord attached to the collar that I slipped around his neck after all us girls got him down on the tiles. He could not get away: the impromptu lead was tied to the leg of my heavy desk and he could not see much through the hexagon shapes in the side of the steel wire bin, especially as every spare inch of that container on his pompous head was stuffed with the silky, soiled underthings of the ladies who worked on this floor. We had a 'whip-round' earlier, right after the rumour filtered down from above, concerning the CEO's imminent visit to investigate reports of bullying and intimidation carried out by female members of staff. I'd never seen so many skirts raised, so many pairs of high-heeled feet stepping out of panties, and so many painted fingernails sliding down sheer hose during the collection for his Christmas helmet. My idea, naturally. I mean, the audacity of the man! Believing he could just stroll down here and put us all to rights.

'Get this off! Immediately!' But with us all drunkenly laughing and shrieking, as if there was a male stripper inside the room, we could hardly hear his cries from inside the lingerie-upholstered tin-hat. It seemed these modern women had found a new form of titillation for a special occasion.

When his leash pulled taut – about one foot from the closed door – he made a coughing sound and slid down to his elbows. A pretty little secretary called Sylvia, with a shiny red bob of hair, immediately teetered over to him and struck his backside with a metal rule. Strom Reynolds gasped and clutched his cheeks with both hands. Sylvia, who'd donated those lovely black see-through panties to his party hat, squealed with delight and clapped a manicured hand over her mouth. Another woman, Mrs Bish, dressed in pinstripes, snatched the ruler from her younger colleague's hands and struck the CEO even harder to make a lovely wet sound. All the girls applauded.

'Get 'is trousers down,' Penny, a heavy-set blonde in knee-boots, shrieked.

'Get 'is cock out!' Amanda, the petite brunette PA, cried out, as she drunkenly wobbled about in her suede stilettos.

More laughter. All the girls were flushed in the face and wild of eye. Plastic cups of champagne were knocked over in the scuffle around Strom Reynolds's crawling body. Four pairs of clutching, scratching hands tore his trousers down his thighs, then flipped him on to his back, to pull the trousers inside-out over his feet. Kicking, writhing Reynolds clamped both hands over his groin.

'Look!' someone said, in awe. 'He's got a hard-on.'

Painted faces jostled over the crotch of their fallen leader. His hands were pulled away from the front of his underpants. Two painted fingernails slipped inside the waistband of his briefs and stripped them down to his knees.

'Ooh,' Penny in the boots said. 'You should be proud of that, sir. No wonder your secretary's always got a smile on her face.'

Some of the younger women became helpless with laughter at this remark and had to sit down. But an eager tension braced the trio of older women who stood over Reynolds. Old scores needed to be settled. I believe two of these women, Janet and Pam, had been overlooked for promotion by younger things he favoured with both his eyes and his expense account. The third, Dee, he'd disgraced with a very public one-night stand. So they rolled him over onto his stomach to hide his erection. Using the belt from his trousers, Dee, with an intense but faraway look in her eyes, began to lash his buttocks. Janet joined in and, between Dee's strokes, lashed Reynolds with the detachable strap from a Louis Vuitton handbag.

Once the girls had worn themselves out, while the rest of us counted the blows like coxes of rowing eights, Pam kicked off her shoes and then began to tickle Reynolds under the arms with her hot, silky toes. One, two, three and then four plastic cups full of champagne were thrown over Reynolds's half-naked and smarting body. As he struggled to free himself of the tickling onslaught, two of the office juniors in charcoal trouser suits stripped off their own belts and the flogging began again.

Crying and laughing at the same time, demented with pain and mirth, Reynolds jerked around the floor, his hat banging against office furniture with a tinny racket.

Two more pairs of panty-hosed feet began to trample him and roll his head around on the carpet tiles while slappy hands and stingy belts lathered his buttocks and thighs from both sides. A stiletto heel jabbed his left buttock and made him howl. The last two buttons on his blue shirt popped free.

'Ees pissin' 'isself!' Penny in boots cried out. Poor Reynolds had been tickled to such distraction that his firm cock began to spray a yellowy rope into the air, wetting shoes and sprinkling dark droplets of liquid onto sheer tights like rain splashed up from a wet pavement.

'Dirty sod.'

'Dirty, filthy old man. He's pissed on my shoes.'

'Give us a hand,' Penny said, as she forced her tight skirt down her big, smooth thighs. Off came the tights too, before she squatted her large backside over the caged head of the CEO. Gushing from between her bushy sex lips, a heavy stream of urine spattered the chest, neck and head of Strom Reynolds.

'Go on. Give the greedy bastard a good soaking, girl,' the lady from the canteen said.

Lighting up a cigarette, I turned on my swivel chair and smiled at my two employees. Naked and trussed up with masking tape, their mouths stuffed with my gym socks, they keenly watched the humbling of

Strom Reynolds. It came as no surprise to me that neither of them could contain the swelling muscle between his legs. I never gave them permission for arousal, but I let it go this time. After all, it was Christmas and at these parties those of us in charge have to overlook a little unconventional behaviour.

And right then, on the last day before the firm closed down for the holiday fortnight, I realised just how far the revolution had spread from my office. Those male employees who had been unable to flee the building when the drinking began two hours earlier had been dealt with in a particular style: two male accountants were gagged in the ladies' toilets of this floor; another executive was locked inside a cleaning cupboard in the dark, and was left in there for the duration of the festive celebrations after watching his suit, shirt, tie and underwear fed through a shredder; the post-room boy was trapped inside his rubber buggy with a pair of secretary's tights stretched over his head; and the chairman was lying very still on the back seat of his Mercedes, muttering about the loss of his clothes.

And poor Reynolds was the last of them to hold out, which is probably why the girls were so hard on him. But eventually they tired of the flogged, wet wretch with the bin on his head. They needed fresh sport. Eyes still wild with drink and a strange lust, clothes dishevelled, breathing hard so their breasts rose and fell inside their silky blouses, they gathered around my chair to stare at my two boys – Creech and Brown – tethered beside their mistress's desk.

Crossing my legs at the thigh, so neither man could fail to see that their boss's sex was naked above her black stocking tops, I said, 'Go ahead, ladies. It's Christmas. Treat yourselves.'

10

Archivist 5

Total sensory deprivation was never the purpose of the device. Inside the sarcophagus I could both hear through invisible ear grilles and see through the discreet eye-slits. Whoever was originally put in here by their mistress was able to both hear her voice and see her when she was standing before the sinister case, perhaps to taunt or insult or temporarily block the mesh covering the nose and mouth. There was a strong smell of hard rubber inside, and it was not long before the heat of my breathing body raised the temperature inside the man-sized cabinet. Wearing tight knee-boots and a tight black dress did nothing to ease the not altogether unpleasant discomfort when confined. My pale flesh dampened my sheer black underthings, and the sensation of being mummified by successive layers of nylon, silk and the harder outer rubber of the sarcophagus I found sensual. Of course, it was designed for the bodies of men, but despite my height, my being of a slighter construction than the physiques of most men afforded me a little more room in which to flex my toes and limbs to maintain circulation.

Unable to consult my watch, I could not say for how long I was entombed in the sarcophagus before the first guests arrived, but I estimate the period of my self-inflicted entrapment to have lasted for at least three hours.

Earlier that afternoon, after bidding goodbye to the Director through the closed door of his office, and wishing him a good weekend, I opened and shut the front door of the museum before returning to the basement, boots clutched in my hand. Down there, my stomach alive with nerves, my breath quickening, I smoothed my mask into place and proceeded back up to the main gallery to slip, undetected, inside the sarcophagus.

It seemed the secret patrons who sat on the board of the Neretva collection met on the last Friday of each month. Once again, I had been infuriatingly dismissed early for the weekend by the Director. When he called my desk from the phone in his study to tell me to go home, I was halfway through the preparation of a new exhibit, provided by a socialite and her maid, that would occupy one corner of the mezzanine, replacing the dentist's chair and accoutrements that had been gathering dust in that space for years. I was barely able to contain my annoyance at this interruption in my work, and my frustration was increased by my exclusion, yet again, from one of these gatherings. As curator and archivist of the collection, I thought it scandalous that I should be left out of discussions on policy concerning the museum. Who was more intimate with the material than me? For the last two months I had not only familiarised myself with the extraordinary hoard, but had made some notable additions and alterations to the exhibition space. The Director and members of the Board, apparently, were deeply impressed with my work.

My impatience to know more of the collection's history, and to know every one of the secrets of the strange society that maintained it, impetuously compelled me to hide inside the sarcophagus on the ground floor and to spy on the meeting. I presumed the discussion would be held in the Director's office. But even if I could not hear what was being said through the door, I would at least get a look at who ran and financed this operation. Perhaps even overhear some revealing detail as they strolled past my hiding place. Once I had gathered all the intelligence that was both available and safe to gather, I could slink away, out of the museum. And there was another reason I imprisoned myself in the bizarre mantrap. Since first putting on that curious face of fine rubber – or maybe since the very moment I first set foot inside the museum – a narcotic appetite for thrill-seeking and deviance had begun to motivate so many of my thoughts, feelings and actions. Reason had been deserting me of late. It was as if some other motivation, buried beneath my consciousness at an instinctive level, was now in control of me. I just could not help myself. And did not want to stop.

But nothing I had seen or experienced since my association with the Neretva collection had begun could have prepared me for what I witnessed that evening.

They arrived individually. I counted ten women. Five of the women brought men who carried the scarves and coats discarded by all the women at the door. Young men in dinner suits, cashmere overcoats and old-fashioned but elegant hats. Well-heeled men who followed their female escorts in absolute silence, with eyes lowered. A posture I had become quite familiar with in recent weeks. But it was the women who excited my interest. As they passed my position, sometimes pausing to admire the cabinet full of braces, ankle hobbles, skull caps and skin clamps that stood directly across the room from the sarcophagus, it became immediately obvious to me that it was these ten women who were the power behind the Neretva collection. They exuded absolute authority.

They were simply but elegantly dressed in two-piece suits of the finest, most supple latex I had ever seen. Fabric that moved like silk but reflected the electric light like polished onyx. Their jewellery was discreet, expensive. Hair invariably styled like presidential wives from the 1950s. Heels patent and unfeasibly high. Stockings seamed and sheer. Torsos compacted by strangling foundation wear they wore beneath their jackets without a blouse. But their faces? Who could tell how old any of them were? Beautiful, cruel, regal, humourless masks above long, impeccably dressed bodies. And such pale skin. The very presence of these latex wraiths filled me with a terror so profound I could not swallow or blink. A perceptible chill filled the room. I shivered. Lights flickered, as if to splutter into extinction, then seemed to grow in power until the museum was filled by an almost blinding white light. Instantly, I was certain of two things: that I should not be here; and that the presence of so many of these ghost-like despots in one place had produced a tangible energy that was practically unbearable.

I could not see him, but I heard the Director. He called each woman 'Your Eminence' as he greeted them on their arrival. And within his servile tone, I recognised both fear and awe. Cultivated voices drifted around my prison – some faint, others so close I felt they were inside the tomb with me, speaking directly to me. These rubbery confines were disorientating.

'Darling, the new exhibit of the consultant's tools has a sparse, though wonderful aesthetic. I can almost smell the surgery.'

'The Manor grows from strength to strength.'

'There is a long waiting list of patients.'

'And it's not even open to NHS patients.' Laughter.

'I hear they are recruiting more staff.'

'Yes, a delightful Russian chiropractor has been in receipt of a mask. She joined them last week.'

'And word has spread. There are many applications from medical facilities for receipt of out-treatment. My staff are working around the clock to complete the assessments.'

'I am having the same problem with the legal profession.'

'Excellent. One day, there may well be a new kind of justice in our institutions.'

'Well, you should see the advances we are making in higher education. The suitability of the female academic for our creed is, quite simply, astonishing.'

'There have been another five queries from intermediaries of members of parliament also.'

There were mutters of approval.

'The new girl has done marvellous things with the new displays.'

'Indeed.'

'She takes chances.'

'I'll say.'

What did they mean?

'Her arrangements enhance the overall effect.'

'She has fulfilled our expectations. Sooner than we predicted.'

'I hope she knows her efforts are appreciated.'

'I have made her aware of this, Your Eminence,' the Director said.

The voices of the women, and the sound of their high-heeled shoes on the marble floor, faded away. 'All of you,' was the last thing I heard – a command made in a curt tone of voice, 'go down and make yourselves ready. Prepare the temple.' Immediately, this was followed by the sound of the trellis door of the elevator being rattled open, then closed. I heard the clunk and then the whirr of the lift moving down to the basement. The command must have been issued to the men. But what did it mean: *make yourselves ready*; *prepare the temple*?

Further away, inside the Director's study, I heard laughter – sadistic, cynical laughter – and more voices that were muffled before the door was shut. I breathed out and pushed the sarcophagus open. Unsteady on my feet, I tiptoed out and massaged my lower back. To spend more than a few hours in there must be truly gruelling. But to sit nearby enjoying a glass of wine and to just know that a living, immobile figure was trapped inside? I could only begin to imagine the delights.

Walking on my toes I moved along the main gallery and stood beside the study door. The familiar dusty-waxy smell in the air had gone. Instead, it was drenched with the smell of many strong perfumes competing for dominance. But, outside the door, I heard nothing. I moved closer. Still nothing. Swearing under my breath with frustration, I briefly considered just barging in there and making some phoney excuse about leaving an umbrella at work. When wearing the mask, I hardly even recognised myself. Locked doors and recalcitrant people, courtesy and good manners were things I could have little patience with if they hampered my new desires, my wants, my needs. But I took a moment to remember the way in which the air was electrically charged by the presence of these creatures, and I thought of my stolen glimpses of their hard, beautiful faces, the absence of compassion, the emotional void that could only be filled with the debasement of others, and I contained my impetuous desire to become the uninvited guest.

But then I heard something. Shocked, I whispered 'No!' But there it was again. The snap of a thin, hard piece of wood against the solid meat of a human body that carried through the solid wooden door from the chamber within. And then a deep moaning sound after the fourth blow. The thumping sound continued; it made me wince. Now a man was weeping, but still the blows fell at regular intervals. His cries rose. It was the Director! He began a shameful blubbering. Then there came bumping sounds, as if the furniture was being angrily rearranged, and then a harsh voice, full of malice – the incomprehensible words spat at the recipient of the flogging. The Director was being caned! Then silence. The door handle turned.

Gasping, I stumbled away from the door and flattened myself in an alcove, around the corner from the study. Pressed against the glass front of a cabinet that displayed a depraved clown outfit with iron shackles attached to a pair of preposterous shoes, an outfit designed to reveal the bare buttocks and hanging genitalia of the wearer, I held my breath and tried in vain to slow my thumping heart. Had I been heard, skipping away from the door?

No more than a few feet from where I stood, shivering, the first of the women came through the door of the doctor's study. She was covered to her feet in a long purple robe of silk, and I realised it was the hood pulled over her head and face, obscuring her peripheral vision, that had saved me. And then the others followed her, also clad in the long priestly vestments, with just their pale hands, blood-red fingernails and the pointed tips of their high-heeled shoes visible. Each of them carried a long black candle that was lit and flickering. As they turned towards the emergency staircase that led down to the basement, I saw, to my horror, the same terrible saturnine face from both the stone feature on the front of the building and the door knocker of the museum, woven into the back of each robe.

Panic – a sudden clawing, suffocating desire to flee the building and never return – overwhelmed my brief relief at not being discovered. Not even my imagination would dare to dwell on what these satanic priestesses of this blasphemous place would be capable of doing to a trespasser. And when I peered inside the study and saw the Director, I clapped a hand to my open mouth.

Face down on his elegant desk, the Edwardian lamp angled at his head – now gloved inside a clinging mask of black latex – he had been hauled from his wheelchair, stripped of his tweed suit and brown waistcoat and caned into near unconsciousness. A thin layer of frost prickled over my entire body.

A sudden, mad compulsion urged me to shriek with laughter at the helpless and thoroughly disciplined shape of this once-proud scholar. To think he sat up here and had the temerity to assume authority over my work. And whatever his position was, he could not even cope with that and had to be corrected by such brutal means. And he was nothing more than their administrator. A figurehead, a stooge who now sucked on rubber and dared not move for fear of the welts on his back causing even more discomfort. How could I respect this man – this kind, elegant, courteous figure?

How infuriating that guilt should try and make an unwelcome appearance in my heart before this spectacle. Had we of the masks not gone beyond such trifling impediments? I must be stronger. We had created a new morality by wearing these faces of latex. Our will was the new law in our lives. This place housed historical accounts of a new philosophy that began at the very roots of female emancipation. And now, in homes and offices and surgeries and hotels and restaurants and places of learning, beautiful doll-like faces were taking control. Had our sex not always wielded a subtle but significant power through our sexuality? Was it not merely a matter of time before we became organised? Before man became enslaved by his inability to resist our power?

Drunk on the euphoria of revelation, the exaltation of the visionary, I found myself walking to the stairs that would lead me down to further enlightenment.

11

Diva

Written Statement. Submitted March 2003. Archive number 8973. Following items also submitted: one latex mask; two pairs of high-heeled sandals; two pairs of boots – one knee-length, one thigh-length; two corsets; two used pairs of fully fashioned, seamed stockings; three fabulous silk gowns; three wigs; one cane; one leather body harness and ceiling suspension apparatus; one flight case containing Fender guitar and fitted with man-size compartment inside; one latex suit for male; one backstage pass on neck chain; three Madam CDs; three Madam tour programmes; one microphone with stand.

Sitting before the mirror in my dressing room, I put my face on. Behind me, a hairdresser teases and back-combs my waist-length hair into a black fountain. My make-up is positively operatic, my lips positively porno in red lipstick that glistens, my eyelashes positively dollish. I am beautiful. I select my jewellery: long silver earrings and black pearls.

'Madam, have you decided on a dress yet for the encores?' It is Ralphy, my dresser, who speaks. 'How about the new purple gown? You just look divine in purple. With the thigh-boots and the studded belt.'

'Not now, Ralphy,' my manager, Seymour, says. 'Madam, I need to speak to you alone.' He is nervous; he sweats too much. He gestures to the hairdresser and Ralphy to leave the room. Neither of them even considers moving without my permission. They look at my reflection and await my instruction. Casually, I spray perfume on my neck and between my breasts. I pout at the mirror, then check my teeth for lipstick. 'What the fuck do you want, Seymour?'

He sighs, then wipes his brow. 'There's just a little snag, Madam.'

'Snag? I don't do snags, Seymour, as well you know. Sort it out and don't bother me again before the show.'

'I know, I know, I know this is a bad time. But it can't wait. It's the promoter –'

'That's enough,' I say to my hairdresser and push her away. I unbelt my long, black silk gown and let it fall from my pale shoulders. In the mirror I admire my new breasts, push them together and blow a kiss at my astonishing face in the mirror.

Seymour clears his throat and twists his fingers, chews the inside of his cheek. I can feel his stare like a draught against my nakedness. 'I tried to speak to you about this situation earlier, but you didn't want to be disturbed until six.'

'Ralphy,' I say. 'I'm ready for the underwear now. Fetch me something black and flimsy. I want to feel good under the dress. It helps my performance.'

'Certainly,' Ralphy says, his eyes wide. The hairdresser picks up her things and leaves the room.

'Bitch,' I say. 'Get me another hairdresser, Seymour. They never get the back right. Where's that girl with the spiky hair I hired?'

'You fired her. Two nights ago. And there are no more hairdressers. They won't work with you any more. But anyway, your hair is the last of our problems. This promoter –'

'No, Ralphy. No, no, no. Do you have shit for brains? What's wrong with you? Not those stockings. I will not tolerate lycra.'

'The promoter,' Seymour says again.

Turning around on my chair I look at Seymour. 'I am not in the habit of repeating myself. I do not want to hear another word about the promoter.'

'Well, you'll have to, Madam. He won't pay the price you're asking. No one gets 98 per cent. Ever. Not even Shania. I told you.'

It happens so quick, he doesn't see my arm move. But the know-it-all smirk leaves his face the moment his tie goes tight around his throat. A split second later his face is kissing the floor by my high-heeled, jewelled slippers. I hold his head against the carpet by wrapping his tie around my knuckles. 'Now, you listen to me, you little pissant punk. I don't give a rat's ass what Shania gets, or Britney, or Maria, or fucking Cher. When Madam wants 98 per cent she gets it, and the pencil-dick promoter is grateful for his 2 per cent.' I place a high heel on the back of his head. 'Now you go back out there and get him to sign the contract or two things will happen. One, I'll put the heel of my shoe through your skull and send your severance pay to the morgue. And two, I'll pull the show and the promoter can deal with ten thousand rabid fans in rubber masks who've paid fifty quid and driven out here to see the woman they love more than their own mothers and wives. And if I'm forced to pull the show, I'll hold you personally responsible. I'll whip you the colour of fucking beetroot just so you can be a red carpet for my high heels at your own funeral. Now do I have to do your fucking job as well as my own hair and make-up because no one can tell their arse from their elbow in this town, or what?'

'I'll do my best. I'll ask. Ow! That hurts!'

'Don't ask, bitch, tell! Or I'll go right through you with this. Now get the fuck out of my sight. I don't want to lay eyes on you again until after the final encore when you have my cheque.'

Rubbing the back of his head, looking as if he might burst into tears and hiding his erection at the same time, Seymour finally leaves me in peace. 'Ralphy, darling,' I say, as my manager closes the door, 'I feel like a massage. Get Thor in here. And tell chef to make me a steak. Make it rare. I need meat.'

Ralphy nods, then hesitates, checks his watch. 'Show time in five minutes, Madam.' Through the walls, along the floor, down the backstage corridors, comes the sound of twenty thousand feet stamping, and ten thousand voices shouting, 'Ma-dam!' clap-clap-clap, 'Ma-dam!' clap-clap-clap, 'Ma-dam!' clap-clap-clap.

I feel the new skin go tight on the refined bones of my face. My eyes narrow. Ralphy swallows and shrinks away from me, back towards the rack of dresses he dare not let anything happen to. I speak slowly, as if to a child. 'Your little playmate, Seymour, has gotten Madam all tense because he cannot do what he is told to do. And when Madam is tense, and hungry, you know what happens. Remember Cleveland, bitch?'

'Right away, madam.' Ralphy bows, then scurries away.

Just as I'm attaching my second stocking to my suspender clip and thinking about which shoes to wear for the first number, the door blows open.

'The promoter, I presume,' I say, without even looking up, just continuing to smooth black nylon over my thigh.

There is a pause, then he collects himself. 'Just who the fuck do you think you are? 98 per cent? No one gets 98 per cent. You expect me to lose money? Fuck you.'

For a moment I close my eyes, and let the madness pass. 'Excuse me?'

The fat promoter looks at the ceiling as if beseeching a god. 'First the catering sucks, so she turns the table over on the TV people. Then the lighting ain't right, so we make last-minute changes. The stage is no good, so we make it higher. She books three hours on a soundcheck so the support get nothing, and she only turns up for the last five minutes to say, "One, two, three, four, this is such a fucking bore," and then walks off the stage. I got three hairdressers in tears, two security men who look like they seen a ghost, and ten thousand lunatics about to start ripping up chairs out there, and she ain't even dressed yet. And now she decides to renegotiate.'

'Those shoes. Pass me those shoes with the silver heels and black straps.'

'What?'

'Shoes. The shoes.'

Exasperated, he looks over the 33 pairs of high-heeled shoes on the table by the fruit and flowers. 'Not those. Do they have black straps and silver heels?'

'What the fuck?' he says, picks out the right shoes and places them on the floor before my feet, wetting his lips when I cross my legs.

'Now hand me that case.'

'Huh?'

'The black guitar case with the silver clasps. Pass it over.'

'What am I? A fucking roadie?'

'The case.'

Belligerent, he slides it towards me. Slowly, I slip my feet into the high heels and buckle the teeny spaghetti straps around my ankles. Moving across to the full-length mirror, I admire the way my figure looks better when I'm standing in the shoes. '98 per cent.'

'You outta your fucking mind, lady?'

'98 per cent, or I walk back to the Holiday Inn and get an early night.'

'Do you know who I am? Do you know why they call me Mafia Sam? Do you realise I could have Madonna on her knees, opening wide just to get 10 per cent? You need therapy. Think you can just . . .'

Oh, he just goes on and on. I stop listening to him and click open the locks on the guitar case.

There is a knock at the door. 'Come in,' I say.

Chef appears with a tureen. 'Madam, your steak.'

I nod at the coffee table. Then I open the guitar case with the lid facing the promoter so he can't see what's inside. The promoter goes off again with both barrels. 'Oh, so now she's gonna eat. You deaf, lady? Don't you hear that sound out there? That's the friggin' audience. So why don't you get your over-priced 50 per cent ass down there and start hollerin' into a microphone instead of breaking my balls?'

It makes a good sound, a stainless steel tureen coming down hard over a bald head. Like a gong, but more hollow. Blinded by steam and metal, he stumbles against the couch. Snatching his hands from the air, I cuff his thick wrists tight into the small of his back. I take off his silly metal hat and plunge his

205

face into the sofa, jamming it between the cushions. His feet slide out at angles. I stuff my left foot against his cheek so the point of the heel touches his lips. In seconds I have his belt undone and drag his trousers down to his knees. He makes a whimpery sound.

In and out the cane goes, all over his ample buttocks. And what a glorious sound this hickory makes on so much flesh. After every blow there is a muffled echo from down there in the cushions, a little 'oof,' and each time I leave a long red mark that'll keep him on his toes for days. 'Oof, oof, oof.'

'Who's on their knees now, chubs? Mmm? Mafia Sam? Bitch Sam, that's who. Sam the weeny bitch.'

'Oof, oof, oof.'

'I could record this sound. Get your fat arse on a record taking stick.'

'Oof, oof, oof.'

'You're a star, Sam the weeny bitch. A real star. I'm going to put you on stage tonight. Dangle you like a puppet.'

'Oof, oof, oof.'

'I think you'll like it.'

'Oof, oof, oof.'

'Big swinging dick like you needs a firm hand every now and then. You're no different from all the others. What do you say, darling?'

'Oof, oof, oof.'

'That's why your dick's nice and hard now. Good and hard for Madam. Just how she likes it.'

'Oof, oof, oof.'

'And she always gets what she likes.'

'Oof, oof, oof.'

'So unless you want 98 of these stripes on your backside, bitch, you'd better cough up the 98 per cent fee.'

'Oof, oof, oof.'

'What? I can't hear you.'

'Oof. OK. Oof.'

'I still can't hear you, Sam. Scream for me, Sam! Scream for me!'

'OK. Oof, oof.'

'If you stop licking my shoe for a minute you might just be able to communicate, Sam.'

'Oof. OK. Whatever you say. Oof, oof.'

'Would you please welcome ... recording live for Bitch records ... all the way from London, England – Madam!'

One hour later I teeter onto the stage and the crowd sounds deafen the drumbeat to 'What I Need Makes You Bleed'. I look out at my audience, but can only make out the faces in the front rows. Some of the men are crying. Some of the men faint. All of the men are wearing dog collars from the Madam merchandise stand. I love them all. They put my album in the top ten last week and have filled every stadium so far on the *Kiss the Boot* tour. They're nothing without me.

Just to get them warmed up, I do three classics: 'Stiletto Strut', 'Into the Dark, Boy' and 'Hurting You Softly'. I don't even get to 'Going Back to School' and already they're throwing hundreds of roses onto the stage. Under my high heels, the stems crunch and the petals squash. The hot air smells like a greenhouse at a botanical garden. When I play any town, the florists' shelves are cleared in hours the day before a show.

Keeping a respectful distance at the back of the stage, my masked and muscle-bound musicians keep their eyes lowered and concentrate on playing; my three backing singers in black funeral dresses and veils stand on pedestals to the right, leaving me with the entire front of the stage to strut and sing and to crack my whip above the heads of the lucky boys who got tickets down the front. Sometimes I catch one with the whip, but they don't seem to mind.

I take a quick costume change after 'Hell is Other Women', and then walk back on stage to do 'Just Walking My Dog'. It's always a crowd pleaser, and two of my lucky fans from each city get to crawl naked on stage with me, with collars and leashes, down there by the spikes of my thigh-boots. I always wear thigh-boots with seamed stockings for this number, and a corset with matching elbow-length gloves that I reveal on the first chorus after throwing my black cape off. When I teeter close to the front of the stage, some of my fans start to masturbate. Security start to drag them out, but quickly get overwhelmed by the rush of others trying to get closer to my heels. I put one foot on the monitor to sing the final chorus. The lights fade to black when I let my doggies nuzzle between my thighs as I stroke their little black hoods.

When the lights come on, the crowd know what to expect: me lying on the long white piano in a pinstripe jacket, panties, stockings and heels, nothing else. It's becoming a tradition now, my boys out there singing all the words to the ballad 'Tied Down by Love', with me joining them on the chorus. Never fails to bring a tear to my eye, all those lighters held in the air.

After the third costume change to a black latex floor-length gown with side splits, the guitarist starts the riff to 'Pets' and the crowd starts jumping up and down. Tonight I have a surprise for them. 'My darlings, would you please welcome a very special guest. A man who once made the mistake of displeasing me.'

I pause and listen to the many raised voices at the front: 'Take me, Madam.' 'Walk on me, Madam.' 'Hurt me, Madam.'

'And you know what happens to naughty boys who displease Madam?'

The crowd finishes the sentence for me. Ten thousand voices scream: 'They become my pets!'

'Darlings, would you please welcome my very special pet, Mr Ninety-eight per cent.' And, backed by a drum-roll, Mafia Sam is lowered from the ceiling in a leather harness and leather underpants. Blindfolded, a ball gag between his teeth, his hands and feet strapped together, he just hangs up there and gently sways as ten thousand pairs of envious eyes look up.

Tonight, I'll give them three encores.

Of the ten thousand fans who attended the show, only twenty were given backstage passes by Helena, my booted PR girl. During the show, she weaved among the crowd, out there in the arena, like a leopard in a herd of nervous goats, seeking suitable candidates to provide entertainment for me and my entourage at the after-show party. Men and women who sought out and accepted those of us with extreme tastes in sensual fulfilment. They were not ordinary music fans that Helena selected, but individuals who found themselves compelled to gravitate towards the lifestyle reflected in my work. All of them had been touched and then seduced, despite the conflicting warnings of reason, by the imagery in my videos, the photo shoots in magazines, the lyrics of my songs, and the rumours that circulate about my reputation. And, by accepting the backstage passes that hang on the little chains around their necks, they realised they were absolving themselves of control and freedom and responsibility; they were submitting to my authority. Until they were released, maybe even a week later (it had been known to happen), they belonged to me.

Blindfolded but excited, they were led by my security into my penthouse suite back at the hotel. Bowls of fruit, sprays of fresh roses, plates of exotic canapés and cases of chilled champagne filled the tables. Helena herded the fans into a long single file facing me. I lay on a long couch with my backing singers – the widows – beside me. Our red lips moistened at the sight of the groupies – fifteen men and five girls. The latter had done their best to imitate my style for the show: long, wild hair; lots of make-up; tight and revealing latex dresses; seamed stockings; high-heeled boots. Nice try, girls. But they were only cheap imitations, mere sluttish parodies of their precious Madam, whom they vainly hoped to emulate. And the male groupies in their dog collars, little pants and leather harnesses? How many of these semi-naked articles had I dealt with so far on my tours? How many of them had willingly debased themselves for my enduring glory? No biographer would ever believe the excesses committed by me during my life on the road. But one has to do something to relieve the boredom of a one-night stay in their hopeless towns. Night after night I indulge my whims and darkest fixations, lining their bodies with autographs they would feel for ever.

'I think these girls should entertain us first,' I said to the widows, who smiled with approval. Excited at the prospect of so much fresh meat, so shapely and sweet and youthful, the speed at which we drank increased and each of us loosened inside. 'Helena, dim the lights and go. There are to be no interruptions.'

'Yes, Madam.'

I left my place among the dolls on the couch and took a stroll around the file of tense, trembling groupies. 'Among ten thousand men, this was the best I could get?' I said before the men and watched the disappointment replace eagerness on their faces. 'I've seen worse, but I can't remember where.' The widows smiled and began to flex their latexy limbs. From their vanity cases they selected the appropriate equipment. Behind the fans I walked slowly so they could hear my heels on the marble floor. They were chilled by my presence and received the first sign of what they were about to receive as I trailed my sharp claws against their buttocks. When I reached the five girls, I said, 'Madam wonders if you know how to please her.'

They murmured their approval, then tried to outdo each other. 'Oh, yes, Madam,' a young blonde girl said, 'I'm your biggest fan.'

'As if,' another muttered.

'Maybe if you got the hair right,' another quipped.

'Girls, girls,' I said with a giggle, delighted with the competition for my favours. 'You are all precious to me. And Madam treats all of her girls equally.' I kissed each of them on the cheek and they immediately reached out for me, touched me, stroked my latex arms, put their fingers against my lips, stroked my plastic cheeks.

'Oh, Madam. You looked fabulous tonight.'

'You looked so sexy.'

'You played my favourite songs.'

'I've seen you nine times on this tour. It's making my boyfriend crazy.'

'I have your face tattooed on my ankle.'

I could only smile at the devotion; it never failed to touch me. 'Girls, before you are released in the morning, I want you to give your names to Helena. I want to put the names of such pretty girls in the *For Those Who Serve I Salute You* section of my new live album.'

Overcome, one girl began to sniff. Another tried to hug me. But I stepped away from the girls and turned to face the widows. 'Fetch the musicians from their cases. Then cum-slut these pretty little things.'

Shock and astonishment appeared in each pretty, blindfolded face. 'Madam?' 'What?' But two of the widows were already leading the girls away from the men to place them in a kneeling cluster on the black rubber sheet spread out in the centre of the room. 'Kneel down, all of you,' the widows commanded in uncompromising tones, clipping the odd hesitating backside with horse crops.

'I want to take the blindfold off,' one of them said, unease in her voice.

'No. Best if you leave it on. Just sit still and open your sluttish backstage mouths for Madam.'

'I'm not sure about this,' the redhead said.

'I just wanted my records signed,' pleaded the girl with the thin nose and curly black hair.

'Silence!' I commanded, and the sound of my raised voice made them all flinch. 'You are here for Madam's pleasure. And you will pleasure Madam's band. These boys play hard for Madam, six nights a week. And they haven't been emptied for at least five days. They get restless.'

The female groupies leant against each other and started to whip their blindfold faces about, sensing the approach of the band, so recently sprung from their large flight cases, where they are stored with their instruments after each show. The eager band jostled around the girls, flexing their muscles, breathing heavily through their rubber hoods – in my presence they may never show their faces. Extending my cane toward the group of kneeling girls, I issued the command, 'Take them. Take the sluts. Chuck it all over them.'

With their long white fingers, the widows unbelted and unzipped the band from inside their pinstripe trousers. Turning the girls face up, holding their chins between finger and thumb, the widows then moved each thick cock between the trembling lips of a kneeling girl.

'That's it, my darling girls. Eat the food from Madam's table.'

The groupie girls were nervous at first, screwing up their noses at what was on offer, so that the widows were forced to hold the back their heads and to push their faces onto the long cocks. But their desire to please Madam soon took over. Their heads quickly developed an on-and-off sucking rhythm. Three of the girls even began to use their hands to stroke the shafts plunging between their cheeks. 'Oh you lucky girls,' I said. 'Can you believe it? You are actually sucking Madam's band.' The suggestion added weight to their resolve. They moaned and began to lavish the anonymous cocks with even more tongue and lipstick. Soon, mingling with their perfumes and hot struggling breaths was the salty tang of fresh cock. The widows and I stood over the girls and swigged champagne from the neck of a bottle. We coaxed and encouraged the sucking groupies until the band begin to ejaculate. One by one, they splattered and pooled their seed over the wet mouths and warm, painted faces of the kneeling girls. Laughing, we shook up more bottles of champagne, and directed the foam all over the kneeling groupies until their hair was soaking and their make-up running.

'Good boys,' I whispered to my musicians. 'And when you're ready again, I want you to fuck these little sluts harder than they have ever been fucked before. Do you understand?'

'Yes, Madam,' they muttered in low voices, leering through the eye-slits of their masks at the coughing and spluttering girls on the rubber mat.

'Get those gimps on their hands and knees,' I commanded the widows, pointing my cane at the long line of patient men, who stood shoulder-to-shoulder sniffing at the air. 'You boys will not be so lucky. The only thing you'll get to suck on is the air between your gritted teeth.' The widows used canes and harsh words to get the men on the ground, their buttocks pouting upward.

'Ladies,' I said, with a smile, to my widows – all so tight of mouth and narrow of pretty eye. 'Will you join me?'

'Yes, Madam,' they said in an enthusiastic chorus.

And with the kneeling slaves we became busy with our evil, stinging sticks. From the first to the last, we wore our arms out. The widows breathed hard all around me, in between the curses they threw at the whining slaves. 'You little shits! Did you think you were going to touch Madam? Aye? You're not even worthy of looking at her face!' Lash, lash, lash: lashings of hard wood against their thighs and buttocks until our shoulders ached. And the boys would never forget Madam's touch. Sudden flashes of white lightning across their rumps and behind their

214

eye-masks. Oh, how they howled – especially the younger ones with the tighter buttocks. And the anticipation of those who waited their turn, as we flogged their neighbours, was exquisite to behold: the trembling; the attempts to see under their blindfolds; their wincing at the sound of a cane cutting into flesh so near.

Tired but exhilarated by the thrashing of another fifteen fans, I retired to the couch with another bottle of champagne to direct events. 'Make it worth their while, girls,' I said to the widows. 'It's not every day they get backstage.' It would be a long night for these young men, because the widows had curious tastes and, after indulging themselves at a show, would sleep all day like pretty bats in a dark cave.

Back over on the latex mat, spread across the marble tiles like an oil-slick, my musicians had sufficiently recovered to begin penetration. I could soon see five pairs of high-heeled boots pointing toward the ceiling; leathered ankles gripped tight by five pairs of hands and spread wide to allow a remorseless, thrusting access between the thighs. There were moans and whimpers and small heartfelt cries from my female fans. Positions were swapped and two of them were arranged on all fours. They looked over their shoulders at me, eyeliner running, lipstick smudged, and I blew a kiss at their young faces.

One of the girls began to noisily climax, her voice warbling after every stroke from my bass player's solid meat. A second massaged her breasts together to provide a target for several long, hot white ropes of cream from the perspiring drummer. And some of the musicians changed girls, withdrawing and then passing a pair of booted legs to each other, swapping places. It was not long before I noticed two of the girls kissing and swapping hot seed between their lips.

And soon the air was filled with the sound of canes striking flesh again. The widows had stretched three of the male groupies over the couch and continued to test the new hickory canes they had picked up in New York. Others had been tied into strange, tight, constricted shapes with white twine – arms strapped together behind their backs, ankles attached to wrists by ropes taut as guitar strings, apples stuffed into their mouths – and then positioned like strange sculptures in a submission gallery. One of the widows had lined five of the men, face down, along the floor, head to toe, and proceeded to slowly walk across their bodies in a pair of sharp heeled sandals, before turning on the last pair of shoulders and walking back the way she had come. Another of my curious backing singers sat in a chair and drank champagne as if it were sparkling water. Legs apart, eyes sultry with drink, she allowed two of the lucky groupies to first remove her shoes, then massage her silky toes, before commanding them to lick the soles of her tired feet. And these hot, eager, male tongues must have pleased her, because she then guided them up to her sex. Holding the back of their heads, she bucked and writhed and pressed her sensitive lips over their faces until she had reached her peak.

And so the guests at our little backstage party were relentlessly used and exhausted through the night until our extreme fancies were satisfied. When the sky outside bruised a dark bluish colour, my thoughts turned to the next show in the next town and my eyelids became heavy. So I untied one of the figures on the floor, whose cock possessed a length and girth that I found appealing, and I led him by the collar into the bedchamber. Soon I would sleep. But not that soon.

12

Archivist 6

Written Statement. Submitted March 2003. Archive number 8974. Following items also submitted: one latex mask; one pair of high-heeled sandals; two pairs of boots – one knee-length, one thigh-length; two corsets; two used pairs of fully fashioned, seamed stockings; one pair of cuffs; one pair of ankle hobbles; one black cane; three latex dresses – red, black, electric blue; one pair of elbow-length latex gloves.

How can I say how much of it was real or how much of it was a dream?

When I finally came round, I found myself lying in my own bed, back at the flat. The sun was rising behind cloud and rain, pooling a greyish light through the blinds that struggled to live as my memory did, sluggish as if blurred by the vapours of a fading anaesthetic. How had I come to be here? The last I remembered, I was back at the museum.

Down the stairs I had walked from the main gallery of the Neretva collection to the darkened basement, determined to see what mischief those cowled queens and their manservants were about to engage in, the thrilling shock of the Director's plight still so fresh in my mind.

None of the lights were switched on in the archive, but I could still see. The shapes of my desk, the library, the packing crates and viewing machines were indistinct, but from somewhere there seeped a reddish glow. A thin, flickery light that made shadows move and the eyes dart after them.

There! Behind that little oval door to the sealed room that was damp with river gas, the light was issuing from inside there. And so was the rhythm – the low, thrum of sound; hypnotic, trancelike, alien. Between the pulses, I heard voices too, incanting a low chant. Lines of prayer in an old language to something that had to be worshipped beneath the ground. As I had long suspected, the Director had lied about this room and its use. I thought of the presence that spied on me while I worked alone, the sound of its laughter, and I very nearly turned back.

Things became hazy thereafter. Even though my instincts screamed for me to turn away, I was pulled toward those sounds. In a place of antiquity and mystery it was not in my nature to falter, and besides, who could resist that primal drum? Beats made in the middle of circles through the centuries, in dark woods and secret cellars. Candlelight and incense and the electric waiting for a guest of honour to arrive – manifesting from out of the moving darkness around the pale, vulnerable flesh of its disciples. Through the blood-light I teetered in long boots, to get closer, to hear the words, to mouth the same sounds with my own glossy lips. Swaying to the strange rhythm, I placed my hands on the little door and drank in the vibrations from within, like some nocturnal plant that found succour in moonlight. Did the door open, or into my mind were terrible images transmitted?

Did I really see a large chamber made from red brick with a concave roof and candles fitted inside narrow alcoves? Were there really five pale bodies of beautiful young angels tied by rough ropes to the wooden crosses bolted into the bricks along one wall? Naked angels who wore white silken veils over their faces and crowns of flowers on their heads, who hung in silence, engrossed in the liberating stings of the flails that were being flung against their young skin by the robed priestesses, in time to the beats of that old leathery drum? Did I dream of the ten tall figures in the pope's robes, that disgracefully fell open, as they exerted themselves, to reveal thin dark under-things on their supple bodies? How could eyes be so black even in such faint light? And what manner of ritual demanded that they milk the hard cocks of these tortured youths, into that black goblet passed from one ghostly hand to another, their red nails clicking against the blackened pewter? And then, was each of the five angels actually bled with a long silver knife, ever so discreetly from a small incision over the left nipple, so they could give a few dark drops of blood to the chalice already heavy with their young seed?

Was it an altar at the far end of the chamber? That table draped in black silk upon which candles and a long rectangular mirror were supported? Before which the warm chalice was briefly decanted by a robed woman, who then bowed in reverence and offered the cup up to the mirror.

The wind! I remember a terrific wind. Hot and gusting with a howl through subterranean canals and crevices to blow and billow and swirl through that place of brick and candlelight. Up went the robes. Flung about the bodies of the white-limbed coven, who shrieked and laughed with abandon and guzzled from the chalice. Holding each other upright in the violence of the air, so that they could sup and clean each other's unclean mouths of the vitality drained from the bodies of the captive angels, their strength and vigour and vitality and fertility restrained, enslaved, farmed and devoured. Oh, how I longed to sip from that cup!

And when all but two candles were doused in the storm, and when the ten women dropped to their knees and bowed before the altar, was it a figment of my imagination that something came out of the mirror?

Came out laughing like a countess who bathed in blood, or a queen that lay beneath stallions, or an empress that asked an empire to service her cravings? How did my mind survive the merest impression of her: something so beautiful, so terrible, so hungry, that came into that room dancing? Something so impossibly long and feline. Before I closed my eyes or fainted did I see full breasts more beautiful than porcelain perfection transformed into flesh? Were those claws on hands so beautiful it hurt even to look at them? And why did the face that peeked through the luxurious folds of long, black hair falling to her knees need to be concealed by a mask? Was it for our protection? And if I did sense her getting busy about those angels on the crosses, because I certainly saw nothing, will I ever forget the cries of those youths? It was as if five souls had been suddenly ripped from their mortal vessels and clutched to the body of a goddess, who then moaned in such a way as to make me weep with a happiness so profound it hurt.

That was the last of the night I remembered until I awoke in my bed and opened my eyes, but quickly shut them tight. My head hurt. The muscles around my stomach ached. My limbs felt heavy with fatigue. An impenetrable thickness swaddled my mind. But, curiously, I felt young all over again, as if my body was shedding a tired skin and was now recovering to be stronger, invigorated. But part of me felt strangely aged too. As if I had seen too much and my excesses had left an indelible mark. I fingered the skin of my face. Soft, smooth, but no longer coated in a film of latex.

After a shower and a cup of strong coffee, I knew what I must do. At my desk in the living room, I opened the cover of my laptop computer and began to type. And I have been sitting here alone, oblivious to the ordinary world outside, until the confession is complete. I have become the doctor who has operated on herself, the scientist who has experimented on herself, the zealot who has worshipped herself. I have become a living part – a mere cell in a new, mutated strain of life, a revolutionary member of a forbidden party – of something that is destined in time to change everything so it will never be the same as it was before.

And then I gathered the mask and the rubber clothes I had worn, and the underwear, the boots, and the shackles and cane I had used on my overnight guest, and I packed all of them into a case, ready for the museum, where they now belonged.

Whether chemical agents have influenced my behaviour and my perception, whether I have actually seen these things or hallucinated like some guinea pig on untested pharmaceuticals, or whether I have been influenced by the oldest science of all – the occult – I know that the masks will continue to be worn. If it is possible to do something, it will be done. Indecency is irresistible.

13

Lady

Written Statement. Submitted March 2003. Archive number 8974. Following items also submitted: one butler's diary; one black butler's suit; one latex mask; one pair of high-heeled shoes; one set of see-through lingerie – garter belt, brassiere, French knickers; two used pairs of fully fashioned, seamed stockings; one cane; one riding crop; one pair steel cuffs; one photograph album.

On the high stool in the hall, beside the front doors I sit and wait for you. Looking out from the glass panels in the doors I suppose I should be admiring the elegant square where we live – the pink and red sprays of colour in the flower beds and window boxes, the stone mansion blocks, and the ladies in hats who walk their little dogs past the iron railings, with the solemn-faced men trailing behind, laden down with bags. But these days, nervous with anticipation of your return, I look at nothing but the road.

Much later than I expected, your car pulls up outside, idling engine an air-cooled hum, the expensive tyres whispering to a stop. A black car with dark windows. I cannot see you through the glass but I can sense you inside. A demure, petite shape. I can even sense the faint chill and palpable tension that braces the air in any space you occupy, no matter how briefly.

When the horn sounds – persistent, insistent, a note of impatience – it makes me start. Forehead prickling with heat, I rise from my chair and instinctively adjust my tie. Swelling up inside me, a great bolus of pent-up frustration and rage expands. 'Bitch,' I say aloud, insulted, degraded and humbled that I should be made to wait and then be summoned by the sound of your horn. My fingers go white on the door handle. I go out to greet you, my jaw clenched too tight to speak or smile.

Moving around the warm bonnet to the driver's side, I open the door. Gushing out to stun me comes the fragrance of your perfume mixed with the smell of expensive leather seat covers. My anger escapes from my body like heat in a poorly insulated house. The stiffness of irritation in my spine melts, becomes fluid. My heart beats faster. My mouth goes dry.

Inside, you take the tight leather driving gloves off your pale fingers. I stare at the dark clots of red paint shining on your fingernails. They rattle the keys and then remove them, silvery like trout lures, from the ignition. 'Bags are in the boot.' You remove your sunglasses. Below the sheen of your leather skirt I stare into the footwell and look at your legs. Your stockings are black. A ray of sunlight makes them shine. They make your legs look solid as if they are made from glass. 'Put the car away. I won't need it again today.' One slender leg is raised to step out of the car. My breath catches in my throat and I quickly peek inside your skirt; sheen on the thigh; black suspender clip on the dark band at the top of your stocking; there for just a moment, then gone. A foot in a high-heeled shoe is placed on the tarmac. I admire the ankle and think of how your slim, white legs – so girlish, so innocent in the morning – can be transformed so much by the shoe and the nylon, and of how everything else changes when you dress and fix your hair and prepare your face. You change, the world around you is changed and everyone's reaction to you is changed too. If only I could be immune to such things. If only all men could be.

You drop the keys into the palm of my hand. From the dark interior of the Mercedes, you uncoil the rest of your thin body. Hair freshly tinted dark red and newly set, lips a wet claret in the pale surround of your delicate, pretty, ageless features, you emerge into daylight. What brief independence I experienced in your absence is instantly replaced by my second-guessing your wants, needs, thoughts and feelings. Any residual day-dreaminess is petrified by a frosty fear of displeasing you.

Standing before me in a simple ensemble of black jacket, leather skirt, white silk blouse, handbag looped over one shoulder, you reach out and touch my hand. I inhale you – perfume, moisturiser, bathroom lotions, secret potions – and feel dizzy. Your fingers are cool, the touch soft. I twitch: afraid, surprised, hopeful. My eyes dart up to your too bright, too clear, too green eyes. You fold my fingers over the car keys and crush them into my hand. I gasp, step back.

On the pavement, a young woman pushes a man in a wheelchair. His legs are covered by a tartan blanket. He looks at me and winces. The young woman who pushes him smiles to herself.

'I will not tell you again. Stand on the other side of the door when a lady alights from a vehicle.' Your

225

lips hardly move. I blush from head to toe and begin to sweat from guilt and shame. And then you are gone, past me, through the front door. Sweat cools under my shirt collar. I shiver.

I'm at the door – bedroom-peeking – and will treasure this little indiscretion, safely stored in my mind where you can't go yet, as though the memory is an underground film that passes between enthusiasts.

After putting the car away and struggling up from the garage with all those bags, I carefully make your lunch, like a neurosurgeon cutting and slicing and stitching irreplaceable, fragile bits together in a porcelain skull, because your salads have to be just right in both composition and presentation. Then I run your bath, using a thermometer to gauge the right temperature, before retiring to the kitchen so you can bathe in peace. Always be there but not there. But when you go into your room, your thoughts preoccupied with an afternoon liaison with a married man, you are careless and leave the door ajar. And up I come in my socks, silent on the marble tiles, to haunt the corridor outside your door. With the mirror opposite the bed angled just right, I can watch you dress through a crack in the door. I don't stop to think. I can be disgusted with myself and remorseful later, but for now, like an addict, I just have to get a fix streaming through my electric veins.

In the reflection I can see you sitting at your dressing table, applying your make-up. Then the face, that invisible screen you press to your bones – the plastic shield of illusion that I have often thought of destroying in my most petulant moments. And what will the lucky barrister with three children get from his mistress this afternoon? You've been seeing him for months; he phones you all the time; soon he will be discarded. 'Love is better if it destroys. So much more is at stake,' I once heard you say to a friend on the phone. And you must be nourished by the desperate feelings you incite in men. How else can you remain in power?

Now the underwear. Ah! The black brassiere with the transparent cups and straps that cross your gentle shoulders and are clipped into place in the middle of your smooth back. And the see-through French knickers, over the garter belt with the four straps to each thigh. Then the stockings, barely visible, like smoke trailing from your fingertips when you raise them in the air, then fold them over and over into a manageable roll before dipping your red-nailed toes into them. And the shoes? My lady, I know you so well: high-heeled sandals that barely weigh a few ounces when they sit in the palm of my hand, with just two straps thin as spaghetti; one for the ankle, one for the bridge of those delicate toes. One strap may as well be tied around my manhood, the second around my throat, for you could lead me into the very fires of hell when your body is mounted on those spiky pedestals. The silk dress completed with pearls, a thin gold bracelet for the wrist and a dab of perfume at the side of your neck. Drop, drop with the glass stopper and my nostrils flare like an ape downwind of an explorer's wife. And now you are ready for another man. I leave your shrine, queen, and lurk back down to my lair to suffer.

But not for long. While you are away and having your creamy skin gouged by rough fingers, and your svelte limbs bent this way and that in a hotel bed, I am chasing your ghost back here, trying to steal your soul, like an old witch who collects locks of hair, for a spell to cast over myself, to further bewitch myself.

My movements quick and jerky and my eyes wide, as if I could be discovered at any moment, I move through your bedroom and touch your things. Inside my throat and mouth I can feel the thuds of my excited heart. I close the curtains and turn on the lights, for such rummagings are best conducted in a sealed, artificially lit space. It brings the euphoria of night, and enhances the self-indulgence of containment. Like a suspicious, cuckolded spouse, I ease open your drawers, both terrified of and eager for revelation. I dry my fingers against my trousers and then touch the frothy, lacy things you wear so tight against your breathing, sweet, sweet skin. I hold a pair of small panties against my cheek and briefly decant a chemise under my nose. I let a pair of long black stockings dangle from my fingers and peer through them to see the world turned into a dark and silky and magical place that can only ever be glimpsed through the veil of a woman's private things.

I pause for a moment and try to still my mind. A maelstrom of thoughts, memories and visions boils in my head and absorbs my consciousness inwards.

Breathing more evenly, I drop to the floor and brush my nose over the carpet where the pinkish soles of your feet have recently walked. Like a pilgrim looking for a cure in the dust of a saint's footprints, I crawl to the wardrobe where your precious relics are stored. In there, behind the mirrors, I gaze in wonder at the treasure of your shoes. Leather so soft and supple and glossy, straps and heels and uppers so beautifully cut and fashioned, soles so unblemished by contact with dirty surfaces – dainty cages for your perfect feet. I turn your boots into respirators and lick the pale leather soles like a cow looking for salt. I am a big, clumsy, trembling animal among such fine things. I try to leave no fingerprints as I rustle through tissue paper in hollow hatboxes, my fingers stroking silky gowns and animal furs – even the small creatures of forest and field must suffer for your glory – everything gently scented by your perfumes, your long black cigarettes, and by the places you go while I wait here for your return.

I lick a diamond ring and wrap a chiffon headscarf around my erection. Crouching on the floor, away from the mirrors so that I cannot see my own disgrace, I inhale the smell of your nails from open polish bottles until I feel dizzy and dreamy. And then, drunk on your aromas and fabrics and all the visions contained within them, I make a spectacular discovery. A lump forms in my throat. My fingers shake. Something peculiar happens with my vision – I can't focus, my sight goes jumpy. No! Not you. How can you own such things? Do you use them? I cannot believe it!

This private hoard you have kept from me. Safe in a black case with a steal trim. So fat on your power over me, you have carelessly left this unlocked, and into it my wretched hands go. A life undisclosed to me but revealed like shocking revelations from the diaries of the dead. For whom are these heavy steel cuffs? Your own slender wrists or the hairy thickness of a barrister or diplomat's arms? And the dehumanising hoods of thin, black latex. Whose once human eyes are turned into red-rimmed, flitting, animal orbs through these holes? Stretched by the square jaws of men. No doubt about it. I rummage further, my shirt stuck to my back. This cruel stick with the silver handle, wrapped in black silk, and the evil density of the horse crop, make my skin shiver in vulnerability as if I am anticipating a blow.

And the little elegant album made from black leather? I am too scared even to hold it in my hands, let alone open it. No, I am not in control of my fingers as they unclasp the covers.

You photographed them!

I am angry. Feeling at once betrayed and cheated. How can this have been kept from me? So the barrister may never even get to heave his chunky body, so reddish and meaty on a hotel bed, between your white thighs. Instead, you tie him this way and that, choke him on the rubber bit, and punish his buttocks. Those are your red-nailed toes peeking from the peephole shoes that walk on his hirsute back. I would recognise those toes anywhere. And who is the man in the mask who kneels naked and sucks your heels into his mouth – the redness of his mouth grotesquely disembodied in that surround of clinging latex on his chin, his eyes startled by the flash of the camera? Like a war criminal you have documented your cruelty, but an investigator has broken open your safe. How will I ever look at you again without giving away what I know?

Downstairs the phone rings. My heart stops.

Quickly, trying to remember the pattern of how these secrets were arranged, I stuff everything back inside the case and close the lid. Slipping it up inside the wardrobe behind the hatboxes and your riding outfit, I quickly glance about the room to make sure everything is as it was. I rush off to the distant trill of the phone.

* * *

When you returned in the cab with your two friends, I was trying to sober up in the kitchen. Of course nothing works – strong coffee, cold water over the head, fresh air. You just have to let these things take their course. So, with a tremendous effort of concentration, I walked to the front door. And as I was not out there ready to open the door of the cab, you were displeased. The reek of toothpaste and mouthwash only served to make my inebriation more noticeable: spearmint is such a squealer.

When I opened the front door to admit you and your well-heeled friends, I bowed, but not before they had exchanged quick knowing looks and sly smiles. You looked at me only once. It was enough to make my testicles tingle, then shrink.

But I couldn't help myself helping myself to your drinks cabinet! I wanted to cry out. Not after what I found in your room. The whisky went down so easily and now I can't stop the world from spinning. But you still expect the best service: cocktails and little sandwiches for your glamorous friends. 'G & Ts?' you asked them.

'That would be nice. If he's left us any,' said the one in the tweed suit with the short white hair. I have met her before and she always looks at me as if I am ridiculous; a slight mocking smile on her face. Excuse me while I take off the clown make-up, bitch.

The other woman with the shiny blonde hair and violet lipstick sat with her fabulous legs crossed, looking idly around the living room, and nodded. They could be your sisters. Immaculately presented, chic suits from the best designers, porcelain complexions a little glossy beside the windows. But the similarity is greater in attitude. Do you ever crack genuine, warm smiles? Do any of you ever speak without detached irony? Have you nothing positive to say about anyone? Is it only misfortune that makes you laugh? Are you all impossible to please?

I wasn't thinking straight. When I came back from the kitchen there were problems with co-ordination. Residual shock from earlier had become a surly sullenness I was at a loss to control. I was resisting you; dragging my feet. Never being able to relinquish the promiscuous freedoms of a wealthy woman's lifestyle was one thing, but to indulge in such perverse role-playing with your conquests – though it should have come as no surprise – I confess to feeling more wounded by my recent discoveries than by anything else since being in your service. The tray heavy with glasses, tonic bottles, ice and cucumber sandwiches must have become caught on something. It was not a deliberate action to upset the silver tray and to send it clattering and splashing its contents to the floor – though my mind was on other things and your silent friend's elegant legs were quite the distraction I find irresistible.

'Shit,' I said. The word just blurted itself out of my numb mouth. A man in my condition could not be thought too badly of for swearing in polite company, surely? And was it a disorientating embarrassment, or the drink, or some act of psychic interference that made me plunge forward into the lemon slices and melting ice cubes? I had no control of my legs – it was as if I had been willed down, on to all fours among your spiky heels and shiny shinbones, shirt untucked and climbing up my back under the waistcoat. There followed a terrible period of inarticulacy in which I could not speak. The link between mind and mouth had been severed.

'Oh really!' the tweedy woman said, batting a hand at her skirt to knock away droplets of gin. The silent

232

woman exhaled with annoyance. You looked at me. And it seemed all the antipathy in the world was concentrated in your beautiful, stiff mask of a face. 'Get out.' You said nothing else, but your hands? Your pretty hands, and the way they twisted and writhed in your lap. I had to look away.

And there is something about falling and failing in formal company, especially when you are a subordinate, that brings on the hysterics. Everything seems suddenly absurd: the delicate gestures, the manners, the assigned roles, the hierarchy, the permissible discourse and behaviour. I had transgressed them all. I felt as if I had taken a shit in your prize roses before the panel of judges, but I could not stop laughing. My body shook with mirth at the utter hopelessness of it all. And that lemon slice hanging from my knee? Surely that would soften your hard faces. But no.

They left soon after. After my disgrace, any further attempt by you or me to regain face would have been a sham. So I just waited in the kitchen for you to come down for me. You took your time. Enough time for me, infuriatingly, to enter a period of sobriety. No more laughter now, only tears.

You asked me to 'please accompany' you to the study. You may as well have said guillotine, because this was the end for me. In this place where you sat so still behind the desk with the perfect posture, you usually paid me. And it was the same place you interviewed and hired me: a short and deeply uncomfortable occasion in which I could not break my stare from your mouth – so red, so wet. This time I looked at your pale hands as they wrote the cheque, because I could not meet your eye.

'You employment is terminated. Gather your things –' you said "things" as if I kept ripe garbage in my little room beside the kitchen '– then leave the premises within the hour. You can go now.'

'No.' Who said that? Did I? The word just seemed to appear and then hang, suspended in the cool, clean air like a tangible object we could both see and were surprised to discover between us. I cleared my throat. 'My position is a staff appointment. There must be a period of notice.'

You leant back in your chair, a look of dollish surprise on your previously haughty face. 'Drunkenness in service results in immediate dismissal. Read your contract.'

I smiled, but it felt clumsy and ugly on my face – a terrible and inappropriate reminder of my earlier disgrace. I killed the smile. 'And where could I possibly go in one hour?'

'That's not my problem.'

The way you said that – as if delighted by my plight – gave me a sudden, incautious and blustery confidence. I recalled, with an uncanny clarity, all of your disrespect, rudeness, unpleasant tones and spiteful remarks since I had come to work for you. I was finished here. I had nothing to lose. But eloquence deserted me; I was too emotional. Too many hot, desperate ideas tried to squeeze through the same aperture of tense mouth all at the same time. 'How dare you treat me like this!' Churlish, clichéd and wholly ineffective and ridiculous as a result.

Your little nose twitched and you uttered a short, mocking laugh.

'After all I have done for you.' Just getting worse. Where was this stuff coming from? Where would one start?

You shook your head. 'Don't be tedious.'

'Tedious? Oh, I'm such an inconvenience to you now. Bet you'd like to hit me with that cane. Eh? Just your style.' But my voice was losing strength. I had been given a chance to leave with some dignity, but the opportunity had been wasted.

The sun outside must have just moved behind a cloud. It was as if a shadow had passed over your face. I became suddenly uneasy at the sight of what I can only describe as a studied nonchalance in your expression, as though you were pretending to concentrate on me while listening to a far-off voice at the same time. I had never seen you like this before. I thought you mad. I should have left right then. But the narcotic curiosity I have always felt about you, coupled with a childish desire to be the one to accuse and humiliate, for once, kept me standing before your desk.

'Well then, you leave me no choice,' you said, quietly, after a long silence.

'What?'

'There is nothing left to say.'

'Madam?' To my consternation, my old submissive tone of voice returned; the tone I employed when I still had a job.

'This period of notice, of course. I had forgotten. We'd better begin today.'

I felt awkward, as if I had been awarded a gift I did not deserve from someone I had wronged. You should have been furious with me. And yet you seemed to have merely arrived at some trifling decision.

I crept back down to the kitchen, confused but shamefully grateful. As I sat in that room with my elbows on the table trying to make some sense of all that had been said and done that day, you came for me.

How quickly you moved. More of a glide than a walk, even though the heels of your boots were so high. And the determination in your eyes, the intent to do someone harm in your beautiful wax-dolly face, gave you the moment of surprise required. You overcame me so swiftly I never had time to cry out or struggle. I only managed to open my mouth, as if to speak, and to swallow a medicinal gust of whatever chemicals were soaked into that wad of cotton wool.

Purged of obstinacy, of thought, of speech by the sudden obliterating pain of each stroke from your thin cane, I can only pant and sweat and groan. The hot stinging discomfort is completely contained within my body that is bent over the foot of your bed. I cannot distribute this pain, or alleviate my suffering, because you tied me so tight I cannot move. All I can do is concentrate on the whipping of my flesh with the instrument of correction. And I am being corrected – I am being absolved of petulance, of resistance, of rivalry, of delusion. All the things that made me fight you, resent you, desire you. You are emptying me of any further competition to your absolute mastery and beauty.

As the caning continues and the endorphins rush to my rump to anaesthetise the lacerated, stricken flesh, I feel light-headed, almost dreamy. I let go of any sense of self, of ego, of identity – I begin to exist purely for the sensation of your touch and for the notion of your supremacy in this space. I am entirely in your care. I cannot act or think for myself. You control me with sensation. It is liberating to accept complete defeat; to have my choices so totally reduced to nothing. Freedom was always my problem; the unshakeable notion that I was still your equal and should have been treated with respect. In your employ, I could be nothing but a machine, an automatic gratifier of your needs; there was no more room in your life for another personality with all its wants and ideas and habits. You were the sun and I was in your orbit. You have money, you have style, you have beauty; how could I have kidded myself that anything else matters? The best I could have hoped for was a pride or satisfaction that I had served you well.

My saliva bubbles on the rubber bit between my teeth. I look over my shoulder and see your face: pale, discreetly painted, deep in concentration. Gradually the enormity of my treason and the weight of your anger will be reduced with every successive stroke. But now I am past the worst of the acute discomfort. I feel as though I could go on for ever – biting rubber, my limbs squeezed by metal cuffs, my anus stretched by the big steel fist, an eternity of cleansing pain. You are reducing me, then reshaping me. Will all men one day be transformed by this absolute design?

And how hairy and flabby I feel, how despicable and deserved of punishment, when I look at your streamlined contours and shiny surfaces. You are plasticated, glossy, aerodynamic. Every inch of you has been re-coated by a thin layer of latex. The human shape with all of its imperfections has been artificially rendered into living sculpture. To see you is to understand power – total dominance over the natural world, the triumph of materialism, the superiority of one will, unburdened by compassion or pity.

Down to the floor of your room you tug me by the collar – inert, offering no resistance, broken – and upon my nakedness you then stand with your cruel shoes. Pale feet, skinned in ultra-fine nylon and then re-skinned in supple rubber, mounted on spikes thin as pencils; your contoured density is applied through these nails that drive into my skin and crush me whimpering to the floor. I can do nothing but bellow, then take shallow breaths as you begin to walk. Sweaty, unshaven, lacking in muscle tone, undisciplined, I can only look up at the glossy perfection of your slender body and dolly face, as if I am an old version of something, being replaced by the new.

It was hard to keep track of time while I was living without the usual routines of day and night, work and rest, week and weekend. Suspended inside the harness in the dark bedroom, swaying at the foot of your bed, or shut inside that trunk, and all before you even put me to work, I guess it must have been one month before I went outdoors. The period of notice I demanded was given and served.

So much isolation in the first two weeks gave me much time to think, and in time my longing for companionship was satisfied by the stroke of your cane, the heel of your shoe, the flat of your hand. Curiously, it began to feel like a form of intimacy between us. We had a relationship and the punishment was sex. I depended on your whims for a release from solitude if only to feel pain, or to devour simple foods and water served in a steel dog's bowl. And during those brief periods of trampling and spanking and whipping, you knew I would have done anything you asked, without thinking.

In the third week, you put me to work. Crawling about the marble floor on that length of chain that

238

stretched from your bed, while naked save for my head (totally coated in that hot hood), a cloth in my hand, cleaning and polishing every square foot of floor, was worth the few minutes of your inspection at the end of the day. Showing no emotion, but a slight disdain in your perfect face as you examined the gleaming results of my slow, exacting, meticulous labours, you would teeter about on your spike heels as I crawled behind, ready to polish any spot I may have missed as a result of exhaustion. But every hour of hardship was worth each of the minutes I spent on all fours, trailing behind your glossy calf muscles and tight-skirted bottom. And not once did you permit me to walk on two legs.

In the fourth week you sealed me from head to toe in the tight rubber suit. All identity erased, my mouth stoppered with a ball gag, I cooked for you, served you food, washed your dishes, ran your baths and changed your bed. I executed your demands without question. You never once thanked me, you barely even noticed me – the dark, glossy shape darting about to fetch and carry, or bowing out of a room once dismissed. Three times I even drove for you, my perverse rubbered head and body hidden behind dark glass, while you made phone calls from the backseat of the Mercedes. And life was so much easier: I had no cares beyond the execution of my duties. And despite the drudgery and the unthinking servitude, I would always look forward to the thrill of your presence. Just being in the same room as your high-heeled shoes, occupying the same space with the severe-looking woman in a leather suit, became all the reward and payment I needed.

Of course, technically I was fired. My P45 was issued and the authorities were notified that my position had been terminated. I was no longer on your payroll. My existence as an individual in his own right ceased abruptly. What few relatives and friends I had were promptly informed that I could no longer be found at your address. My old self and life were effectively dead. But you kept me.

And I believe you will keep ownership of me, as long as I do not speak, or assert myself in your company. Just yesterday, I had to swallow a lump in my throat and I must confess to have become all teary-eyed when you suggested that my old black livery may be returned in order for me to take care of shopping and other duties outside the apartment. Soon, I would be able to show my face to the outside world again. But what a different face it will be. A handsome but emotionless face. The face of a man humble but reliable. A man indispensable in the service of his lady. A man not prone to excitability, nor to unclean antisocial habits. A man with no interest in strong drink or gambling. A man indifferent to all women beyond her whom he serves. And the new mask will help, you said. It will make everything so much easier. I will look better than I have ever done. I will look younger and more handsome. And I will finally be relieved of all those stubborn, unattractive qualities that have handicapped my sex for so long. And it'll practically be invisible, you said. Only under strong lights can it be detected. All the girls are going to get them for their men, you said.

NEXUS NEW BOOKS

To be published in July 2004

THE PLAYER
Cat Scarlett

Carter, manager of an exclusive all-female pool tour, discovers Roz in a backstreet pool hall. When he sees her bending to take her shot, he can't resist putting his marker down to play her. But, when he signs Roz up to his tour, she discovers that the dominant Carter has a taste for the perverse, enforces a strict training regime, and that an exhibition match is just that.

£6.99   ISBN 0 352 33894 6

THE ART OF CORRECTION
Tara Black

The fourth instalment of Tara's series of novels chronicling the kinky activities of Judith Wilson and the Nemesis Archive, a global network of Sapphic corporal punishment lovers dedicated to chronicling the history of perverse female desire.

£6.99   ISBN 0 352 33895 4

SERVING TIME
Sarah Veitch

The House of Compulsion is the unofficial name of an experimental reformatory. Fern Terris, a twenty-four-year-old temptress, finds herself facing ten years in prison – unless she agrees to submit to Compulsion's disciplinary regime. Fern agrees to the apparently easy option, but soon discovers that the chastisements at Compulsion involve a wide variety of belts, canes and tawses, her pert bottom, and unexpected sexual pleasure.

£6.99   ISBN 0 352 33509 2

To be published in August 2004:

THE PRIESTESS
Jacqueline Bellevois

Gullible young solicitor Adam finds himself attracted to Megan, his beautiful fellow employee, and dominated by worldly-wise workmate Donna. The owner of a slinky, City-based fetish club finds she is being defrauded by a mysterious regular, known as The Priestess, and the three of them must learn to serve their client well. Submitting their own sexual tensions to the rules of the club, and discovering its association with a bizarre 'sanatorium', the trio discover that their lives will never be the same again.

£6.99   ISBN 0 352 33905 5

TICKLE TORTURE
Penny Birch

Jade, confident but submissive, is struggling to come to terms with the demands of her lesbian lover, AJ, to become her lifestyle slave. Matters aren't helped when her participation at a wet, kinky cabaret goes too far, bringing its shifty management after her, intent on sexual revenge. With the added distraction of her lewd friend Jeff Bellbird, and extra toppings from Doughboy the pizza man, Jade looks less likely than ever to resolve her dilemma.

£6.99   ISBN 0 352 33904 7

EMMA'S SUBMISSION
Hilary James

This fourth volume of Emma's story finds its very pretty heroine back in the thrall of the sadistic Ursula, who is now supplying well-trained young women as slaves and pleasure creatures to wealthy overseas clients. Having been trained by Sabhu – Ursula's Haitian assistant and slave-trainer – Emma is hired out to the cruel wife of an African dictator who uses her in the most degrading ways. Emma soon discovers that the woman has acquired a painting which has been stolen from Ursula. Ursula wants it back at any cost and if Emma fails in her mission to retrieve it, she may never see her beloved mistress again.

£6.99   ISBN 0 352 33906 3

If you would like more information about Nexus titles, please visit our website at www.nexus-books.co.uk, or send a stamped addressed envelope to:

Nexus, Thames Wharf Studios,
Rainville Road, London W6 9HA

NEXUS BACKLIST

This information is correct at time of printing. For up-to-date information, please visit our website at www.nexus-books.co.uk

All books are priced at £6.99 unless another price is given.

THE ACADEMY Arabella Knight ☐
0 352 33806 7

AMANDA IN THE PRIVATE Esme Ombreux ☐
   HOUSE 0 352 33705 2

ANGEL Lindsay Gordon ☐
£5.99 0 352 33590 4

BAD PENNY Penny Birch ☐
£5.99 0 352 33661 7

BARE BEHIND Penny Birch ☐
0 352 33721 4

BEAST Wendy Swanscombe ☐
£5.99 0 352 33649 8

BELLE SUBMISSION Yolanda Celbridge ☐
0 352 33728 1

BENCH-MARKS Tara Black ☐
0 352 33797 4

BRAT Penny Birch ☐
0 352 33674 9

BROUGHT TO HEEL Arabella Knight ☐
£5.99 0 352 33508 4

CAGED! Yolanda Celbridge ☐
£5.99 0 352 33650 1

CAPTIVE Aishling Morgan ☐
£5.99 0 352 33585 8

CAPTIVES OF THE PRIVATE Esme Ombreux ☐
   HOUSE £5.99 0 352 33619 6

CHALLENGED TO SERVE Jacqueline Bellevois ☐
0 352 33748 6

CHERRI CHASTISED	Yolanda Celbridge 0 352 33707 9	☐
CORPORATION OF CANES	Lindsay Gordon 0 352 33745 1	☐
THE CORRECTION OF AN ESSEX MAID	Yolanda Celbridge 0 352 33780 X	☐
CREAM TEASE	Aishling Morgan 0 352 33811 3	☐
CRUEL TRIUMPH	William Doughty 0 352 33759 1	☐
DANCE OF SUBMISSION £5.99	Lisette Ashton 0 352 33450 9	☐
DARK DESIRES £5.99	Maria del Rey 0 352 33648 X	☐
DEMONIC CONGRESS	Aishling Morgan 0 352 33762 1	☐
DIRTY LAUNDRY	Penny Birch 0 352 33680 3	☐
DISCIPLINE OF THE PRIVATE HOUSE	Esme Ombreux 0 352 33709 5	☐
DISCIPLINED SKIN £5.99	Wendy Swanscombe 0 352 33541 6	☐
DISPLAYS OF EXPERIENCE £5.99	Lucy Golden 0 352 33505 X	☐
DISPLAYS OF PENITENTS £5.99	Lucy Golden 0 352 33646 3	☐
DRAWN TO DISCIPLINE £5.99	Tara Black 0 352 33626 9	☐
AN EDUCATION IN THE PRIVATE HOUSE £5.99	Esme Ombreux 0 352 33525 4	☐
THE ENGLISH VICE	Yolanda Celbridge 0 352 33805 9	☐
EROTICON 1 £5.99	Various 0 352 33593 9	☐
EROTICON 4 £5.99	Various 0 352 33602 1	☐
THE GOVERNESS ABROAD	Yolanda Celbridge 0 352 33735 4	☐

THE GOVERNESS AT ST AGATHA'S	Yolanda Celbridge 0 352 33729 X	☐
GROOMING LUCY £5.99	Yvonne Marshall 0 352 33529 7	☐
HEART OF DESIRE £5.99	Maria del Rey 0 352 32900 9	☐
THE HOUSE OF MALDONA	Yolanda Celbridge 0 352 33740 0	☐
IN FOR A PENNY £5.99	Penny Birch 0 352 33449 5	☐
THE INDIGNITIES OF ISABELLE	Penny Birch writing as Cruella 0 352 33696 X	☐
INNOCENT	Aishling Morgan 0 352 33699 4	☐
THE ISLAND OF MALDONA	Yolanda Celbridge 0 352 33746 X	☐
JODHPURS AND JEANS	Penny Birch 0 352 33778 8	☐
THE LAST STRAW	Christina Shelley 0 352 33643 9	☐
NON-FICTION: LESBIAN SEX SECRETS FOR MEN	Jamie Goddard and Kurt Brungard 0 352 33724 9	☐
LETTERS TO CHLOE £5.99	Stephan Gerrard 0 352 33632 3	☐
LOVE-CHATTEL OF TORMUNIL	Aran Ashe 0 352 33779 6	☐
THE MASTER OF CASTLELEIGH £5.99	Jacqueline Bellevois 0 352 33644 7	☐
MEMOIRS OF A CORNISH GOVERNESS	Yolanda Celbridge 0 352 33722 2	☐
MISS RATTAN'S LESSON	Yolanda Celbridge 0 352 33791 5	☐
NON-FICTION: MY SECRET GARDEN SHED £7.99	Ed. Paul Scott 0 352 33725 7	☐
NEW EROTICA 5 £5.99	Various 0 352 33540 8	☐
NEW EROTICA 6	Various 0 352 33751 6	☐

THE NEXUS LETTERS £5.99	Various 0 352 33621 8	☐
NURSES ENSLAVED £5.99	Yolanda Celbridge 0 352 33601 3	☐
NURSE'S ORDERS	Penny Birch 0 352 33739 7	☐
NYMPHS OF DIONYSUS £4.99	Susan Tinoff 0 352 33150 X	☐
THE OBEDIENT ALICE	Adriana Arden 0 352 33826 1	☐
ONE WEEK IN THE PRIVATE HOUSE	Esme Ombreux 0 352 33706 0	☐
ORIGINAL SINS	Lisette Ashton 0 352 33804 0	☐
THE PALACE OF EROS £4.99	Delver Maddingley 0 352 32921 1	☐
THE PALACE OF PLEASURES	Christobel Coleridge 0 352 33801 6	☐
PALE PLEASURES	Wendy Swanscombe 0 352 33702 8	☐
PARADISE BAY £5.99	Maria del Rey 0 352 33645 5	☐
PEACH	Penny Birch 0 352 33790 7	☐
PEACHES AND CREAM	Aishling Morgan 0 352 33672 2	☐
PENNY IN HARNESS £5.99	Penny Birch 0 352 33651 X	☐
PENNY PIECES £5.99	Penny Birch 0 352 33631 5	☐
PET TRAINING IN THE PRIVATE HOUSE £5.99	Esme Ombreux 0 352 33655 2	☐
PLAYTHINGS OF THE PRIVATE HOUSE £6.99	Esme Ombreux 0 352 33761 3	☐
PLEASURE ISLAND £5.99	Aran Ashe 0 352 33628 5	☐
THE PLEASURE PRINCIPLE	Maria del Rey 0 352 33482 7	☐

PLEASURE TOY £5.99	Aishling Morgan 0 352 33634 X	☐
PRIVATE MEMOIRS OF A KENTISH HEADMISTRESS	Yolanda Celbridge 0 352 33763 X	☐
PROPERTY	Lisette Ashton 0 352 33744 3	☐
PURITY £5.99	Aishling Morgan 0 352 33510 6	☐
REGIME	Penny Birch 0 352 33666 8	☐
RITUAL STRIPES	Tara Black 0 352 33701 X	☐
SATURNALIA £7.99	Ed. Paul Scott 0 352 33717 6	☐
SATAN'S SLUT	Penny Birch 0 352 33720 6	☐
THE SCHOOLING OF STELLA	Yolanda Celbridge 0 352 33803 2	☐
SEE-THROUGH £5.99	Lindsay Gordon 0 352 33656 0	☐
SILKEN SLAVERY	Christina Shelley 0 352 33708 7	☐
SISTERS OF SEVERCY £5.99	Jean Aveline 0 352 33620 X	☐
SIX OF THE BEST	Wendy Swanscombe 0 352 33796 6	☐
SKIN SLAVE £5.99	Yolanda Celbridge 0 352 33507 6	☐
SLAVE ACTS	Jennifer Jane Pope 0 352 33665 X	☐
SLAVE GENESIS £5.99	Jennifer Jane Pope 0 352 33503 3	☐
SLAVE-MINES OF TORMUNIL	Aran Ashe 0 352 33695 1	☐
SLAVE REVELATIONS £5.99	Jennifer Jane Pope 0 352 33627 7	☐
SOLDIER GIRLS £5.99	Yolanda Celbridge 0 352 33586 6	☐
STRAPPING SUZETTE £5.99	Yolanda Celbridge 0 352 33783 4	☐

THE SUBMISSION GALLERY £5.99	Lindsay Gordon 0 352 33370 7	☐
TAKING PAINS TO PLEASE	Arabella Knight 0 352 33785 0	☐
THE TAMING OF TRUDI	Yolanda Celbridge 0 352 33673 0	☐
A TASTE OF AMBER £5.99	Penny Birch 0 352 33654 4	☐
TEASING CHARLOTTE	Yvonne Marshall 0 352 33681 1	☐
TEMPER TANTRUMS £5.99	Penny Birch 0 352 33647 1	☐
THE TRAINING GROUNDS	Sarah Veitch 0 352 33526 2	☐
UNIFORM DOLL	Penny Birch 0 352 33698 6	☐
VELVET SKIN £5.99	Aishling Morgan 0 352 33660 9	☐
WENCHES, WITCHES AND STRUMPETS	Aishling Morgan 0 352 33733 8	☐
WHIP HAND	G. C. Scott 0 352 33694 3	☐
WHIPPING GIRL	Aishling Morgan 0 352 33789 3	☐
THE YOUNG WIFE £5.99	Stephanie Calvin 0 352 33502 5	☐

------------✂------------------------------

Please send me the books I have ticked above.

Name   ....

Address   ....

           ....

           ....

           .... Post code....................

Send to: Virgin Books Cash Sales, Thames Wharf Studios, Rainville Road, London W6 9HA

US customers: for prices and details of how to order books for delivery by mail, call 1-800-343-4499.

Please enclose a cheque or postal order, made payable to **Nexus Books Ltd**, to the value of the books you have ordered plus postage and packing costs as follows:
    UK and BFPO – £1.00 for the first book, 50p for each subsequent book.
    Overseas (including Republic of Ireland) – £2.00 for the first book, £1.00 for each subsequent book.

If you would prefer to pay by VISA, ACCESS/MASTERCARD, AMEX, DINERS CLUB or SWITCH, please write your card number and expiry date here:

....

Please allow up to 28 days for delivery.

Signature ....

Our privacy policy

We will not disclose information you supply us to any other parties. We will not disclose any information which identifies you personally to any person without your express consent.

From time to time we may send out information about Nexus books and special offers. Please tick here if you do *not* wish to receive Nexus information.   ☐

------------✂------------------------------